THE TEMPERING

THE MACKENZIE DUNCAN SERIES

The Tempering
Mackenzie Duncan Series
By Adrianne James

Copyright 2013 by Star Bound Books

Cover Design by Gonet Design
http://www.facebook.com/gonetdesign
Editing by Rogena Mitchell-Jones Manuscript Service
http://www.RogenaMitchell.com

Dedication

This may be the hardest dedication I have ever had to write. Not because I don't know who to dedicate this novel to, but because my heart is breaking just thinking about the fact that he will never be able to read it.

To my big brother, Duane. This one is for you. You have always believed in me and my work. You have been my friend, my mentor, my tutor, my confidant, and my protector all rolled into one. You never put yourself before others and you never let anyone put you before themselves either, no matter how many times we tried.

Thank you for holding on long enough to give me two days with you. Thank you for holding on long enough to meet your neice and nephew who fell in love with you in those two days and tell everyone about their Uncle Duane and how awesome he was and how much they miss him. Thank you for always being there for me when I needed you. Thank you for scaring off all the rotten boys who tried to get my attention when I was younger and thank you for not threatening my husband when we started dating.

Thank you for every memory I have of you. I will treasure them forever.

Acknowledgements

There are a few people that made this book happen and it's time for me to say thank you. A big thank you to my beta Cherylanne. Your helpful comments and suggestions helped make THE TEMPERING what it is today.

Thank you to Rogena Mitchell Jones who took my novel and made it shiny.

Thanks to JC Emery who listened to my ramblings of werewolves on many occasions, including a few late night phone calls.

And Finally, thanks to Vanessa from New Adult Tours for getting THE TEMPERING in front of so many new readers.

Chapter 1

The crisp October wind whipped through the Harvard football stadium, sending a shiver down Mackenzie Duncan's spine. She was always the one to feel the chill of fall first, and first to freeze come winter. Mackenzie did not like the cold weather of Massachusetts.

The roar of the crowd was almost deafening and the scent of spilled beer and over- priced hot dogs filled her senses, making her wonder why she ever thought coming to the big game was a good idea. Perhaps it made her feel like she could fit in. Perhaps she felt if she could just make it through one normal outing in her first year of college, she had a chance of the amazing experience her mother continued to rant about since she received her acceptance letter back in the spring. *"Remember to find the fun in college,*

Mackenzie. Despite what you think, college is not all about books!"

She tried telling her mother that she enjoyed books. As long as she could remember, she had immersed herself in fantasy worlds provided by the wonderful imagination of authors. Her lack of typical teenage behavior did not impress her mother.

"TOUCHDOWN! Harvard takes the lead!" The obnoxiously loud commentator yelled into the microphone, sending his shrieking voice cascading through the sold-out stadium. The crowd cheered and Mackenzie stood with the rest of her classmates and clapped along, taking in the scene before her. Beers were clinked, others were chugged, but mostly they were spilled during the celebratory hugs between the Final Club members that acted as if they ruled the school. For all Mackenzie knew, they probably did. Final Clubs were clubs for the elite, the rich, the students who had the money to go to Harvard without ever having to apply for financial aid or scholarship. Most of them were legacies, third or fourth or even fifth generation Harvard men. Everything in life had been given to them, and Mackenzie hated the fact that she was jealous.

Mackenzie stood to move farther away from the group, hoping the distance would allow her to pretend that they were not even there. If she could make it up to the top corner of the bleachers, she could sit through the rest of the game—have that one "normal" college experience—then get back to her studio apartment in time to get her paper on the mythology of ancient Egypt finished. If that went well, she might even get a full five hours sleep before having to get up for her shift at the local coffee shop.

She took two steps then remembered the scarf she had brought, knowing she would be cold. As she turned around, she bumped right into Todd Nealy, president of the most affluent of the Final Clubs.

"Sorry, I didn't mean to run into you. I just need my scarf and you can have the seat." Mackenzie avoided his face. He had the bluest eyes and the blondest hair. He was muscular and tall, and damn near perfect. The problem was he knew it.

"No, it's my fault. I should have seen you, I mean, there is just so much of you. How did I miss you, right?" He smirked at his buddies, as Mackenzie's face grew warm with embarrassment. Then the embarrassment was gone and she was left with rage. Mackenzie had a temper. She knew she wasn't the perfect size two that all the guys seemed to want, but she rarely considered herself a large woman.

"You're right; there is just so much woman here that you really wouldn't know what to do, would you? You claim to have not seen me. I just think that you have never had the luxury of touching a real woman; you had to find the opportunity to do so. Now, if you will excuse me, I will be going." She grabbed her scarf from the seat and tried to leave. Todd grabbed her arm, his fingers digging into her skin, keeping her from moving. "I don't know who you think you are, but you better apologize for speaking to me that way. Do you know who I am?"

"Of course, I know who you are. You make it your mission in life to make sure every student here knows exactly who you are, who your father is, and who his father was. Here's a little hint. You. Are. An. Ass. You have a rich father who gives you free reign to spend whatever you want. Any girl you have ever been with has known you were an ass and just really liked that pretty pocket book of yours.

"Oh, one last piece of advice, NEVER touch me again. My daddy did teach me a thing or two before he landed himself in prison. So I suggest you remove your hand now."

Mackenzie's little speech did nothing to help the situation she found herself in. The look on Todd's face went from annoyance to sheer murderous anger. His grip tightened on her arm. "Bitch, I suggest you find a dark hole to spend the rest of your time here because from this point on, this is war."

She smiled and noticed the audience that had gathered. She wretched her arm from his grip, while bringing her knee up at just the right angle and velocity to bring Todd to his knees with a high-pitched squeak. "I don't want war. I wanted you to let go of me. Honestly, what kind of man puts his hands on a woman?"

The echoes of a few girls cheering helped slow her heartbeat as she left, removing herself from the situation. Had she overreacted? Maybe she was just like her father— temperamental and violent when there was no real need. She should have ignored his comment. She should have been a lady and walked away. She should have done anything but knee that asshole in the balls like he deserved.

~*~

Instead of climbing the bleachers as she had intended, Mackenzie descended to the bottom and slowly made her way through the thousands of drunken football fans to the exit. She waved a friendly goodbye to the guard at the gate who looked at her as if she were insane for leaving with a full quarter to go. Maybe she was, but she wasn't enjoying this "typical college experience." She would rather be at home, working on her paper, and enjoying a cup of hot cocoa.

Walking down the street toward the JFK Bridge, Mackenzie thought back on the last three months at Harvard. Not only did she choose the strangest major at Harvard, but the country as a whole. Mythology and Folklore doesn't tend to gain popularity like business or law. But she was okay with that. She knew what she wanted to do with her degree, she would write the next great mythological series and would consult on any games, shows, or movies that required any mythology or supernatural elements. A degree would surely put her leaps and bounds above any other consultant out there, and companies contacted her department all the time for that stuff. Any job that didn't require the question of "Would you like fries with that?" would be a step up for her and a first in the family.

She was the first to go to college, but she couldn't just go to college, she had to go to the best college. She sent a letter to her father the day she received her acceptance letter. His response was almost immediate.

He demanded to know where the money came from that she used to bribe the "bitch who looks at applications." It wasn't as if she had seen him in the twelve years he was locked up. Where did he get off responding like that? She was lucky she was even being admitted after being held back in elementary school because of the amount of time she was kept out of class by her parents for one court hearing or another. She knew then that she had to rise above her family. She had to cut them all out if she ever wanted a real life. A mother whose priority in life was mediocrity and fitting in with the social norm, and a father who solves any problem he comes across with his fists or drugs, were not exactly great role models. She hadn't spoken to either since she left for college. Without any siblings to worry about, she was on her own and that was perfectly fine by her.

Mackenzie pulled her coat tight around her as she took the first few steps onto the walking path along the bridge. Looking out over the Charles River, she smiled at the beauty the lights created when they reflected off the water. The sky had an almost bluish purple glow and the full moon was high in the sky. She may have been better suited to sit inside and work, but if she were able to admire the beauty the world had to offer through a window, that was what she considered perfect.

Stepping off the bridge, Mackenzie checked her watch and was shocked that it was already ten-thirty. She looked down the well-lit street that held a throng of students partying with the game blaring on their radios, and then to her left at the quiet park. She loved the park. It had plenty of trees and most of the time it was completely deserted. It reminded her of Colorado at times. Even though she didn't like to admit it, she missed her home state. She quickly made the left turn and found herself walking amongst the tall maple trees. Had there been any light, the beautiful oranges and reds would have created a kaleidoscope of color in a canopy above her. The trees stood so closely together that almost no light was able to break through the leaves. It was pitch black with the exception of one clearing about thirty feet in front of her where the moonlight was shining in like a spotlight.

The sounds from the street behind her slowly faded away with every step, but at the same time, her unease grew. Looking over her shoulder every few moments to confirm that she was still alone, she quickened her pace. She didn't know why, but she felt as if she were being watched. When a noise from the tree line echoed through the area, her heart began to race. Goosebumps erupted on her skin and fear gnawed at her.

The rustling from the trees had Mackenzie on high alert. She stopped and searched the trees as best as she could, but without any added light, she knew she had little chance of seeing anything. *Just walk quicker. It's just an animal.*

Swallowing down the fear that threatened to engulf her, she tried to look in all directions at once, not wanting to be surprised from any angle. With every step she took, the noise in the trees never faded. *It has to be an animal. It has to be an animal. Animals are not scary. It's probably a raccoon or something.*

Raccoons are nocturnal, so are possums. That's it. Nothing to be frightened of. Just another few steps and I will be in the light, then another five minutes and I'm out of the park. Just a few more minutes. She wanted to believe anything except the truth– that she was in danger.

Time seemed to slow in those last few seconds before Mackenzie reached the light-filled break in the trees. The noise she heard was growing stronger, louder, and she didn't know what to do. She began walking backwards, trying to keep an eye on the tree line, but in doing so, she tripped over a large rock.

A menacing growl sounded from the trees and when she turned to look behind her, a giant wolf leapt at her from the darkness. The fear overtook her, making her feel trapped within her own skin and unable to move or scream.

The wolf had a large head with strange yellow-green eyes. Its brown fur was matted and for some reason, its size reminded her more of a bear than a wolf. When Mackenzie realized the wolf's mouth had opened and she could see the razor sharp teeth, she flew into protective mode. Her arms rose up to cover her face and she tried to push herself backward, away from the beast. Within seconds, the pungent aroma that was the beast's hot breath seeped around her arms and over her face. Her stomach wretched but before she could heave what little lay in her stomach up, the beast bit down on her arm. The sharp teeth pierced her flesh and she could feel the tearing of her skin as the beast flung his head back and forth.

As Mackenzie's blood filled the wolf's mouth, she finally let out a blood-curdling scream. She tried to pull away. She pounded against the side of the beast with her free hand while kicking her legs about hoping to make contact, but everything she did was useless against the giant monster as it continued to tear her arm apart.

Mackenzie had to do something, or she knew she was going to be killed by the wretched wolf. Her thoughts swirled around, trying to think of anything she could do to free herself. She pushed and pulled at its muzzle with her free arm, trying to dislodge the teeth embedded in her flesh. The sharp pain in the mangled limb became an incredible burn, but the wolf must have severed a few nerves because she could no longer feel anything but numbness from her shoulder down to her fingertips.

Remembering what had put her in this position to begin with, Mackenzie reached behind her and grabbed the damn rock and swung it at the wolf's head. With a loud crack, the rock connected with the top of the wolf's skull. Briefly shocked, the beast's grip released as her arm fell from its mouth. Before he could go in for another bite, Mackenzie gouged her thumb straight into its freakish yellow-green eye. With a loud yelp, the wolf retreated and snarled once again, baring his teeth. She had angered it, and she was suddenly more frightened than she had been when her arm was being shredded in its mouth. Pure rage marred its face. She quickly threw the rock, hitting it square in its bloody snout. A loud crack resonated through the park before the beast turned and ran off.

~*~

As she lay on the cold grass in the middle of the moonlight unable to grasp what had just happened to her, the numbness in her arm began to dissipate. The pain did not slowly creep back in, but came with a vengeance, and was like no other pain she had ever felt before. The cold air surrounding her stung her skin and when she tried to pull her coat closer to her body, she looked down at her arm. Before her was a tattered mess, from her shoulder to her wrist, of fabric all stained a muddy red from the blood pouring from her wounds. Her skin and muscle were ripped apart, with bones showing through. It looked as if she had been made up to look the part of a zombie for one of those horror movies.

Mackenzie tried to stand, but was hit with sudden dizziness and collapsed. As soon as her injured arm collided with the ground, a slight burning sensation began to emanate from the middle of her wound. As if her torn flesh were kindling, and catching fire inch by inch, the heat grew in intensity and size until it engulfed her entire arm. Screaming out in pain, tears streaming down her face, she brought her arm against her chest, cradling it, hoping it would help with the pain long enough for her make her way home. She moved to her knees and then slowly, using all the strength she had left, she stood up carefully as not wanting to end up on the ground yet again. She took a sluggish step. Each one harder than the last, she began chanting to herself to keep going.

"Don't stop. Just a bit more. Keep going. Don't stop." There was no one around to hear her and honestly, she was speaking aloud just to hear her own voice, to know that she had really made it out of that encounter alive, even if she may never have use of her mangled arm again. Daring to look once more, she moved the tatters of her coat back to reveal the gaping hole in her arm. Not only was her flesh torn to the point of seeing bones, but also she was able to see the long marks from the wolf's teeth etched distinctly in her bones. Dizziness began to cloud her vision again, and she forced herself to look up at the street just ahead.

Mackenzie fell to the ground as soon as she stepped onto the lit sidewalk. She could hear the partying from the few blocks away. Just a half hour before had seemed like the worst possible choice she could have made. She laughed to herself due to her sheer stupidity. Then she laughed at the fact she was laughing when she desperately needed a hospital. Then she laughed until she sobbed. There was nothing funny about the situation in which she found herself. Nothing funny at all.

It was then she felt a harsh painful tingle throughout her body. It wasn't a feeling of limbs falling asleep but something else. The fire that had been stationary in her arm flamed hotter as it crept up over her shoulder and began to lick at her collarbone, then down her chest and up her face, seemingly at the same time. The tingle grew more intense deep within her bones, as a buzzing rang loud in her ears, also. The burning, tingling, and buzzing all rushed through her body until she was entirely consumed. Then, as if it had never happened, the flames were extinguished, and all was quiet. There wasn't a rush of cooling relief, nor was there a grand finally of pain. It just stopped.

She looked back to her arm, through water-laden eyes to see what couldn't be. She slowly lifted her arm higher to get a better look. Before her, Mackenzie watched as her muscles and tendons and veins began to re-grow and knit back together. Her skin sealed itself over the newly healed muscle tissue, starting at one end and working its way to the other. It almost looked like a piece of fabric being zipped up, leaving no trace of any wrongdoing behind.

Not knowing what else to do, she stood, and then forced herself to look away from her now perfectly healed arm. Totally confused but not wanting to be in the dark any longer, she walked home hoping a good night's sleep would put everything in perspective.

She was fooling herself. Nothing would ever make sense in Mackenzie's life again.

Chapter 2

It had been a rough night for Mackenzie. Not only had a ridiculously large wolf attacked her, but also something strange had happened to her, and she hadn't a clue what. Follow that with a sleepless night and the music from her neighbors pounding through the walls, the few hours of sleep she did get did not leave her rested. In fact, she felt worse that morning than she had the night before.

Mackenzie groaned as she tried to roll out of bed. Everything inside of her was aching. She had never felt so sore not even after her first 10k back in high school. She may have been overweight, but she loved to run as much as she loved to eat. Just the thought of eating sent a wave of nausea through her. Knowing she wasn't making it into work, let alone class, she decided to call the manager.

Rolling over just enough to reach the phone on the bedside table, she squinted at the tiny dial pad before punching in the number to the coffee shop. Her hands were trembling so that just holding the phone was difficult, let alone pushing the tiny little buttons.

The phone rang at least 10 times before it was answered. Worrying that the length of time it took them to answer meant they were swamped, she braced herself for a bad conversation.

"Cafe Crimson, Can you hold please?" Susan, the manager, answered. She sounded stressed as she put Mackenzie on hold before the question could be answered.

Mackenzie listened to the school's fight song play on loop for at least five minutes. She could feel her eyes growing heavier with each passing moment and continued to shake her head to wake herself up. *Just a few more minutes, then I can go back to sleep.*

"Thank you for holding, How may I help you?"

"Hey, Susan, it's me. I am not going to be able to make it in to work. I'm so sick, it isn't even funny."

"Sick? Mackenzie, we are swamped and it is not my fault you decided to go to the game and party last night. Hangovers are not an excuse to call out of work. If you're not here in the next hour, you will have to look elsewhere for employment." With that, she hung up the phone.

Mackenzie lay in bed for a few more moments, trying to process what had happened. It wasn't as if she called out of work often. Hell, she had never called out of work before. But she knew that finding another job half way through the semester would be near impossible and she relied on that paycheck to survive. Sure, she had some money squirreled away, but it would only last so long.

Deciding she needed to go to work, but knowing she would never make it through the whole day, she dialed her friend, Jordan's number.

"Do you know what time it is?" Jordon whispered in a groggy voice.

"Sorry, would you mind taking notes for me in Lit? I won't be making it." Mackenzie knew her voice sounded horse. Her throat was sore and scratchy.

"You won't be in class? Really? You're missing class?"

"Yeah, I'm sick and I have to go into work but I can't see me making it much passed that. I will call you later tonight. I can probably pick them up tomorrow."

"Okay, no problem. Feel better and try not to cough in anyone's coffee." Mackenzie hung up the phone and lay in bed a moment longer.

Finding the strength to stand up and walk to the bathroom to get ready for work seemed harder than climbing Mount Everest for the amount of energy she had to use. Opening the bathroom door, she rested against the frame for a moment before slowly moving to the sink, holding onto anything that could bear her weight. From there, she half-walked and half-fell onto the closed lid of the toilet. She tried to turn on the water in the tub to clean herself up using a washcloth.

Before she could complete the task, a wave of nausea passed through her. Flinging herself onto the floor, she opened the toilet seat lid just in time to expel the small amount of water that was left in her stomach from the previous night before promptly collapsing to the floor. Then everything turned dark around her.

~*~

A loud banging sounded throughout Mackenzie's small apartment, startling her awake. Taking in her surroundings, she realized she had fallen asleep in the bathroom, lying on the floor in front of the toilet.

Standing, she felt whatever bug had invaded her system must have gone because now she felt wonderful. More than wonderful, she felt better than she ever remembered feeling. She was well rested, and she felt like she had so much more energy than normal.

"Be right there!" She went to the sink to brush her teeth to rid herself of the foul taste in her mouth. She paid little attention to her reflection when she opened the mirrored medicine cabinet to grab her toothbrush. When the cabinet door clicked shut, she did a double take.

Dropping her toothbrush into the sink, Mackenzie grabbed both sides of the reflective glass and pulled her face as close as she could while still able to focus on herself. Staring back at her were not the blue eyes she had looked at every day for the last twenty years, but the same yellowish-green that she had seen reflected in the wolf's eyes the night before.

Not able to look away from her eyes, time lapsed without her realization. The knocks on the door resounded through her apartment yet again. Pulled from the magnetism of her eyes, Mackenzie began to exam the rest of her body. She could find nothing else that was out of the ordinary, except that she had full control of her arm, and there wasn't even so much as a bruise left from the horrifying attack.

Her gaze returned to the mirror and her curious-looking eyes. She began thinking of any illness she may have ever read about, heard about, or had seen on those crazy doctor shows. Nothing could account for a change in eye color and what she could only assume was regeneration of her arm tissue.

The banging at her door hadn't stopped, reminding Mackenzie that someone had been waiting for a while now. Leaving the mirror and the question of her mysterious eyes behind, she ran to the door to stop the incessant pounding.

Swinging the door open revealed a very irritated looking woman. She stood a good five- foot, ten inches and her long blond hair swung behind her. Jordon's hands were on her tiny hips as she waited to be let in.

Stepping back to allow her friend to pass through, Mackenzie noticed for once she wasn't looking up at Jordon.

"Where have you been? I only agreed to take notes for you once, so you're welcome for the extra notes, even though you weren't considerate enough to ask for them." Jordon looked around the apartment, as she always did. Jordon grew up with the best of everything, even though her parents didn't have anything themselves. Her family would eat on less than fifty dollars a week just to make sure she had the designer jeans she wanted, or let their car be repossessed just to buy her a two thousand dollar prom dress. Jordon never saw anything wrong with it. In her opinion, parents were supposed to provide and sacrifice for their kids. She just didn't understand how anyone could have parents like Mackenzie had. That's why she befriended her to begin with. Part of her felt bad for the girl, the other part really just wanted to study the effects of such a horrible childhood for a psychology paper. After the paper was complete and Jordon had her A, she just couldn't walk away. Mackenzie knew it was because she felt bad for her, but she didn't really care. She was used to that kind of friendship, but at least she had someone to talk to.

"What are you talking about? I called you this morning. I didn't ask you to go to my other classes." Mackenzie was truly confused. They only had the one class together on Fridays, why would she think she was asking or expected her to go to her other classes?

"This morning? Try two days ago. You called on Friday, today is Sunday. Sunday afternoon to be exact. What have you been doing? And what the hell is up with your eyes?"

"You're crazy. No way has it been two days! I was sick, tried to take a shower, puked, and fell asleep."

"You mean you have been sleeping for more than 48 hours? Seriously, your eyes?"

"I have no clue what's up with my eyes. It must have something to do with whatever made me sick. I feel fine now, but something is still going on. I wonder if that wolf had some kind of weird disease or something."

"What wolf?"

Mackenzie began the tale of her long walk home. She told Jordon everything she could remember and by the end, Jordon was looking at her as if she were insane. There were no wolves in Massachusetts.

"Honey, I think you should see a doctor. Between the hallucinations, the eyes, and sleeping two full days, something has got to be wrong."

And for once, Mackenzie completely agreed with Jordon. She had to be imagining everything. There had to be a logical explanation.

~*~

Mackenzie opened the heavy glass door and stepped through. She never liked having to see a doctor. Not only did she not like the poking and prodding, but also the fees were insane. For the first time she was glad for the Student Health Fee she paid at the beginning of the year as it covered her appointment.

The room was meant to be inviting. The chairs that sat in lines were colorful and looked to have a fair amount of cushion on them. The walls were painted a soft yellow and framed pictures lined them. However, the one thing they couldn't mask with some cheery colors was the sterile odor. The scent told everyone that this was a clean environment, but this time it made her nose itch whenever she breathed in. It was stronger than she had remembered from other doctor's offices.

Maybe the college just used extra strong stuff to combat the myriad of germs that the student body managed to carry.

After checking in with the receptionist, Mackenzie took a seat. The magazines on the table next to her provided entertainment for the first fifteen minutes, and then boredom hit and she began to fidget. Finally, a nurse stepped out from behind a thick wooden door.

"Mackenzie Duncan?"

"That's me." She stood and followed the nurse back. She set her things down on a table in the room and proceeded to get her height and weight checked.

"Let's see, 165 pounds and five foot eight." She began writing in the chart in her hand.

"I'm 5'6". I have been since I was 12."

"No dear, see here?" the nurse gestured to the height portion of the scale, "Five Eight on the nose. Perhaps you grew and just never realized it?"

"I grew, all right." In her mind, she was adding yet another symptom onto her list of weird and wacky things to ask the doctor.

The nurse left Mackenzie alone in the room to wait for the doctor on duty. She slowly walked around the tiny space, looking at all the pamphlets and posters that advised the students of the dangers of drugs and unprotected sex. It just so happened that when the door opened and the doctor walked in, Mackenzie was holding a pamphlet titled 'You Got Drunk and Wound up in A Stranger's Bed. Now What?'

Scrambling to put it back in the pile where she had found it, she ended up knocking the whole stack over. Before she could even chastise herself for her clumsiness, she reached out and caught most of the pamphlets, righting them before picking up the few that fell to the floor. Quick reflexes were not usually in her repertoire.

"Ms. Duncan, nice to meet you. My name is Dr. Mallson." The older gentleman held his hand out for her to shake. She glanced down at it quickly, before placing her hand in his. She wasn't sure why she was so wary of him, but there was something that told her not to trust him.

"Hello."

"So, what seems to be troubling you?"

Mackenzie took the few steps to the bed and hopped up. But when she hopped, she went a few inches higher than she had intended, which made landing on the bed much louder than she expected. The bed let out a groan and slid slightly along the floor, bumping into the wall.

"Sorry about that," she said with a slight grimace. Embarrassing moment number two in all of twenty seconds. The day just kept getting better and better.

"Don't worry about it. How about we just talk about what brought you in? Did you see any of those you would like to take with you?" he asked as he nodded toward the pamphlets on the table.

"No, I think I'm good without them, thanks. I came in because I was so sick over the weekend, that I don't even remember it. Apparently, while I was throwing up I passed out and didn't wake up for a few days. Oh, and my eyes. I have had blue eyes my whole life, up until this morning, that is. Oh, and I grew two inches over night."

"Can you remember anything from the night you started to feel ill?" He moved to the wall beside the bed and pulled down a tool that looked like a little thin hammer but with a light shining out of one end. "Look straight ahead."

As Dr. Mallson started to point the light in Mackenzie's eyes, she tried to recall all the details of the attack. She also wasn't sure she should tell him. He wouldn't believe her anyway.

"I was at the football game, got in an argument with one of the Final Boys and left. When I was walking through the park, I thought I saw something, got scared, and ran. I did fall and bump my head though. You think that has something to do with it?"

"Well, I don't see anything wrong with your eyes aside from the color change. You can make an appointment with your optometrist, if you would like. As for the sickness and fatigue, we can run some tests. Mackenzie, when was the last time you were sexually active?"

Mackenzie laughed at his question. She could count the number of times she had sex in her entire life on one hand, and none of those times had been even remotely recent.

"Not for a long time. About two years ago." The doctor made a note on his paper with a little grunt, as if he didn't believe her. She watched as he scratched down whatever drivel he thought important enough. The sound of the pen on paper as he was writing down what were most likely lies irritated Mackenzie's ears, much like nails on a chalkboard. She didn't stop to wonder why she could hear each stroke so clearly; all she thought about was ripping the pen from his hand and throwing it across the room.

"Ms. Duncan, for me to help you, you have to be honest with me. Now, if the sex wasn't consensual, we can get you any kind of help you need. But you must tell me the truth."

Not only was he lying about her on paper, he was calling her a liar to her face. Mackenzie's temper flared and she jumped from the bed and knocked the file and pen right out of the doctor's hand. The terrified look on his face snapped her back, making her realize what she had just done. Grabbing her coat, she hurried out the exam room door.

"Sorry!" She yelled out just as the doctor made his way into the hallway to watch where the disturbed young girl had gone.

Chapter 3

Three weeks had passed since Mackenzie ran out on the doctor. She still didn't understand why she got so angry. The more she thought about it, the more she realized he was doing his job. She wanted to return and apologize, but she just couldn't bring herself to face the embarrassment. She did, however, take Dr. Mallson's advice and schedule an appointment to have her eyes checked, not that it was any help.

The optometrist told her to see her general practitioner after testing her eyes and finding nothing wrong. Apparently he didn't listen well either because she told him the doctor sent her to him. In fact, there was not only nothing wrong but her eyesight had improved to better than 20/20. She was now able to see at thirty feet away what people with normal vision had to be at twenty feet to see.

With her eyes still the strange color, Mackenzie decided it was time for some real research. Being at Harvard had its perks besides a degree no one would turn away. The university had a library that held every law book, every medical book, and any other book one could think of.

Standing at her desk, she tripped on the strap of her purse that had been sitting on the floor. She threw her hand out to catch herself on the shelf, but when her hand grasped the wood, it cracked. Growling in frustration at the broken shelf, she cursed the old piece of furniture. She didn't have the money, or the time, to deal with anything else.

Losing her job after her two-day Sleeping Beauty act had hurt. No amount of begging received any sympathy from her boss, and no one else in the area was hiring. She knew because she had gone to every store, restaurant and bar hoping to find something but not one job was available. Her funds were dangerously low and while she knew she had enough for rent for the next month, she wasn't sure if she would have enough to eat and she really didn't want to have to call her mother for help. She hadn't called once since she left home and calling to ask for money was not the best way to make contact. She had to fight her mother to convince her that she was responsible enough to attend Harvard. Her mother thought she should go to the community college down the street first to make sure she could cut it, as if getting into Harvard wasn't an academic accomplishment enough. That was her mother, so very supportive.

If she had been able to take her typical route to the library, the walk would have lasted all of ten minutes. Having to avoid the park all together added another twenty on top of that. She couldn't bring herself to go back to the place that changed her life. She couldn't handle the thought that the wolf was still there. She got the feeling it had been after her, that she wasn't a random chew toy. It wanted to hurt her, to kill her. It might have been silly, as Jordon pointed out to her, but it was how she felt.

By the time Mackenzie reached the library, she was pulling off the layers of clothing she wore. It must have been an extremely nice day, she was never hot after the leaves began to turn, and she was typically freezing once the first snowfall covered the ground. Both of those things had already occurred, yet here she was, walking into the building in a simple tee shirt and jeans that were slightly too short due to her sudden and unexpected growth spurt.

She walked quietly over to a table in the back of the medical section and put down her bag. Looking around at all the stacks of books, hoping that one of them held the answers she desperately wanted, she pulled her laptop out of her bag and set it on the table.

When she went to lift the screen, her thumb broke right through the casing with a resounding crack that echoed through the silence. Blood droplets splattered against the broken computer and when she turned her thumb to see the damage, she let out a shriek as the inch long cut slowly sealed itself right before her eyes. She hadn't been hallucinating the night the wolf attacked her. She really had watched her arm heal itself just as she watched her thumb return to a perfect state.

The other students surrounding her looked around wildly before seeing no immediate danger. They threw scowls at her with a resounding "SHHH!" Mackenzie ignored them. She was still in utter shock and terrified. Her thumb just crushed through her laptop. Her skin looked like it zipped itself closed, sealing the slice in her finger as if nothing had happened, not even a scar remained. And to top it all off, she didn't even feel her skin being ripped open.

Even though she wanted to run away and hide in her little apartment and pretend that the last few weeks had never happened, she knew she couldn't. She had to find an explanation.

Carefully opening the lid of the broken computer and hoping for the best, Mackenzie pressed the power button and waited for the hum that would tell her it wasn't headed for recycling. More than two minutes passed before she gave up, slamming the lid closed and watching it shatter beneath her hand.

"SHHHH!" A small girl with a stack of books and a million papers in front of her said while glaring at her, "This is a library!"

Mackenzie could feel her blood boiling. How dare that girl speak to her like an idiot? She knew it was a library. What kind of dumb ass wouldn't know they were in a library?

"Mind your own damn business," Mackenzie growled out. She was pretty sure it was an actual growl after seeing the girl's eyes widen in fear and scamper away. Reminding herself that she was not her father and did not need to lose her cool, she took a deep breath. Breathing deeply for a moment allowed her time to collect herself, and to feel bad for snapping at the girl. Sort of.

Stowing her broken laptop away in her bag, Mackenzie headed over to the computers available for student use. Sitting down while eyeing the keyboard warily, she wondered how on earth she was going to use the keyboard without destroying it. As she hoped the surge of strength had passed, she placed her hands ever so lightly on the keyboard and began to type.

The library's medical database wasn't much help. Not one medical text had each of the symptoms she was presenting. Mackenzie was about to give up when a group of girls walked by, giggling and talking about some new movie and how gorgeous the actors were. It would have been a completely irrelevant conversation to overhear, except when she heard the name of the movie, it was as if everything clicked.

"So, are you going to see *Beneath the Moon* with me tonight or what?" The girl whispered to her friend.

"Absolutely, I mean, who wouldn't want to see half naked men who just happen to turn into wolves?" Then they both giggled and disappeared between the stacks.

Wolves. Why hadn't she thought of that before? She was a mythology major after all! Could the myths actually be true? Could she really have encountered a Werewolf? Frantically, Mackenzie opened up a different search program, one that found books from the schools complete catalog, not just the medical journals she had been searching.

A quick search on Lycanthropy produced seven book results and three online journals. Writing down the call numbers for the books before clicking on the links to take her to the journals, she felt, in anticipation, her heart was pounding faster than a racehorse.

The page before her read more like a medical journal than one written about the paranormal.

DAY 1: Subject tells of a vicious attack by a large animal but there are no signs of injury. Will continue to watch and take note of any abnormalities in subject's mental well-being. Subject appears very lethargic, sleep coming within moments of lying down.

DAY 2: Subject wakes with a high-grade temperature and the symptoms found in strains of influenza. Subject slips into what looks to be a coma, but only has the symptoms of a deep sleep. Fever persists.

DAY 3: Subject still unconscious. Fever still present, body changing. Must be terribly painful as the screams and moans break through the coma-like state. After thirty-two (or 32) hours, fever breaks.

DAY 4: Subject wakes, no signs of fatigue or feelings of lingering sickness. Irises have changed from brown to a yellowish hue. Subject no longer requires the use of eyeglasses and is three inches taller and seven pounds lighter.

DAY 5: No new symptoms to report

DAY 6: Subject's emotions, especially anger, are surfacing when typically would not...

Mackenzie stared in disbelief at the screen in front of her. She could remember the attack and feeling like death the next day, but surely if she had been in the kind of pain the journal spoke of she would have remembered it, or at least dreamt about it, but she couldn't remember anything.

She returned her attention to the screen in front of her that was telling her that her life was forever changed. She knew where this was going and she was not happy about it.

DAY 30: Subject was extremely irritable and restless, wanting to be outdoors but could not explain why the urge was there. Subject broke a window to get out of the lab and promptly sat in the grass, rubbing their hands and feet through the blades. When the moon reached its peak in the sky and the light fell upon the subject, they crumbled to the ground in pain, crying out as their body transformed right in front of me. Subject was no longer a human, but a very large black snarling wolf. I was not able to get away. I have yet to decide if I would rather it have killed me, or to have become one of them.

Mackenzie tried to close out of the webpage while trying to stand up and get away from the computer as fast as she could. Did she really believe this crap? Was someone playing a cruel joke on her or was this for real? She looked around wondering if those boys from the Finals Club had been behind the whole thing. She had gotten into a fight with their leader the same night as the wolf attacked her. Maybe they drugged her or something. At that point, she would accept any explanation other than the fact that she was turning into a Werewolf.

The distance between the computers and the stacks in the far back corner with the old bookshelves and dusty tomes reserved for the few books related to mythology and the paranormal world was only a few feet, but to Mackenzie, it felt as if she were moving in slow motion. She felt every stare and heard every snicker as she made her way to the books that could either go along with the journal of a supposed Werewolf, or find all sorts of contradictions and let her breathe easy.

The first book opened with a cloud of dust. Searching through the index until her eyes landed on the chapter she needed. She slid down one bookcase until she was sitting, her knees pulled up to her chest and the heavy book resting against her knees.

Unfortunately, the book was of little help to her, that is, little help to providing her with the information to hold onto her human status. Everything in the book could relate to what she was experiencing. Throwing the book to the side, she returned to the shelf and pulled another, and when that one spoke of the same symptoms, she returned again.

She knew she was looking in vain. She had studied mythology for years, first on her own and then as one of Harvard's very few mythology majors. Her mother told her how it was a waste of a Harvard degree, but she had plans for her life with a degree in what she had always loved and found fascinating. Was any of that even possible? Could she continue in school and life as if that one night each month were just a simple affliction? The only thing she knew for sure was that she had to find out when the next full moon was and how to stay away from everyone.

Chapter 4

In the weeks that followed, Mackenzie searched for a place safe enough to turn, that is, if she were going to turn. She still wasn't quite sure that she wasn't going crazy but she wasn't going to take any chances.

With just a single day left until the full moon, Mackenzie had to find somewhere to go. Although on the trip north, she did pass a mental institute, she considered that might be her best option.

Middlesex Fells Reservation was a somewhat popular place for parties and camping among the students at Harvard. She knew about where it was from their descriptions and after an hour of walking, she found herself surrounded by tall trees. The leaves had mostly fallen, blanketing the ground in a mix of beautiful oranges and horrid browns. Crunching under her feet with every step, Mackenzie traveled deeper into the forest. If this place was going to work, she had to go off the beaten path, deep into the woods and the thought terrified her.

Nights in Massachusetts, especially in late fall, were very cold. Frigid even. What if she went so deep into the trees she couldn't find her way back? She could die out there! But then that niggling thought of 'what if' joined in. What if she did turn into a vicious Werewolf? She might kill someone. As her mental battle raged on between what she had believed was simple fantasy and the horrifying realization that it might truly be her new reality, she found herself in front of a large cave. Glancing back over her shoulder, she could see that the sun was still high enough in the sky that she could have a small look around inside without needing a flashlight.

The mouth of the cave wasn't very large and just inside she could see that a boulder sat to the side of it. A careful look at the ground showed grooves where the boulder had been rolled back and forth, almost as if someone had used it as a door. But that couldn't be, because it was huge. It would take someone with incredible strength to even move it an inch.

She could see the bones of a few dead animals lying about and realized that she had most likely stumbled into an animal's den. Not wanting to confront yet another wild animal so soon, Mackenzie quickly left the cave and found her way back to the well-worn path.

Breaking through the trees, she heard a man's voice calling out. Down the path a ways, stood a tall man wearing what looked to be some kind of uniform. Mackenzie stopped when she had both feet firmly planted on the dirt, right beside the 'Do Not Wander Off Trails' sign.

"Miss, you need to stick to the trails. It isn't safe for people to go any further. There are wild animals out there and if anything were to happen, should you fall or get lost, we wouldn't even know you were out there," the man said.

"Sorry, won't happen again." She turned and headed the way she came in, knowing she had just lied to the man. If she had stayed and if he had pressed the issue, she knew she most likely would have lost her temper again. It seemed to be happening a lot more often in the past few weeks. Hell, all of her emotions were off the charts. She went off on her professor when he told her she had answered a question wrong and she was certain she was right. She bawled like a baby when watching a Lifetime movie in the student center with a few of the girls from her class, and she became so happy that she giggled and began shedding happy tears when she found out that her favorite restaurant from back home was opening up a location near campus. Yeah, maybe she really did need to see the mental health advisor.

Mackenzie tried to act normal the next morning. She knew that after that night, she would know for sure if she was no longer fully human. Shaking her head and mentally rolling her eyes over how crazy she sounded, she dragged herself from bed and through all of her typical morning rituals. Maybe she would get the mental hospital's number ready just in case.

Something in her felt off. She couldn't place what it was, but it was as if her skin were crawling like when she would watch a scary movie. It had to be all in her head. She just wasn't certain where her life was going and that terrified her, not to mention the possible murderous animal that lay beneath her skin. If she could just get some fresh air, she would feel better. That's what she needed. She was sick of being confined and wanted to get out and run. She wanted to blow off class and spend every minute of the day outdoors. Unlocking her door and stepping out into the hall, she decided that was exactly what she needed to clear her head and return to normalcy.

"Hey! Mackenzie! Where the hell have you been?" Jordan ran up beside her and instantly began the interrogation she knew was coming. "I have been trying to catch up with you for weeks now. You come to class and then bolt, not answering the phone even. Seriously, why haven't you gotten those creepy eyes fixed yet?"

It was true, she had been blowing her off, but she didn't want to tell her that nor could she explain what she thought was happening. She didn't want to hear the comments on her eyes or her temper, and she didn't want Jordan to look at her as if she were insane. Jordan didn't believe her, after telling her about the attack the morning she came to check on Mackenzie. Jordon had chalked it up to a hallucination.

"Sorry, I've been trying to figure some things out. I needed some time to myself. And there is no fixing my eyes apparently. They don't know why they changed color, but they did and now this is it."

"But Bailey told me you watched a movie with her and her girls the other night. Not too busy for them?" Jordan stopped walking and stood with her arms crossed and hip out. It was her typical 'I'm pissed and you better fix this' look. Honestly, Mackenzie didn't really care.

"Not that it's really any of your business, but I was already in there reading when they came in and turned the big screen on. So yeah, I watched it. It's not as if I chose to hang out with them. When the movie was over, I went back to my place. That was it. Look, I have a lot on my plate right now and I don't have time for this." Mackenzie had to speak through gritted teeth and clenched fists. Her anger was on the rise and she had to retreat quickly.

Storming off from her only friend, she felt like an ass. Jordan worried about her and lost her temper. Again. Mackenzie continued to walk away, even though Jordon was yelling her name. And some other colorful words she knew she better ignore. She figured it would be easier to apologize tomorrow if she didn't make things worse by arguing further with Jordan. Or what she really felt like doing—punching her square in the nose. Then again, if what she thought were going to happen that night really did happen, maybe it would be for the better if the friendship ended over a stupid argument. If Jordon was so pissed that she never wanted to speak to her again, she wouldn't be around and accidentally get hurt if Mackenzie lost her temper.

Mackenzie realized she had been spending all her time planning on how to handle the turn, should it happen. She still wasn't ready to completely accept that it was going to happen, but she had spent no time whatsoever on what to do after, if it did happen. Would she stay and try to make it work? Would she run away? No, she was a strong woman; she didn't run away from anything. Even when she was younger with an over-critical mother, a father in jail, and no money to even buy new clothes at Wal-Mart, she never gave up. She always fought for what she wanted and was as headstrong as they came.

She could handle it. She just knew it.

As the day continued, her strength became harder to control, her sense of smell had her running for a toilet to puke when she walked by the boys restroom and the door opened, sending out a whoosh of pungent air. She was able to hear the faintest moans that came from her neighbor's apartment from the downstairs entryway, and she was angry all day. The tip on her pencil broke in class and it infuriated her so much that she threw it across the room, promptly followed by her explosion of curse words when the professor asked her to leave his classroom if she was going to act like a toddler. She knew she should have blown off classes and gone for a run.

When her final class concluded, she practically ran to her apartment to pack a bag. She had never been camping and she wasn't even sure that she would stay the whole night. If the books were right, the change would happen the minute the full moon rose to the highest point in the sky.

Stuffing a few water bottles, some energy bars, and a blanket into her backpack she headed out. Looking at her apartment one last time, she closed and locked the door, wishing she could go back inside and hide under the covers. As she left her building, she was filled with dread. She really hoped she was just insane. It would honestly be the better option of the two.

With every step and passing minute she moved closer to Middlesex Fells, she felt more and more like she was walking in someone else's skin. Her heart was heavy and tears spilled down her face as she thought about everything she might be losing—how she might be losing herself in the whole thing, too. When she finally got to the first trail of the reservation, she started to get angry. Angry at the damn wolf for biting her, angry with the doctor for not listening to her, angry with Jordan for not believing her, but mostly angry at how stupid she had been to wander through the park at night alone.

Why couldn't she have just stayed at the stupid game? Why had she let her temper flair up and piss off The Final Club? Why hadn't she just pissed them off more by actually staying for the rest of the damn game? So many things could have happened differently to make this easier on her. Why did she have to be the one with everything working against her?

As the sun was setting, Mackenzie worked through some of her anger and frustrations by smashing through the trees. She ripped plants from their roots, destroying anything that stood in her path. Rocks were picked up and thrown and she screamed out in a strange almost animal like noise she had never made before. Somehow decimating anything that came into her path made her feel better.

The cave came into view just as Mackenzie realized she had been walking in the dark and that time had gotten away from her. Looking up, she saw that the moon was nearing its highest point. Not knowing what else to do, she stepped forward until she was bathed in the moonlight and waited. After a few moments, she decided she was indeed insane. She turned to walk back, but before she could go more than two steps, the worst possible pain shot through her body. As she fell to the ground, pops and cracks resounded from her arm and her neck twisted off to the side. Her heart raced and sweat bathed her skin.

She had to get to the cave. If she could, she could try to push the boulder in front of the door and keep everyone, including herself, safe. Crawling and clawing her way through the forest floor, she cried out with every bone and every muscle that was slowly torturing her from the inside out. The pain was so excruciating that she nearly tried to twist her own neck, to stop the pain and end her life so she would never have to feel it again. Except, when she tried, it felt like it clicked into place.

As she crawled through the mouth of the cave, her spine snapped. That was the moment that Mackenzie fell to the floor, the fight gone from her as the animal inside took over.

Chapter 5

Snarling, the beast that had been Mackenzie just moments before stood. Taking a step out of the cave, the scent of the woods and all the animals that lived there woke her wolf from its stupor.

Racing through the trees, knocking anything small enough out of the way and dodging around the others, the large black wolf with yellow-green eyes was hungry. It could smell the blood and the fear of something close.

The forest went silent, with the exception of the thundering paws and heaving pants that the wolf left in her wake. Grinding to a halt, her eyes narrowed. Her vision was superb in the dark, her hearing so sensitive she could hear the ants scurrying beneath her feet. She focused on a copse of trees just across the way.

Then she smelled it. Blood. Once she smelled it, all of her senses honed in on it. She could hear the animal breathing, and hear its heartbeat. She could see the glint of its eyes hiding behind the brush. Without a moment's hesitation, she darted after it.

Not able to match the speed of the wolf, the deer had no chance. The wolf clamped down on the animal, the blood spurting into her mouth. Ripping the flesh from the bone, the blood flowed until the creature was no longer breathing.

The blood and meat had done nothing to satisfy the beast. It needed more, wanted more. With every animal taken down, with every drop of fresh blood, the wolf grew stronger. The night wore on and as the sky began to lighten with the rising sun, the wolf grew tired, falling asleep in the middle of a kill, muzzle still buried deep in the hide of a bear.

~*~

Mackenzie's eyes fluttered open. Every muscle in her body was sore and every joint ached. Her teeth were chattering and her skin was covered in goose bumps. Other parts were numb. Pressing her hands into the damp earth, trying to sit up, she saw that she was completely naked. That wasn't the most disturbing part.

She was also covered in blood.

Letting out a scream, she tried to stand, but only slipped in the remains of the animal she must have killed the night before. She sobbed, sitting on the dirt with her knees pulled to her chest and rocked. She had no memory of the night. The last thing she could remember was the excruciating pain. She stood, wiping the tears from her face, but smearing blood along the way.

"I'm sorry. I hope you didn't have a family," she whispered to the bear. Carefully stepping around the animal, trying not to look at it for too long, she searched for anything that might look recognizable. She hoped to find her way back to where she changed; maybe her backpack with the spare clothing had survived.

Every birdcall or wind-whipped tree set her on edge. What had happened to the heat her body was throwing off the day before? She was burning up the whole day and then, as if she went from the Sahara to the North Pole in a single day, she was freezing. Of course, being outside in the middle of November without a single stitch of clothing on her body could have something to do with it.

Finally, after two hours and many cuts (and subsequent healing) on her feet and legs, she came upon the cave. Lying off to the side were the tattered remains of the clothing that had adorned her body the night before and her backpack, completely unharmed.

Diving for the bag, she stumbled and fell onto the leaf and needle covered ground. The zipper couldn't open fast enough for Mackenzie to pull a water bottle out and drink the whole thing in one gulp. Tossing the bottle to the side, she opened up a second, this time, drinking a little slower.

Deciding she needed to wash the blood off before trying to head back to civilization, she also decided not to put her clothes back on right away. She remembered there was a small stream not too far from the cave. But when she slowly turned in a circle to remember which way to go, she couldn't believe what surrounded her.

The more she looked around, the more devastation she saw. Trees were felled, claw marks marred the ground that wasn't covered in fallen leaves, and as she followed the trail of destruction, blood and animal remains began to lead the way like a grotesque version of breadcrumbs. However, it did lead her to the stream. Whatever blood-crazed monster she turned into the night before had the instincts of an animal, and it knew it needed water.

Mackenzie dipped a toe into the still water and pulled it out quickly, the frigid temperatures too much to bear. Staring down at her body, the brown dried blood mixed with the red of the still slick blood from what she assumed was her last kill, she wretched. Her stomach ached and her throat constricted, coughing, and gagging until she expelled all of the water she just drank. She couldn't stand the nauseating thought of killing anything, let alone eating an animal that had been breathing just moments before. She had eaten meat that her father had killed on hunting trips, but by that time, it was already cleaned and usually cooked, looking nothing like its live counterparts.

She couldn't stand the idea of their blood covering her any longer; she plunged into the water all at once. When she had rubbed herself raw, when the only red left on her body was the irritation of her skin from the friction of the water plant she had found to use as a washcloth, she emerged from the water. Quickly pulling the sleeping bag she brought with her from the backpack, she wrapped up, pulling it as tight around herself as she could, urging her body to warm back up to a normal temperature, her new normal temperature.

Sitting on a large rock as time passed by, she tried to remember what had happened. She searched her memory, but not a single moment of the night before was there. She could only imagine what monster she had become. Every time she attempted to force herself to leave, she couldn't. Facing the human world when she wasn't sure she qualified as one anymore was not appealing. It could have been minutes or hours later, she really didn't know, but she finally worked up the courage to return to the well-worn path back to civilization.

Sadness flooded Mackenzie as she crossed the barrier that kept people from wandering off the trail. It was there to keep them safe, safe from wild animals and creatures they didn't even know existed. She was one of those creatures and there was nothing she could do to change it. She knew she would never be able to keep her life as it was. She continued to lose control of herself when she did look like a normal person and who knows what she did when she turned.

"Hey! You! I thought I told you to stay out of there!" The man from the day before had run up to her. Mackenzie couldn't stop the tears from springing to her eyes. His look of utter annoyance softened as he placed a hand on her shoulder. She flinched and his hand vanished.

"I'm sorry. I am so sorry. I had to. I didn't have a choice. No choice." Her words were mashed together and half covered by sobs. She wiped at her tears for who knows how many times since she woke and started to walk away. The man followed her for a few steps, but stopped abruptly.

Her hearing was apparently still quite sensitive as she heard the crack of a walkie-talkie being turned on and the man behind her hurriedly speaking into the microphone. "I need an immediate search of the east quarter of the reservation. If there is anything out of the ordinary, report it immediately. Send the sketch artist, too."

Mackenzie couldn't figure out what had sent the ranger into panic mode. She didn't want to turn around to look at him, but instead began inspecting every piece of herself that she could see. Nothing looked out of the ordinary, but then again, it wouldn't. She had scrubbed every inch of skin she could see in the water. Immediately realizing she may have missed something she couldn't see, she pulled her backpack around to the front of her body to retrieve her mirror. She saw what had alarmed the man. Her bag had bloodstains all over the front pocket where she had opened it to get her water bottles.

Taking a deep breath and quickening her steps, Mackenzie cursed under her breath. What if when they went into the woods, they found more than just the animals? What if she happened upon some poor soul who wandered off the trail and her wolf killed them? They would find her and arrest her and she would wind up in prison just like her dad. She wasn't her dad. She refused to believe it, and had worked her whole life against it. She had to leave. Even if she did allow herself to be found and sent to prison, what would happen the first full moon after incarceration? If she thought the possibility of killing one person, who may just happen to cross her path in the woods was horrifying, the idea of being surrounded by them in a confined building was damn near petrifying.

No, she had to run. She had to leave everything she had worked so hard for her whole life because a fucking wolf got hungry when she was stupid enough to wander off the lit path on the way home from a game she never wanted to attend in the first place. For the first time since leaving home, she wanted her mother. She wanted to be able to curl up in her arms and pretend none of this was happening to her. She may have had her faults, but there was nothing like a mother's embrace to make the big bad scary things in life vanish, even if only for a moment.

Chapter 6

The walk back to campus was a blur of thoughts and plans and what if's and of what was to come in the days to follow. How would she tell her mother her plight without earning a padded cell and white straightjacket in her future? How would she pay back the loans she borrowed for the first and only semester she ever attended Harvard University? A semester she wouldn't even be able to finish.

Sliding the key into the lock on her apartment door felt surreal. Would this be the last time she opened it? Sighing, she realized that yes, it was.

She wandered around her room for a while, just taking in the memories she had created in her short time at Harvard. The school pennant hung above the bed that was decorated in crimson. Getting into college, not to mention an Ivy League like Harvard, had been a huge accomplishment. She was the first to attend college at all on her father's side, and the first to go beyond a community college on her mother's side. She had received letters from family she didn't even know existed congratulating her. It was nice, but it also amped up the expectations and now, she realized how many people she would disappoint when they found out she had quit.

There was no way she would be able to take everything she had with her. Her backpack and a duffle bag were the only luggage she had and she needed to be able to get around on foot. Without a car, taking anything more than she could carry was out of the question.

Mackenzie packed a few personal items and plenty of clothing before zipping up her duffle. Not knowing where she would end up, she knew she had to have as much cash as possible. Dragging a small end table into her closet, she climbed up. Along the ceiling in the small hall closet that led to the bathroom was a loose tile. It would pop up and slide over just enough to hide a small box in. When Mackenzie moved in, the tile was slightly ajar, and when she went to investigate, she found a handful of joints, covered in dust. When she moved the tile back into place, she realized that it was the perfect place to save her money. Once she bought a small box with a little lock, she began to hoard away all her tip money and as much of her pay checks as she could.

Mackenzie pulled the box down and left the tile slightly open, just as someone else had for her. While in the closet, she grabbed her Harvard jacket and an extra pair of shoes. Once she had packed, she sat down on the bed and cried. Again.

Forcing herself to stop crying and to deal with her life was not an easy task but she was never one to dwell on her past. She would rather deal with the reality of her life and move forward in whatever direction fate led. As a child, Mackenzie learned to adapt to whatever life threw her way—new schools, disappointed family, and a father who was in and out of jail. She may have never wanted this life, but this was the life she had.

She knew before she could leave for good she needed to say goodbye to Jordan and to withdraw from school. She wanted to be able to go back one day and failing out of every class in her first semester would not look good on any school application.

Jordan lived in the student dorms on the east side of campus. The walk there was cool, and much to her surprise, stayed that way even while carrying what had to be close to fifty pounds in her bags. She passed by students and faculty, none of which paid her any attention. They would never miss her. She never made a name for herself at the school. She hadn't had the chance. But it was better that way. If no one would notice her absence, no one would think anything was out of the ordinary.

Climbing the stairs one-by-one, running her hand along the polished wooden handrail up the thirty-two stairs to Jordan's floor, her heart filled with dread. She was going to lie to the one person who took the time to get to know her. She was going to say goodbye, and most likely never see her again. She didn't like the idea, but kept reminding herself that it was for the best. If she stayed, she could hurt someone.

When she finally stood before Jordan's door, her hands began to shake and her stomach rolled, sending a wave of nausea through her. She could do this. She would do this. She had no choice. How was she being so rational yet so emotional? How could she concentrate on so many different things at once? Thoughts of leaving, packing, saying goodbye and all the emotional shit that went with it. Not to mention, turning into a giant wolf that, if the morning taught her anything, had a craving for blood and violence. Every bit of it was running through her head since she had got up that morning.

Mackenzie took a deep breath, raised her hand, and knocked on the door in front of her. When neither Jordan nor her roommate answered, she felt relieved. She wouldn't have to say goodbye face-to-face. She wouldn't have to try and explain what she didn't understand herself.

Quickly pulling out a notebook from her bag, she used the door as a hard surface and wrote a letter to Jordan. She could say everything she needed to, without having to answer any questions. The only thing she could think to tell her was exactly what her mother told her from the beginning. She couldn't handle the high expectations of Harvard. She wasn't ready to be completely submerged into an adult world. Mackenzie apologized for leaving on such short notice, that she was leaving her key with the letter and to feel free to go and take whatever she wanted, and then to please leave the key on the dresser when she left. The school would take care of the rest. They owned the apartment anyway.

Folding the letter into thirds, she slipped her key in, and then folded the ends up, creating a pseudo-envelope before slipping it under the door. One goodbye down, one to go.

After an hour in line at the registrar's office, the woman at the desk finally called Mackenzie forward.

"What can I do for you?" The woman had dark brown hair with a few strands of grey starting to poke through and very ornate glasses resting on her nose. She smiled at Mackenzie while she stood there, staring ahead, not saying anything. "Miss? Are you all right?"

"As much as I can be. I need to drop out." Mackenzie's voice was just barely above a whisper. She never in a million years thought she would say those words. But there she was, quitting. She was a quitter. She was running away. Just like her father.

"Of what class?"

"All of them."

"Are you sure? You don't seem so sure. Let me get a counselor for you. I am sure we can help you with whatever academic problems you're having." She stood and began to walk away, but Mackenzie couldn't talk to a counselor.

"NO!" She banged her hands against the counter in front of her, startling the poor woman. Quickly softening her voice and removing her hands, she added, "I'm sorry, but no. It isn't academic. It's personal. I wish I could stay but I can't. Can you please just pull me from the school? And is there any way to get a partial refund of the money I paid out of pocket for tuition?"

"All right, let me just pull your information up. What is your name?" She sat back down in a huff, no longer being overly polite. Mackenzie didn't blame her after the way she had exploded.

"Mackenzie Duncan." The woman began typing away and within a few minutes the printer began making noises. Reaching behind her, the woman grabbed a small stack of papers and a pen and placed them in front of Mackenzie.

"Sign here, here and here." She pointed to all the places marked with an X. Reading the document was nearly gibberish. A lot of legal stuff that she had no clue what it meant until she saw the word voluntary. She was leaving the most prestigious school in the country voluntarily. If only she felt like she had a choice. Mackenzie signed each and pushed the papers back to the woman.

"Thank you, about my tuition?"

"Take your copy of these and go see Financial Aid. They should be able to tell you if you are early enough in the semester for a partial refund." Mackenzie smiled at the woman and began to walk away, when she heard, "Whatever personal issues you have going on, please remember you can always reapply. A college education is important and throwing away a chance at Harvard may just haunt you for a long time to come." She was being haunted all right, but leaving Harvard was the least of her worries.

The financial aid office was a bust as she had missed the deadline for any sort of refund by three days. She would just have to make do with what money she had on hand and figure out the rest of her life before the next full moon.

Chapter 7

Day after day, the sun rose and set, and the moon high in the sky sent shivers through Mackenzie. Her sleep was no longer sound, as she would wake up crying and sweating, from the nightmares that plagued her. Every night was the same thing. She was running around the woods, looking for campers, and killing them with her bare teeth, ripping them apart as if they were made of paper. When she would go to the water to take a drink, her reflection would not be that of a wolf, like she knew she was, but of herself, enforcing her fear that she was the monster.

Mackenzie had taken a few buses east, not caring where they were stopping. Mostly, she walked. She refused to be in a small, enclosed area with anyone, just in case, every myth was wrong. Maybe wolves could turn more often than on a full moon. Maybe they would do something to make her angry and she would "wolf out" as she started calling it.

Any time she happened to pass by a library, she would go in hoping they might have stocked different books than the last. It was a shame that the only books that featured Lycanthropy were considered fiction. Even so, she combed through them. Any piece of information to help her cope, help her learn what she was, and help her learn what that really meant.

Without any idea of what town she had wandered into, Mackenzie slipped into a little bagel shop for breakfast. She had been walking since eight that morning and she was starving. Standing in line, she couldn't help the shiver that ran along her skin. Someone was watching her. Glancing around the shop casually, she hoped to spot whoever it was.

When no one seemed to be paying any sort of real attention to her, Mackenzie turned back to face the short line ahead of her. Her stomach growled loudly just as she stepped up to the register.

Since the change, Mackenzie seemed to be constantly hungry. She would eat three times the amount she used to and it was doing very little to help her dwindling cash reserve. Ordering three bagels, all with cream cheese and lox, she paid and thanked the woman. Mackenzie picked up her breakfast, finding an empty table in the back of the shop. If no one could sit behind her, she would be able to see if anyone was really watching her.

Whatever that park ranger did, didn't actually affect her at all. At least that was working in her favor. She supposed she should be grateful for the fact that she hadn't seen anything to say that she was in trouble. If she had hurt anyone that night, they would be searching for the girl spotted leaving the scene of the crime with blood covering her bag. She had no run-ins with police or anyone searching for her as she thought she might after leaving Harvard.

Mackenzie pulled her notebook from her backpack and opened to the page she had created as a calendar. Three days. She had three days before she would turn again. Suddenly, her appetite disappeared.

Dumping the last bagel into the trash, she walked back up to the counter, which thankfully, no longer had a line.

"Excuse me; I was wondering if you knew of any forests or woods around here? I have a project I need some stuff for." Mackenzie knew it was a lame lie, but throwing something out there was better than them asking and her losing her cool. Again.

"Yeah, two towns over. Granby. They have a huge state park."

"Thank you." Mackenzie walked out of the shop with at least a plan for the next few days. She still wasn't sure about anything beyond that, but she would worry about that if she managed to survive wolfing out again.

There was no public transportation available so Mackenzie had to walk. There was one good thing about her newfound healing powers, her feet never hurt or got blisters from being on them for too long.

However, she would have to invest in some new clothes soon since hers were becoming looser every day. Between all the walking and an apparently incredibly fast metabolism, she was dropping the extra weight she had always carried. She was still far from looking like a fashion model, but being at a healthy weight was definitely in the near future.

With every step, Mackenzie glanced at her surroundings. The paranoia had yet to dissipate. Every person she passed, she inspected and to her utter horror, her instincts kicked in and she would take in a giant whiff to smell them, hoping to gain a better sense of who they were. When she tried to fight the urge, her entire body was on edge.

After five hours of walking, Granby came into view. It was a small town with a lot of little Mom and Pop stores lining the main streets. The houses all had yards and it felt as if by simply walking into this town, Mackenzie transported back in time fifty years. Trees were everywhere, a mix of bare branches, and orange and red hues lined many of the streets. If Mackenzie had been there for any other reason, she might have even reveled in the idyllic quality. Unfortunately, she had things to accomplish. There was time for admiration of the town's beauty later.

First thing, she needed to find a place to stay for the next two nights. She knew very well that she wouldn't be staying anywhere near the town, or the people in it, on the third night. That night was reserved for the beast. She would check into some kind of motel, and then find the state park the bagel girl had mentioned. She needed to learn those woods as best as she could in the next two days to be able to go deep enough to protect anyone from her path.

The further into town Mackenzie got, the more she could see the outline of the trees of the park on the horizon. If she had any chance of even checking them out that night, she needed to get going—and soon.

A bed and breakfast sign swung from a large, white farmhouse with a wraparound porch and a beautiful bay window. The yard was extremely large, but the best part was the land looked to go on for miles, right up to the edge of the state park.

Sighing in relief at yet something else to add to her list of things going in her favor, she knew she had found where she would be staying. Mackenzie climbed the steps to the porch. What looked to be immaculate from the street, actually had signs of wear and tear that only a house loved by its owners can acquire. The house featured paint patches from touch-ups, different colored nails in the floorboards, and a homemade swing hanging from the ceiling that needed a new set of chains and a fresh coat of paint. She smiled, wishing she had grown up in a place that she could call home for more than a year or two at a time. This house had obviously been lived in for many years. At least, she chose to believe that and didn't really care if it were true or not.

Mackenzie pushed open the door and a little bell jingled overhead. A few children ran through the room chasing after a cat. The brown blur darted under a table that sat low to the ground and when the children kneeled to try and coax him out, a hiss resonated through the room. Or maybe it was just Mackenzie who heard it since no one seemed to pay any attention to the children still desperately trying to reach the cat.

As if she knew what the cat was thinking, Mackenzie rushed forward and touched the children on the shoulder, gaining their attention. They pulled their little hands out from under the table just as the cat's paw, its sharp claws extended, swiped forward, missing the children by mere centimeters.

"Hey, I think the kitty might want some time alone."

"But we want to play with him! Mommy said it was okay."

"I am sure it was, but I think the kitty might be a little tired of playing now. I see a checkerboard over there. Maybe that could be fun." Mackenzie pointed to the bay window that overlooked the front yard. It had a bench built into the wall just under the pane of glass with a little table right in front of it. The table had been painted to be a permanent game board for both the checker pieces and the chess pieces that sat in a box on the floor.

"Oh! Good idea!" The children ran off, the cat completely forgotten. Getting down on her hands and knees, Mackenzie peered under the table. Her new amplified eyesight could see more clearly in the dark than she thought was possible, making the outline of the cat as detailed as the individual pieces of fur. The cat spotted Mackenzie and backed up, pressing itself along the wall with its fur standing on end.

"Hey, pretty kitty, the kids are gone, you can come out now." Mackenzie made some kitty calling noises that never actually do any good but everyone does anyway. The cat only responded with a powerful hiss that sent shivers down Mackenzie's spine. "Okay, fine. See if I ever save you again."

Huffing at the cat's attitude, she wandered over to the front desk. She hoped that they had a room available and that it wouldn't drain the last of her cash. The door behind her jingled, and all at once, her senses went into overload. She could smell something, something that made her feel like she was home, that made her feel safe. Her entire body relaxed and she had no idea what had made the change.

When Mackenzie looked over her shoulder, she saw a woman that exuded power, but more than that, the woman looked at her two younger companions with a motherly love. Her own mother often had that look. While she may be critical and they may not actually get along very well, the love was there. That, she never doubted for a second.

The young man who accompanied the woman, who was tall with broad shoulders and a fitted shirt that showed off the muscles of his sculpted chest, had deep brown eyes that just so happened to be looking directly at her. His lips ever so slowly lifted into a lazy half smile and then he winked at her. Looking away quickly, Mackenzie almost missed the girl with them who kept her eyes to the floor and shuffled her feet as they all moved forward.

~*~

Luckily, for both Mackenzie and the trio who came in after her, they still had rooms available. She could feel the young man watching her, but she refused to turn back around. She had no business looking at anyone like that; nothing could come of it anyway. Men complained about a normal woman's time of the month, what on earth would any man think of her *time of the month*?

Taking her key from the man behind the desk, Mackenzie practically bolted for her room. With every step away from the newcomers, she lost that safe feeling and her nerves were on edge again.

Once she reached her room, opening the door turned out to be more problematic than it should have been. She put the key in the lock and when she went to turn it, the key snapped in two. Staring down at the broken piece of metal in her hand just angered her. Why couldn't she get control of her strength? Would it always be like this? What if she tried to shake someone's hand, or hug someone? She could crush them. The more time that went on, the more of life's pleasures that were taken from her without her having any choice in the matter. She hated it.

Returning to the front desk, she tried to breathe deeply, tried to count to ten and back down to one, even tried thinking happy thoughts, to calm herself down before she spoke to anyone. But nothing worked. She couldn't conjure any happy thoughts at the moment. All she could think of was bared teeth, hideous breath, and blood. So much blood.

"My key broke in the lock." Mackenzie didn't wait in line. She didn't say excuse me. Her manners were simply gone and she really didn't care. They were lucky she was clenching and unclenching her fists to give them something to do because all she wanted them to do was crash through the stupid desk.

"Oh my! I am so sorry about that. Let me get you a new room and room key." The woman worked quickly, making the adjustment on her computer before handing over another key. "Room seven, just up the hall and to the right."

Mackenzie just nodded and turned to find her new room when she bumped right into the girl who never took her eyes off the floor. Before Mackenzie could force herself to apologize, the girl looked up with murder in her eyes. Her yellow green eyes.

"Watch where you are going!"

Mackenzie couldn't respond. It was as if cold water had been dumped on her head. All anger left her body but her heart continued to race, beating faster with a feeling of hope that she might not be alone after all.

"HELLO! What are you fucking deaf?"

"Your eyes? Have they always been that color?" Mackenzie whispered.

"What? Oh. Yes, yes, they have now leave me the fuck alone." The girl walked away quickly to find her group.

As if she had never found her cool, her muscles contracted, and her eyes narrowed as she watched the girl with the long blonde hair and slim figure retreat. Mackenzie took a deep breath and when that didn't work, she punched a hole through the wall in the hallway as she walked toward her room. She looked around hoping no one had spotted her and when she was sure she was in the clear, she ducked inside.

Chapter 8

As soon as Mackenzie had calmed herself down, she locked her room and headed for the back door of the large farmhouse. Unfortunately, she wasn't the only one with that idea.

The woman from the lobby was standing next to the door, putting on her jacket. While the woman looked to be in her early forties, she was extremely beautiful. Her light brown hair had been tucked into her jacket and when she reached up to pull it out, Mackenzie saw that the woman's hands were not soft and elegant as she imagined they would be. Seeing her standing there, in designer jeans and a killer coat, with hair that looked to be styled by a professional, she kind of expected to see perfectly manicured fingernails and maybe a ring or two. Instead, the hand had short fingernails with dirt lining the undersides of them without a single piece of jewelry in sight.

"Going out?" the woman asked, opening the door.

The weather was still cold, but it didn't matter. The beauty that was before her took her breath away. The scent of the earth and the moisture in the air drew her forward. Apparently, being a Werewolf really makes a girl appreciate nature.

"Yeah, thanks." The moment that Mackenzie walked through the door her skin began to hum as the fresh air and hard ground beneath her feet worked their way into her system. It took every ounce of self-control she had to not run through the grass to the trees to start exploring. It didn't matter what she was doing, as long as she wasn't trapped inside the walls of the house. It wasn't until she heard the footsteps behind her that she spun around with her adrenaline pumping, ready to strike if she needed to protect herself.

"Whoa, sorry about that. I just wanted to walk the trails in the park. I'm Margret." The woman held her hand out for her to shake and after a moment, Mackenzie took it in her own. Calm seeped into her skin, pushing back her protective nature. As much as she craved the calmness, alarm rang through her. It had to have been Margret that set her at ease, but it was such a sudden change. Pulling back, she stared at this woman, wondering what on earth she was. Was she a vampire? Werewolves were supposed to be able to sense them right? Was she a witch? Somewhere she read that Werewolves were magic and magic could feel other magic. Or was she another Werewolf?

"Mackenzie. Excuse me." Mackenzie took a harsh right as they entered the tree line following one of three paths laid out. Hoping the woman took the hint and didn't follow, she stayed the course. Once she felt she was far enough away, she looked over her shoulder. Margret was nowhere in sight. Taking in a deep breath of relief, she hoped she was just over reacting.

When she felt she was far enough from the entrance, and certain that no one was close by, she ventured off the dirt path and into the thick forest. Large trees, each with its own unique scent, surrounded her. She was really beginning to get the hang of the sensory overload she gained with her change.

The quiet snapping of a twig was common, she had found, when out in the woods far from where people roamed. She was in the animal's territory and they made noises, disrupted the environment around them, and didn't care for her presence too much. But the twig snapping wasn't what caught Mackenzie's attention. Someone was out there, screaming and crying.

Mackenzie sprinted toward the sound. She had to help whoever it was, this far off the path they could be hurt or lost. She at least knew the way back. But when she reached a small clearing in the trees, and found the source of all the commotion, she wished she had never come.

"What the hell are you doing out here?" the bitchy girl from the house yelled without even turning around to look at Mackenzie.

"I heard all the noise, and thought someone might need some help. Sorry." Mackenzie turned to leave and heard the girl mumble something about "no one can help me now." Not knowing what to do, Mackenzie went back. Maybe she could find Margret and tell her where to locate the girl. Maybe Margret would know what to do. She really shouldn't care, the girl was a royal bitch and all, but no one should be alone when they are that upset. But finding the woman who she practically ran from just an hour before wasn't something a practical person would do. But was she even a person anymore? All she knew was that girl needed someone and it wasn't her. Unease settled in her. Mackenzie had always followed her gut instincts and she was questioning it. Looking back at the girl, and hearing her tormented cries, Mackenzie knew she had to find Margret to help her. She couldn't leave her like that without trying to help, no matter how much the two of them clashed.

She could remember every tree she passed and when she didn't recognize the look of one, she stopped and took a deep breath in through her nose. The scent led the way back.

Once Mackenzie found the main trail, she ran. She was pushing herself to run faster and harder than she had in the past. So fast that she had underestimated the time it would take her to slow down and ran right into Margret

"Oh! Sorry!" Mackenzie took a few steps back to give the woman some room. Margret just offered the same motherly smile she gave to the others in the lobby.

"It's not a problem. It's really beautiful out here, isn't it?" Margret took in a deep breath and looked around with wondrous awe. "I love being in nature.

It's like it is part of me. It calls to me. What about you?"

It was as if she read Mackenzie's mind earlier and that didn't sit well with her. "Yeah, something like that. But look, I ran into that girl you came with. She's off the path and seems to be pretty upset. I was worried about her. I think you might want to go find her."

"Analise? Of course." Margret huffed a little in annoyance, like this was nothing new. "You mind telling me which way to go?"

Mackenzie took the next few minutes trying to explain how to find the clearing. A few times, she had to stop herself from giving details that included the special scent of the trees or leaves, or decomposing materials on the forest floor. Margret thanked her and left in the direction that Mackenzie had pointed.

For a group of people she had tried to avoid, she sure was having plenty of encounters with them.

~*~

Surprisingly, Mackenzie slept well that night, better than she had in the month since she learned her new fate. There were a few times before she fell asleep that she thought she heard someone outside her door, but when she opened to look, no one was there. She chalked it up to her increased paranoia leading up to the full moon.

With just one day left until the full moon, Mackenzie thought she ought to eat as much as possible. Perhaps a full stomach would limit the amount the wolf hunted.

A girl could hope.

The dining area inside the house was really homey. Everyone sat at two large tables that could hold sixteen each. Plates of eggs, waffles, bacon, sausage, fruit, potatoes, and every breakfast condiment you could think of, covered the tables. The food was served family-style. When each platter emptied, it was immediately replaced by a full one. When each plate passed Mackenzie, she took at least two servings worth. She ignored all the questioning looks and just dug in.

When she looked around the room and spotted the three people she couldn't seem to shake, she was in shock. They all had taken plates full of food that made hers look like a child's serving. When the man looked her direction, she was caught staring. Looking down at her plate quickly, she tried to hone her new skills and listen to the conversation coming from that side of the room. Blocking out the other noise was harder than she thought. She could easily hear everything in the room, but concentrating on one specific thing, that was not directly in front of her, was a challenge.

With a few moments of practicing on people closer to her, and slowly farther away with every conversation she eavesdropped on, her ears finally were able to pick up on Margret, Analise, and the man. She still didn't know his name, and with as much of her attention as he drew, that was probably a good thing.

"Stop staring, Geoff! I swear it's like you have never seen a pretty girl before." Analise's voice whispered.

"Now, now. Leave him be. If he is finally interested in someone, even if she isn't the one, he is more than allowed to look. It's good for men to explore their options. What would you say if we told you to ignore all the boys you might be interested in?" Margret chimed in.

"You did. If you remember correctly, I had a perfectly good boy back home. Then THIS happened and I had to come with you." This time Analise wasn't whispering. Her voice had risen to a level that was just barely below shouting and Mackenzie had a feeling that she wasn't going to stop there.

"Ana. Chill. The. Fuck. Out." Geoff said slowly, enunciating each word through gritted teeth.

Analise's chair flew out from behind her, screeching against the floor as she stood. Her hands slammed down against the table and she shot a death glare at Geoff.

When Analise realized everyone had stopped eating and was watching her, she turned and left the room. Whispers filled the air in her wake, and it became too hard for Mackenzie to block out the other noise. She decided she had heard enough of their family drama. She instantly felt guilty for eavesdropping and more than a little embarrassed that Geoff's family noticed the interactions between the two, even if they were from afar.

Politely placing her napkin on top of her plate, Mackenzie left the table, making sure to keep her eyes trained forward. She would not look at Geoff.

Okay, maybe just once.

~*~

Mackenzie packed her bag and headed back out to the trails. She was determined to keep to herself. What better way than to familiarize herself with the woods she hoped would keep the wolf occupied and away from wandering humans. Any sane person would not wander the dark forest in the middle of the night, but there were some who thought camping in freezing temperatures was a good idea. Her goal was to explore and identify any campgrounds. If she spotted any, she would turn around and go the opposite direction, to find a place that would allow her to wolf out with the least amount of damage.

A few hours into her hike, she spotted what looked to be an old campsite, but smelling a bit and checking the fire pit told her no one had been there in at least a few nights. Hopefully, they had moved on, but just in case, she turned around and left the trail as soon as she saw a break in the trees.

When the sun had set, she pulled her flashlight out of her bag and after 30 minutes, she left the woods that called to her so strongly. The steps that led up to the wrap around porch groaned under her feet. She couldn't help but think how she agreed with them— groaning was the only way to express how she felt returning to the house. She had seen a rocking chair on her way out and she wanted to sit and rock and enjoy the cold air on her too hot skin. Too bad, it was already occupied.

"Should you really be out in the woods after dark?" Geoff asked, his dark brown eyes penetrating her yellow-green ones. His question and stare annoyed her. Who did he think he was?

"Should you really be talking to a stranger like you are her father?" Her irritation was evident in her tone, but her body language ensured her message was received how she intended. Her arms crossed over her chest, her hip cocked to one side and her eyes narrowed.

"Hey, I meant no harm. There are just a lot of dangers that lurk the woods when the sun sets. A girl like you might want to be careful." Mackenzie scoffed at his statement. She WAS one of those dangers or at least she would be by the next night.

"A girl like me can take care of herself. I have since I was little." Mackenzie wanted out of the conversation and away from the devastatingly handsome man before her, but looking at the door of the house, and imagining going inside was torture. Instead, she took the steps back down and sat on the bottom one.

She tried to focus on the sounds of the night. The wind blowing through the trees. The skittering of whatever bug hid beneath the house to try and hide from the winter's chill. The few animals that roamed at night. But all she could hear was the fast heartbeat and breathing of the man behind her.

Why did she have to be so aware of him? So aware that she knew when he stood and moved closer to her. Aware that with every step down he took, her skin erupted in goose bumps, and aware of the heat he put off when he sat down beside her.

"Can I help you?" she asked, hoping to put him off with her chilled demeanor.

"Nope, I just like being close to nature. Something about being trapped inside a wooden box, no matter how big, doesn't feel right sometimes. Know what I mean?"

She did know what he meant. It was as if he read her mind. But she would never admit it to him. Just one more night and she would leave and find a new place to stay for a few weeks. Maybe pick up a little side job, if possible, to replenish some of her funds before the next full moon. "Nope."

Mackenzie stood up and climbed the stairs slowly. Why did he have to be so nosey? Why couldn't he have left her alone out there? Now she had to go up to her room just to escape the pull he had on her.

Her room was so closed up. It made her feel as though she were suffocating the minute that she opened her door. She ran to her window and threw it open before going back and closing the door behind her. Pulling a chair under her windowsill, she sat and pressed her forehead against the screen. When that wasn't good enough and her irritation took over, she punched through it, sending the mesh and metal to the ground. Mackenzie leaned out the window, resting her elbows on the frame and her head in her hands. That was how she fell asleep.

~*~

Mackenzie's eyes fluttered open the next morning, revealing at least ten feet of empty space before the ground. Jumping back, with one hand to her hammering heart, and the other gripping the windowsill for dear life, she vaguely remembered breaking the screen the night before. She was horrified at her actions. Her impulses were beginning to turn her into a delinquent! Who was she kidding? Running through the woods killing innocent animals was a precursor to being a psychopath. She should hope for delinquent.

Dashing out of her room and down the stairs, she slipped outside and snuck around the building to find the screen. Maybe she could throw it back up and into her room without anyone noticing? Only, the screen wasn't there.

Mackenzie cursed under her breath. She didn't have the cash to replace or repair the damn thing. Maybe if she went in and apologized and offered to work it off they would let her? Walking back around the house, talking to herself, practicing what she would say, she was startled by a little chuckle coming from the other side of the stairs that led to the porch.

She knew instantly that it was Geoff. She could feel the change in the air around her and she could (unfortunately) smell him. She had gotten a good whiff the night before when he sat next to her. The scent of cut grass, and the aroma of pure man, both penetrated her so deeply, it engrained itself into her memory.

"What is so damn funny?" He stood walking around the steps to stand in front of Mackenzie with a cocky grin on his face. It may or may not have been dazzling, not that she cared.

"You. First, you throw your screen to the ground, then you sleep half way hanging out your window, and now you talk to yourself, thinking you got busted. You really think I wouldn't have heard you? The porch is seriously just ten feet around the corner."

He had a point and she knew it. But if she hadn't been caught by the owner, where was the screen. That's when she realized that he must have moved it.

"Where is it?"

"Where's what?"

"You know what. Where is it?"

"I don't know what you are talking about."

He was smirking. She was pissed. He thought it was a big joke and she wanted to wring his neck.

"You know damn well what. The fucking screen. Give it back now! I need to put it back. Why do you even care?" She was so angry she was shaking. Her eyes narrowed and she could feel her fingernails slicing through her palm where her fists were balled up.

"So they can see that it was broken instead of just thinking the last person who stayed in that room did something to it? You put a broken screen back, and they will know you broke it. There is no screen and they will just think you never opened your window to see it. It is really cold out after all. Who in their right mind opens their window when the weather is near freezing?"

Irritation flowed through her blood like lava. Not only had he insulted her, but he was right and that just pissed her off more. He helped her and she never asked for it. She never asked for anyone's help.

"Whatever." It was a lame response, but it was all she could come up with. She turned and walked away from him and into the house just to run straight into Margret.

Margret opened her mouth to speak but even before she could get a word out, Mackenzie said, "Geoff's outside," then pushed passed her.

It was a bad start to what she knew would be a bad day ending with a worse night. When she got to her room, she flung herself onto the bed and stared at the ceiling for what felt like hours. Maybe if she stayed in one place, she would keep her temper, her strength, and her emotions in check. Her skin itched with the need to be outdoors, but she willed it to shut the hell up, especially when there was a certain infuriating man wandering about.

Except, the longer she laid there, the more her mind had the chance to wander to dark places. What did she look like as a wolf? Was she a full animal, or because she was bitten, was she half-human, half-animal? Not one of the articles or books or websites she found on Lycanthropy had the same information. Not one detail was corroborated in all documents. Would she wake up in the morning covered in blood again? Would she be able to clean up before coming back to her room or should she just check out and hide her bag away, hoping that the wolf wouldn't tear into it?

Her bag had remained in tact the last time, so she decided checking out would be best. No one would see her covered in blood and ask questions she couldn't and wouldn't answer.

Packing her belongings back into her bag, what little of them she had, she left her room and headed for the front desk. The children who had been chasing the poor cat were standing quietly beside their parents in a short line, waiting to speak with the woman at the desk.

"Hi." The little girl waved at her, but her energy from the day before was gone.

"Hi," Mackenzie smiled brightly at her, hoping to cheer her up. She didn't know what was wrong, but seeing small children sad always made her heart hurt. It reminded her of her own sad childhood.

"We have to leave. I don't want to."

"This place sure is nice, but don't you miss your own bed and your toys?"

"We're moving. I don't know where my stuff is. Mommy said it's on the truck." Mackenzie knew exactly what the little girl was feeling. They moved around many, many times in her childhood. Before her father got locked up, they moved constantly to keep him from being arrested. After the police caught him, they still moved constantly because her mother wasn't able to hold down a job and they had to go wherever she could find work.

"I moved when I was little, too. It can be scary. Anything that changes can be scary. But you know what? There can be a lot of good to come with change."

"Like what?"

"Well, were there any mean kids at your old school?" Mackenzie waited for a minute and the little girl nodded her head. "Well, you won't have to see them ever again. They can't be mean to you from far away."

The little girls eyes began to open wider and a smile played at her lips. She was almost there. Mackenzie just had to push a little more.

"And is there anything you have wanted to do before? Or maybe other people thought you could only do one thing but you really want to do something else? Like when I was little, before I moved, I really wanted to play softball but the team was full and everyone told me to play basketball instead. I was okay at basketball, but I wanted to try something new. When I got to my new school, I tried out and made the softball team."

"I like math. I heard some schools have math clubs. My old one didn't. Do you think the new one will have it?" Finally, a full-blown smile filled the girls face. Mackenzie's heart melted for her and a stray tear slipped from her eye.

"If they don't, maybe you can ask a teacher about starting one." Before Mackenzie knew what was happening, the little girl threw herself into Mackenzie's arms, hugging her. Smiling at being able to help the girl, Mackenzie wrapped her arms around her, and hugged her back.

"OUCH!" The girl screamed and Mackenzie automatically let her go. The parents turned so quickly and her mother scooped her up while her father approached with fierceness in his eyes that you only see when a protective animal sees their baby in danger.

"I'm sorry! I didn't mean to hurt her. She hugged me. I was just hugging her back."

"Stay away from her. I don't care if she did hug you, you should have backed away. What kind of sick freak are you, hurting little girls?" She could hear his blood thrumming through his veins. His breathing had increased and his nostrils were flaring with every breath he took. His aggressive position did not help her keep her cool. In fact, she lost it completely.

Mackenzie stood abruptly. Taking two steps forward, she went toe-to-toe with a man who had at least two inches on her, staring him in the eyes.

"It was an accident. I apologized. I suggest you back up. NOW!" Mackenzie could feel a growl in her chest begin to rumble forward, just as the man lifted his hands to push her out of his way. Before he was able to connect with her, Geoff stepped in, pulling the man in another direction while Margret placed her hands on Mackenzie's shoulder.

Whirling around to glare at the woman who just squashed her chance to beat the shit out of the man willing to lay hands on a woman, she stopped short. When their eyes connected, she was able to calm down. She began to breathe slower and was able to think about what had almost happened. In that moment, it didn't matter that Margret forced the calming presence upon her. All that mattered was that it worked.

Everyone in the lobby was staring at them. She was thankful that the children had been ushered out by their mother and had not witnessed the argument. Dropping her head into her hands, she let out a small whimper. That was her best attempt at not crying because she had lost control yet again. It was her fault. She tried to help, tried to have contact with someone, and ended up hurting them and almost hurting someone else. She knew then that she had to keep moving as a lone wolf.

"Mackenzie..." Geoff spoke softly, attempting to comfort her but she didn't deserve his comfort. She deserved to feel the guilt and the sorrow.

Chapter 9

Mackenzie turned and ran from the farmhouse, throwing her key to the desk as she passed. She knew she should stop and ask for a refund for her remaining night, but couldn't afford to break down and lose control around people again.

The grass, brittle from the winter, crunched beneath her feet with every step she took toward the cover of the trees. She had always been faster than most. It's what made her an asset to any team she played on, either softball or basketball, but since the change, she was more than just an above average runner. She was FAST. The weight of her bags would hinder a normal person, but they were feather light to her. She realized this when she needed to flee, she was able to do so with ease.

When she broke through the tree line that led to the cleared patch where she had found Analise the other day, she threw herself to the ground. While running at top speeds didn't wear her out, she was winded. She also felt the familiar tingle that meant her body was healing itself from something. Studying her arms and feeling her face proved that while her heart and lungs could stand up to the forest, her skin wasn't so agreeable.

She hadn't even felt the cuts and scratches when she had gotten them. Could the adrenaline pumping through her have helped with that? Mackenzie really didn't know, and not for the first time, she wished she could find the asshole that bit her to explain some of the ins and outs of this new life of hers.

Mackenzie lay on her back in the middle of the circle for the rest of the day and into the night. She had been snacking on the energy bars and beef jerky she had brought until she couldn't stand to eat anymore. When she began to feel a hum under her skin, she knew the transition was about to begin. She stood and removed her clothing.

A crack came from the tree line followed by what sounded like a sharp intake of breath, but before Mackenzie could even respond, the moon had reached its peak. The light danced on her skin as she fell to the ground in agony.

The wolf rose from the ground on high alert. Something was out there. Sniffing the air, her fur stood on end and a snarl escaped. Taking one cautious step after another, she followed the noise and the scent of another. The familiarity of the smell told her to be wary, but the scent of blood, fresh flowing blood, distracted the beast. Forgetting all about what lay behind the trees in front of her, the wolf dashed off in search of the hunt.

The wolf didn't even take the time to notice what animal lie in front of her. All that mattered was it was warm and slow enough for her to capture it within her teeth. Ripping the flesh from her kill, she heard another noise. Turning her head ever so slowly, a growl permeating from her chest, she spotted another.

It was large, larger than her, and all black. As it took two steps forward, Mackenzie latched onto her now unrecognizable kill and dragged it two steps back. All the while letting the stranger know, in no uncertain terms, this was hers.

The black wolf dropped its head, but still kept its eyes on her, then its front legs, followed by its hind legs until in was laying down. Tearing off a final chunk from her kill, Mackenzie wolf bolted in the opposite direction.

More than once, she spotted the black wolf. Each time her hackles rose and growls rumbled in warning, but it never approached her.

In an instant, the watching wolf became more than a tolerance. The scent that echoed through her body was one she couldn't ignore. Howling, declaring her dominance in the blood that called to her, she ran. Knocking down trees and crushing anything that lay in her path, she made it to her meal.

A thin layer of material covered the warm body whose blood made Mackenzie wolf's body vibrate with need did nothing to protect it. Her claws ripped through the material as if it were made of tissue, the scream that laced the air of the forest was cut short as her teeth latched on.

~*~

The sun rose and light poured onto Mackenzie's face. Blinking and holding her hand up to shield her eyes, she was able to see the blood. *Oh God, not again.* Looking away from her outstretched hand was hard; keeping herself from vomiting at the site that lie around her was impossible.

Rolling over onto her stomach, she pulled herself up to her knees as she wretched. The vomit that flowed from her mouth was red. More proof that the destruction and utter terror that she sat in was her doing.

Scraps of fabric covered her and a stray hand lay beside her. She had killed someone. She was a murderer. She was a monster. Mackenzie stood, desperately looking around for something to tell her who it was. Man or woman? Adult or...child?

Before she found the answer to her question, the trees around her rustled. As if her feet were frozen to the ground, she couldn't move. She whipped her head to the tree line, and to her utter horror, Geoff stepped through. Naked.

Chapter 10

Mackenzie was too shocked at what she was seeing to cover herself. Geoff stepped toward her with his hands in the air, as if in surrender. When she saw him look around at the carnage that lay heart her feet, the floodgates opened and she collapsed, sobbing hysterically.

It was only when she felt a hand on her back that she moved, and she moved quickly. She was still naked and this perfect stranger just happened to approach her in the same way. That was when it hit her—why the hell was he naked?

"What is going on?" She thought back on their brief interactions, all of them with Geoff and his family. It was as if the pieces to a puzzle were falling together and she could finally see the whole picture. "Are you...like me?"

"Yes."

Mackenzie wasn't sure if she was relieved she wasn't alone or scared out of her mind. The only other werewolf she had met, had been in wolf form, and it was a vicious beast. As if he could feel her apprehension, he moved back a little more.

"Did I do this?" she couldn't look at him when she asked. She couldn't look anywhere but at the hand. The only piece of the person left behind, at least the only piece recognizable as a person. Bones were broken into small bits. Some looked a lot like her old black lab's rawhide bones she would get him for Christmas. The ground was covered with blood so thick it could have been painted on.

"Yes." Geoff said without a hint of apathy. It was as if it were just a fact of life. But if he knew she did it, why didn't he stop her? Did he try?

"Yes, that's it? Tell me. Tell me what I did. I need to know. Why can't I remember? Why the fuck can't I control it?" She was screaming. She stood and began pacing around the area, picking up rocks or sticks and throwing them with all her strength, shattering wood into a million splinters.

"Because you're new." This time it wasn't Geoff's voice that pulled her from her rant. Instead, it was Margret. When she turned and saw the elegant woman covered in dirt and leaves without a stitch of clothing on her, she knew the truth. They were all Werewolves and for some reason she had a feeling it wasn't all that coincidental that they found her out in the woods.

"Where is Analise?"

"She is cleaning off, the blood bothers her. She's new, too. Only been turning for four cycles now."

"What is happening to me?" the words came out in a whisper, she didn't want to know, but she needed to. "Will I ever be able to control it?"

"There is so much happening inside of you right now, Mackenzie. So much, and I promise to explain everything in detail if you want me to, but basically? Right now, your body is adjusting to its new form. It's like mixing hot and cold. You have to do it slowly, to give it time to adjust without completely exploding. Have you ever poured boiling water into an ice-cold glass? The results aren't pretty. You have to temper it first. Slowly introduce the hot to the cold. Your human body is the glass. The wolf is the boiling hot liquid. You're in the tempering stage. That's why you have no control, no memories of your time as a wolf."

Mackenzie stayed quiet for a long moment. She looked back and forth between the two and knew she needed them. They could teach her what she needed to know, about what she was and who she was going to become. But why hadn't they told her sooner? Why wait until after the change? She knew she needed them, but she wasn't sure she trusted them.

Analise came through the way Margret had come with a scowl on her face.

"Whoa, looks like I'm not your biggest issue this cycle, huh, Margret?" Mackenzie glared at her, felt her body shake with anger, which quickly turned to utter despair. She was right. She was a huge problem and she needed to be locked in a cage. She needed to be put down like a rabid dog. She needed to be a lot of things and a fucking Werewolf wasn't one of them.

"Analise! ENOUGH! We have all had bad cycles, you included!" Analise put her hands up in front of her in mock surrender.

"Geez, can't take a joke? You gotta lighten up or this whole wolfy business is going to drive you insane." *How could she be so nonchalant about the whole thing?* Mackenzie was appalled. Her life was crumbling around her and this girl makes it into a huge joke.

"There is nothing funny about this!" Mackenzie motioned around her, yelling at Analise. "This is murder! I killed whoever it was and I don't even remember it! It could have been a kid or a mother or a preacher! They didn't deserve this!"

Turning her back on the group she began walking around quickly, picking up any piece she could that belonged to her victim. Victim. It was hard to even think the word, but that is what this person was—a victim. She had turned from the victim into the perpetrator.

"What are you doing?" Geoff asked, looking at her puzzled.

"I'm not just going to leave them like this! The least I can do is bury them. Otherwise, some other animal is going to come out here and cart off each piece as some treasure meal. Leave the blood and the tent so when their family sends someone out, they will know something happened and get to say goodbye, but

I refuse to let this body be any more destroyed than it is now."

Without having any tools lying around, she began to dig with her fingers. After a few minutes, there were two more sets of hands helping her. Margret and Geoff just looked at her with pity.

"What? Don't feel sorry for me. Feel sorry for them. They died and I did it. I don't deserve any sympathy."

"Mackenzie, that isn't true. We all have a hard go of it to begin with, but many Werewolves don't have to go alone. There are packs, families that look out for each other. Help each other. You don't have to be a lone wolf."

When the hole was big enough, they began putting the bloody bits and pieces in. The dirt fell in on top of the body with the help of Geoff and the others just stood, watching at least part of the evidence of the night before disappear from sight.

After cleaning up and dressing, they all walked back to the trail together in silence. Mackenzie had so many questions but she just didn't know where to start. Looking at her companions, she figured she would start off with an easy question to get the ball rolling.

"So, why did my and Analise's eyes change, but yours didn't? I mean, that is if her being born with them was a lie and all, which I'm pretty sure it was.

Not that I really know if she is lying but the coincidence is just—"

"You two were bitten, we were born. When you are born as a Were, your eyes only change when you do." Margret interrupted her rambling.

"So only at the full moon?"

"No. Born wolves can change whenever they want. Bitten wolves can only change at the full moon for a while. Eventually, when they gain more control, they can change whenever they want to as well. Part of the whole 'little at a time to keep your human body intact' thing."

"Tempering, right. Can you tell me more about the packs?" Mackenzie really did want to know about them, she just hoped that Margret would tell her about their pack in particular. Margret smiled that motherly smile at her, tipping her head to the side a bit.

"Of course. Our pack is large. We have seventeen living with us in Montana, then another ten in California, and twelve in Alaska. I travel between them all throughout the year. Lucky for you, we got an anonymous tip about a pup—or newly bitten— that seemed to need some guidance. We found Analise at the last cycle, and then just happened to run into you at this one. You know, the Montana house has room for one more."

"For Analise, right?" She shouldn't expect this woman to just offer her up a place to stay. Her luck wasn't that good.

"Analise is going to the California house. It was the only way to get her to agree to come with us."

"Screw snow; give me surfer guys any day!" Analise hooted from the end of the line they were walking in. Mackenzie laughed a little. Her first smile since before the incident with the little girl the day before.

"So what have you been doing for the last month? Why not just go back right away?"

"It took a while to convince her. First to the house, then a promise that I wouldn't be staying there," Geoff said, slightly offended.

"Oh, where do you live?" She tried to be cool and collected like she didn't really care, all the while her insides were buzzing with the thought of possibly living in the same house. She tried to calm herself; there was no reason to get all girly about it. He wasn't going to be interested in her.

"Montana. Someone has to keep the boys from wreaking havoc in town."

Margret and Analise fell back and let Mackenzie and Geoff walk together. Their whispers started to fade as she listened to Geoff go on and on about the winter sports that he was sure she would love. Something about getting the aggression out in a safe and fun way.

"Snowboarding is great, and when you don't have to worry about breaking your neck, you can do all kinds of shit that most people can't. You should see the looks we get, half are in awe and the others are terrified we are going to kill ourselves."

"What about the girls?"

"What about them?"

"You said you have to keep the boys from wreaking havoc, what about the girls? With everything that's happened since I changed, I can't imagine the girls not causing trouble, too."

"Oh, they do, but it's different. Have you ever seen two best guy friends fight? They get into it, knock each other around, get bored, and find something to do. Usually something knuckle-headed that can get them in trouble outside the house. Girls? When they fight, it's emotional warfare. They don't bother with the getting past it by bonding over paint-balling a bowling alley."

"The boys paint-balled a bowling alley?"

"Sure did. They went out in the middle of the night, scaled the buildings surrounding it, and had a blast. When the sirens went off, they ran and since they never touched anything, and are fast as fuck, they never got caught. Margret was pissed. Made them volunteer to help clean up when the local college was doing a community service drive."

"Do you guys go to college?" Her hope was rising that she would be able to return to school someday. She really didn't want the label of drop out. Wasn't Werewolf enough?

"Some do, but only the ones with some years under their belt. Why? You want to go back to college?"

"Yeah, when the chances of me yelling at my professors or breaking desks is a thing of the past."

"I hate to say it, but those will always be possibilities. You can learn to control it, but we all have bad days."

The edge of the forest drew near, and Margret and Analise returned to their side. Mackenzie hadn't realized how long she and Geoff had been left alone to talk. The knowing grin on Analise's face was expected, but definitely not welcome. She tried to plead with the girl with her like-colored eyes to knock it off. She couldn't mess this up just because some boy made her feel safer than she had since her entire life had been turned upside down.

Chapter 11

The three pack members entered the farmhouse, leaving Mackenzie outside where she leaned against their car. She refused to go back in after the scene she caused with the little girl's father. But standing there alone, she couldn't help but try to search her mind for any small memory of the night before. Something had to have stuck. The more she tried, though, the more her head hurt.

I deserve the headache. Without warning, images flashed through her mind. The severed, gnawed on hand, the tent torn to shreds, the bloody remains being buried. Falling to the ground, she cried. She needed to be stronger. This was her life now. She had no control over what had happened in the past. She needed to look forward. She needed to learn everything she could about her new life and she needed to make it work. No more tears. She had to make shit work her whole life. She did it then. She could do it again.

Wiping the salty droplets from her face with her sleeve, she stood. The resolve she had coursing through her made her stand straighter, breathe easier. If her father taught her one thing before he was locked up, it was how to *appear* strong until you *were* strong. Appearance is everything. If you allow yourself to *look* weak, you will *be* weak. She would no longer be weak, no matter how long it took for her insides to catch up with her exterior.

Analise came down the steps first with the car keys and popped the trunk open. The girls loaded their bags before Analise looked to Mackenzie with a sad smile.

"What?"

"I wish I had known that I would meet you. It would be nice to actually have someone to talk to that is going through everything at the same time I am. I know I can be a bitch, and I don't apologize for it, but when they told me we had someone to find, I had no idea it would be another tempering pup. God, I hate that term, pup. I mean, I guess it fits, I am a bitch, and it's only gotten worse since the fucker bit me."

They both laughed at that before Mackenzie replied, "I know. It would be nice to know someone in the house. But, either way, we won't be alone anymore."

"Very true. Come on. Let's get in."

Mackenzie opened the back driver's side door, expecting Analise to take the back passenger side. When she slid into her seat, she looked up and saw that Analise had taken the passenger side, just not the back.

"Why are you up there? I thought we would sit together." Her heart pounded as she thought she would be stuck in the backseat with Geoff. Didn't she have enough to worry about without developing a crush?

"Nah, it's a long ride to the airport and I figure I will need some entertainment."

"Bitch." Mackenzie knew Analise wouldn't be offended. She was proven right by the accepting smile and wink sent back her way.

"Oh, look, lover boy is coming! Better get all those jitters out!" Analise trilled, dancing around in her seat before starting the elementary school kissing song.

"SHUT UP! What if he hears you?"

The doors opened and both Margret and Geoff got in. "Too late. Super hearing, remember?" Margret said with a smile.

Mackenzie couldn't bring herself to look up. No way would she let Geoff see her rattled by Analise's taunts.

To keep herself from doing anything stupid during the car ride, Mackenzie caught up on some much needed rest. The calmness that always surrounded her around these three (unless of course, she and Analise were about to tear each other apart) made sleep come easily.

When the car came to a halt, the sudden lack of movement jarred her awake. Geoff had apparently fallen asleep, too, using her has a pillow. His head balanced precariously on her shoulder. His mouth hung open and soft snores filled the car.

Looking to the front, hoping that Analise had somehow missed it, she was met with a big grin and a shiny camera.

"Tell me you didn't."

"Can't do that. I won't lie."

Mackenzie let out a little growl and shoved Geoff off her. He woke with a startle and sat looking around, muscles tensed as if in fighting mode.

"What happened? What is it?"

The girls in the car all laughed at him until Mackenzie realized her shoulder was wet. "EEW! GEOFF YOU DROOLED ON ME! YOU ARE A DAMN DOG, AREN'T YOU?"

That caused another round of laughter as they all climbed from the car. Geoff got all the bags and Margret turned the keys into the rental company. Walking over to the shuttle, Mackenzie's stomach dropped. She didn't have a credit card. She only had about a hundred and ten bucks left and she knew that wasn't going to be enough to get a ticket.

"Margret, how much is a ticket to Montana?"

"Why?"

"Um, so I can go with you?"

"Oh, silly girl, I already took care of that. You do want to be in my pack, right? As pack leader, that's my job. I take care of my kids. You're now one of them."

A sense of belonging fell over her. It was an odd sensation. She had always been an outsider, never really fitting in anywhere, not really. Sure, the high school teams tolerated her because she was good at what she did, but no one really liked hanging out with the convict's kid or the girl who killed the curve on the test. The more time she spent with Margret, Geoff, and Analise, the more she trusted them. She couldn't believe she had thought they had ulterior motives to begin with. They just wanted to help her.

"Thank you."

"You are very welcome."

Margret and Analise were going to be flying out to the California house after taking her and Geoff home. That sounded so strange to her, yet wonderful all at the same time. Analise couldn't stop talking about what she had been told of the house she would get to call home. Apparently, it was just north of Los Angeles and Analise was beside herself with joy. But before anything, they had to get to the Montana house. Montana had a LOT of trees. Mackenzie could see that much from the airplane.

"You will have plenty of places to run out here. The house is right in the middle of three national forests."

"Three?"

"That's right. I know how to pick locations. Many, many years of practice. When you live as long as we do, you learn a thing or two." Margret said with a smile and a pat on Mackenzie's shoulder.

"Wait, what does that mean?"

"What how to pick locations? It's easy, really."

"No, about living as long as we do?"

"Oh, right. I sometimes forget how little pups know when they weren't changed by someone who planned on sticking around. On average, a Werewolf's life is ten times that of humans."

"Wow."

"Yeah."

They didn't talk anymore on the plane. Mackenzie had a lot to take in. She would be living for a long time. Everyone she knew and loved would grow old and die and she would still look like a young woman.

It was that train of thought that brought her around to Geoff. How old was he? If he was born a Werewolf, has he been able to change since he was a baby? Is he some creepy old man hitting on a nineteen-year-old girl? He sure didn't look creepy, and nothing he had done so far would be even close to considered hitting on her. The disappointment in that did not go unnoticed and she chided herself for the thought.

The plane landed and four hours later, they arrived in Whitefish. It was a quaint little town with that same small town feel as the last place she stayed. The one where she killed and buried the camper. The town so small that everyone had to know everyone else and the citizens surely had gone looking for them already.

Shaking her head and chanting her new mantra, *I am strong. I am moving forward. I will not cry again,* she took in the sights. Geoff pointed out key locations—the coffee shop, the grocery store, the 'best pizza in town,' and the street that led to their house. There were very few houses along the way and they were spread out.

They pulled into the driveway where the house that stood before them was massive. It looked like a log cabin on steroids. It was three stories tall with a large wrap around deck on the second floor. A gigantic stone chimney adorned the front part of the house from the ground floor all the way up. Floor-to-ceiling windows filled most of the front space on the third floor. It could have been one of the sorority houses back at Harvard, no, one of the frat houses. Not the exterior of course, but the feel of the houses. The grandeur of them. The logs looked very rugged. Something that Mackenzie actually liked very much. The sorority houses were always so prim and proper and it drove her nuts. She wanted to go and plant some weeds in the yard just to fuss it up a little. She never did, but it would have been fun.

Snow covered the ground, and in the side yard, she could see a handful of guys throwing it around, trying to pelt each other.

Stepping out of the car, everyone in the vicinity stopped what they were doing and looked to Margret.

"Family meeting in fifteen minutes!" They all called out their understanding and began heading into the house. Mackenzie was marveled at how they listened to her, how they didn't question her or ask who the new girls were.

"Come on, we can get your stuff put into your room before the meeting," Margret said as Geoff ran off to the group of guys, picking up a handful of snow along the way. Before he even got close, he threw the packed ball and it sailed through the air, landing firmly against the back of some guys head.

"Sounds good. Thanks." Mackenzie picked up her bags and followed behind Margret, trying to remember the layout of the house as they passed by each room. A brief look into what she assumed was a living room, or maybe a den, looked to have a large TV and shelves full of either movies or video games. With the throng of men in the room, and the hooting and hollering she heard long after they passed, she assumed video games.

"The boys can get a little excited. Don't mind them. If anyone gives you any trouble, you let me know." Margret smiled looking back over her shoulder at Mackenzie toward the ruckus the boys were making.

"Thanks."

Mackenzie found her room on the third floor. The floor-to-ceiling windows bathed the room in sunlight, giving the amber walls a lovely glow. Although three bedroom suites adorned the room, each enjoyed plenty of space between them. This way, even though the girls shared a room, they wouldn't feel like they were living on top of one another.

"Teresa and Natalie are in this room. Teresa has been with us for almost four years and Natalie for the last three. They tend to... well, let's just say it takes a strong personality to room with them. But, I think you will be fine. You stood up to both Geoff and Analise, so I think you will be able to handle these two better than anyone else will. You have a couple minutes to check out the room, then come on down for the meeting. We will get you introduced to everyone and I will have the girls go over the house chores and rules with you. Okay?"

Mackenzie nodded and watched as Margret left the room, closing the door behind her. When she knew she was alone, she spun in a circle slowly, taking in her surroundings. Obviously, the bed by the massive window was hers and she was more than happy about that. She walked over to the bed, threw her bag on it, and gazed out the window. She could see for what felt like miles. Being on the third floor put her just about level with the tips of the tall trees across the narrow road. With the snow clinging to the trees and the setting sun hitting it just right, she felt like she was in the middle of a winter wonderland.

Sighing, she turned and looked at her new life. Just a month prior she was living a human life in a tiny apartment she had to work her butt off to keep. Here she was a Werewolf but at least she had the perk of an amazing house filled with people who can understand and help her. Accept her for who she is. She would give anything to go back to that apartment and to her life alone, but if she couldn't it wasn't a bad place to be.

The bed sank under her weight, but the mattress was pillow soft and Mackenzie couldn't help but lie back and stare out the window. Sadness flooded through her, and as the tears started to slip out of the corner of her eyes, she wiped them away, reminding herself that she would not cry anymore. She was strong. She would make the most of her new life and say goodbye to her past.

The door to the bedroom opened and two girls walked in, stopping short when they spotted Mackenzie. Sitting up, Mackenzie gave them a little wave and a half smile.

"So you must be the reason for the family meeting." A tiny red-headed girl, with slight blonde highlights, stepped forward with a small smile.

"That would be me. I'm Mackenzie." Mackenzie stood up and walked toward the girls. The second girl, a dark-skinned girl with beautifully shaped yellowish green eyes framed by the longest lashes Mackenzie had ever seen, jumped in place a little and when Mackenzie was within range ran toward her, hugging her tightly. Not sure of what to do, Mackenzie stood still, with her arms to her sides, and her eyes wide, looking at the other girl, hoping for some clue as to how to detach herself.

"Natalie! Chill out! You want to scare her away before she even unpacks?" Natalie quickly let go and backed up. Her face was flushed with embarrassment, and she mumbled an apology.

"Sorry about her. She hasn't quite gotten control of the emotions yet. Everyone conquers the stages differently. Teresa," She said as she offered her hand.

"We better get going. Margret doesn't like anyone to be late to family meetings," Natalie said and motioned toward the door. "Family meetings are at the dining room table."

The three girls left the bedroom and walked down all three flights of stairs. Mackenzie was instantly grateful when she found out the boys were all on the second floor and the girls on the third. If they made the kind of noise at night as they did earlier in the living room, she would never get any sleep.

The dining room was very large with three rectangular tables made out of what looked to be a red oak, pushed together to create one giant table with chairs around the perimeter. Nearly, every seat was full. Thankfully, they were not the last to arrive.

"Mackenzie, you'll sit beside me for this meeting. After today, you may sit where ever you like." Margret stood and pulled the empty chair out for her. Teresa smiled at her and took a seat next to a tall man. When he wrapped his arm around her and kissed her forehead, she knew that this "family" definitely did not have any dating policy. With a quick glance around the room, she wasn't sure if she was happy or sad at that. At least if it weren't allowed, she could give herself more reasons to avoid any feelings developing for Geoff.

When the last seats filled, Margret cleared her throat. The room fell silent and every pair of eyes was on her.

"Today's family meeting is in celebration of a new member joining our pack. This is Mackenzie Duncan. She was alone and confused, and we are just very grateful to have found her when we did. She was turned by a stray and has been tempering without any guidance. I hope you all will help her with any questions she may have, advice you may feel compelled to give, or listen if she needs to talk. Mackenzie has endured two cycles, and I hope before the next full moon that she will be better prepared. Let's all take a moment to welcome her to our home. Mackenzie, dear, please stand."

Margret touched her shoulder and she knew she had to abide. Being the center of attention was never her thing. She stood but looked to the table instead of at her fellow "brothers and sisters."

What surprised her was when she heard all the chairs screeching and looked up to see a line forming in front of her. One by one, each member came up and hugged her, welcoming her. It wasn't until the last member came up, that her heart beat frantically in anticipation of his arms around her. Geoff.

Unfortunately for her, she was surrounded by super hearing Werewolves and she got more than a few knowing grins. One of them just happened to be Geoff. With his arms around her, she felt him breathe in deeply, then whispered in her ear, "Don't worry, I have that effect on a lot of women."

His arms vanished and the heat he put off evaporated as he stepped away to take his seat. Margret smiled brightly at Mackenzie then she herself enveloped her in a hug. Despite her previous embarrassment, she truly felt like she found a home.

"Teresa and Natalie will show you around and explain the chore rotations. The girls will show you were my office is, but you are not to go in there unless you are requested by me. Do not let anyone in here try to pull a fast one. No one has the authority to send you into my office. They did that before, only it backfired since our pup didn't get in trouble, they did. Isn't that right, Max?" The glare Margret sent in Max's direction was playful, but his ashamed face told Mackenzie that when it happened, she was not in a playful mood.

The meeting was dismissed and a few people hung around to say a final word to Mackenzie before going back to whatever it was they were doing.

Teresa and Natalie took her by the arm and led her down the hall. Not only did she learn the ins and outs of the house, but she was filled in on all the members as well.

Chapter 12

Before even opening her eyes, Mackenzie could hear the bickering between Natalie and Teresa. In the two weeks she had been staying at the house, she learned quickly that she didn't need an alarm. Natalie was very much an early riser and was up by seven sharp every morning. Teresa, however, was very much NOT a morning person and preferred to stay up late, sometimes not turning her light off until close to three in the morning. The bickering and the noise level became Mackenzie's alarm clock.

At night, Natalie slept like a log, there was very little that could wake the girl up. Teresa was able to shower and blow dry her hair, watch TV, and through it all, Natalie snored away. However, Teresa was the opposite. The minute Natalie began getting dressed, the noise would wake Teresa up. Mackenzie was just glad she knew how to pretend to sleep when she didn't want to get dragged into what seemed to be a continuous feud.

The noise level at night did bother her. She actually asked Teresa to keep it down on the third night when she worked up the courage to do so. She was, after all, the intruder. The conversation went well and since then Teresa had tried to keep it down. Mackenzie was used to early mornings and she could never hear Natalie anyway. It was the arguing that sometimes grew to screaming that usually woke her.

When the crash of something against the wall sounded through the room, Mackenzie decided to stop pretending to sleep. She had found that while Natalie hadn't conquered her overly active happy feelings, Teresa hadn't conquered her temper. If it escalated any further, she might be separating a fight instead of just an argument.

"Can you two knock it the hell off? T, if you had just let her get dressed instead of yelling, you could be back to sleep by now. Nat, if you had taken your stuff into the bathroom last night, you wouldn't have woken her up. How is it that you two have been rooming together for so damn long and haven't figured this shit out yet?" Mackenzie's rant came without even getting out of bed. She sat up, rubbed her eyes, and then stared at the two who stood there, looking at her, completely dumbfounded.

"Whatever, I'm going back to bed." Teresa crawled back under her covers and proceeded to block out the light with her pillow.

"I'm going for a run, want to come?" Natalie asked with a smile. At least she didn't hold the little rant against her.

"Nah, tomorrow for sure, though. It's been a while since I ran just for fun." *As opposed to for my life or in fear,* she added mentally.

"Sure thing," Natalie whispered when a groan came out from under the pillow of Teresa's bed. Rolling her eyes, Mackenzie stood and gathered her things to get ready in the bathroom. Once she was awake, there was no going back to sleep and she knew it. It was her day to dust and vacuum the living room, which as it turned out, was a completely different room than where the boys were playing their games. The living room had a television and a big sectional couch as well as a wall filled with bookshelves. Pictures adorned the walls, all of the pack members from each of the house locations were in one photo or another. She hadn't looked at each one in detail, mostly just the ones with Geoff. She hated that she searched out those specifically.

Padding down the stairs, she could hear that some of her new family was awake, but most were still sleeping. When she got to the living room, she decided to wait on the vacuuming out of respect for those still in bed and grabbed a dust rag.

She took extra care to dust the pictures with Geoff in them. She told herself it was because they were extra dusty, but the throat clearing in the background told her she was busted ogling again. She couldn't help it. It was as if he called to her.

"I'm pretty sure my face hasn't been as dust-free since that picture was put up."

"There was a smudge. I was trying to get it off."

"Want some help?" Before she could say no, he had grabbed a rag and started dusting at the other end. In no time, they met in the middle and the job was complete.

"Thanks." Mackenzie took the rag from his hand and put them in the cabinet below the bookshelves. When she stood, she saw one of the old tomes with the title Lycanthropy.

Mackenzie fingered the spine, wondering if she would look silly opening it up. She was surrounded by Werewolves and had yet to ask anyone any more questions. Not even Teresa and Natalie, who had become her best friends in the house.

"That's a good one. Some of it isn't actually rubbish. But if you want to know the facts, you should really ask someone. There isn't a single book that gets it all right."

"Why not? Why wouldn't one of use write one? I mean, it would be super helpful to be able to Google 'Why am I turning into a hairy beast once a month' and not have a bunch of PMS Websites pop up."

Geoff laughed loudly, his eyes crinkling as his head fell back. The flutters in her stomach that were always present when he was around magnified and she had to look away.

"Because we want people to think we're myths. Can you imagine what the world would do if they knew we were real? Every unsolved murder, every violent crime, everything would be blamed on us.

They would want to study us. Hell, they might even force people to change by injecting our wolf saliva into their blood stream. It wouldn't be pretty."

Geoff moved to the couch and sat down, looking to Mackenzie as if he were inviting her to join him. She finally moved her feet in his direction when he patted the cushion impatiently. Looking back toward the hallway, as if she were actually contemplating leaving, she sighed and sat down, on the other end of the couch. She was hoping the distance would keep his grass and pure man essence from penetrating her senses and turning her into a giggling fool.

"Seriously? I won't bite. Well, at least not for another two weeks. Unless you want to see me change on demand. Some girls like that, I hear." He grinned as if he were the funniest thing in the world, but Mackenzie just couldn't bring herself to find the humor in the beast. The last time she bit—her whole body shuddered as she remembered the resulting carnage.

"I'm good here."

"Fine. Then I think I will move over there. I really don't want to have to yell." Geoff stood and moved his seat about two feet from where Mackenzie sat. "There. Now, ask away."

"I don't even know where to start." She really didn't. She had been studying mythology for years, but she was so confused about what to believe and what to chalk up to human fears and imagination.

"How about the first thing that pops into your head. We don't have to go in any specific order." The first things that popped into her head were all questions about Geoff. Not the impression she wanted to give off, but damn it, she couldn't help herself.

"How old are you? Like for real. Margret said we live a lot longer than humans."

"We do. Ten times their life spans. I'm afraid if I tell you, you will want to run away. Think I'm some old man."

"Yeah well, I guess you just have to tell me and find out if you're right or not."

"I'm two hundred forty."

"Holy shit."

"Are you running yet?"

"No. Just damn. Two hundred and forty! But you look like a young man. How the hell does that work?"

"It's the healing properties of our blood. The constant healing keeps us looking younger longer. I appear to be in my twenties, but I have been around a long time. Within our pack, you will find a wide range of ages, from you, being the new baby in the house, all the way to our pack leader. Margret is over four hundred years old."

"Wow. What about kids? Do you have any? I mean, two hundred and forty years is a long time to go without starting a family, or you know, accidentally starting a family."

"Why, Mack, I think I should blush! Are you asking if I have had the company of a woman in my bed?"

Geoff may have said he should blush, but she was the one who flamed red. She hadn't meant to ask that. Who would assume he hadn't been with someone in that long!

"No! Of course not! Forget it, never mind."

"I'm just giving you a hard time. No, I have no children. I have enough responsibility keeping the pups in line."

"But, I mean, if there are born Weres, it is possible though, right?" She hadn't realized how badly she wanted a future family until that moment. There were no small children in the house and if the ages were as diverse as Geoff said, did that mean there were no parents?

"It is possible for some. Born Weres can have children with each other and every offspring would carry the Were gene. If a male, born or bitten, impregnated a human woman, the child wouldn't be a Were. They would have extra abilities, like faster reflexes, better hearing, and eyesight, things like that. A male human can impregnate a born female Were and the baby has a fifty-fifty chance of carrying the gene. Female bitten wolves are barren. They can get pregnant, but when they turn each month... it just can't survive that. " He wouldn't look at her. Mackenzie was glad for it, too. The tears in her eyes were threatening to overflow. She could never be a mother. She would never have children. Another thing to add to her list of things she lost because she walked down the wrong fucking path.

"But why?" her voice was barely above a whisper, "Why can a born have children but I can't?"

"It's in the DNA. When a woman is born a Werewolf, her body is different on a cellular level. It has something to do with the uterus and its shape and durability. When a woman is bitten, it doesn't make her exactly like a born. I'm not sure why."

Mackenzie sat in silence. A minute passed. And then another and another.

"Are you all right?" His voice caressed her before she felt his hand on her shoulder. She couldn't answer him. Truth was she wasn't really sure if she was okay or not yet. She knew she wasn't able to verbally answer without losing it.

"Gimme a minute." Standing and moving over to the bookshelf, she took a few deep breaths, hoping to calm herself down. When that didn't work, she started grabbing whatever was within reach and throwing it across the room. She heard things smash, and cursing coming from the hallway as her antics brought other members from the house to see what the commotion was. The only thing she heard that helped stop her tirade was Geoff's voice telling them all to go away, to give her time to let out her emotions.

When she stopped throwing things, the empty bookshelf became a resting place for her forehead, and a really good place to hide her face from Geoff.

"Better?"

"Actually, yes. So, never? I can never have kids?"

"I'm sorry."

"So then why the hell do I still have to have a damn period each month?"

"Um...maybe I should get Margret."

Even through the harsh reality of the situation, she had to laugh a little at his awkwardness. Apparently, his many years on the earth still didn't desensitize him to that of a woman's natural biology.

"No, don't. I just, I need to sit." Mackenzie pushed away from the shelf, stepping over the disaster that lay on the floor, and sat back on the couch. When Geoff sat next to her again, she didn't try to move away. When he grabbed her hand and gave it a supportive squeeze, she refused to read too much into it.

"Do you want to ask anything else? Or should we just maybe clean this up?"

"How about both?" She stood before he could answer and began collecting the books from the floor. As she arranged them back on the bookshelf, she heard Geoff leave the room and return a few moments later.

~*~

"So, are we it? I mean are there other people who turn into other animals besides wolves?" Mackenzie really was curious. She had read at one point that there were just as many shifters as there were animals. Some could even pick and choose what they turned into.

"You mean like people who can turn into dogs or cats or other people?" His voice gave off hints of humor, as if he wanted to laugh but didn't want to offend her in any way.

"Well, go ahead. Laugh it up. Until a few months ago, I thought Werewolves were a thing of make believe, too. Who's to say all the stories don't have meaning somewhere."

"Sorry, sorry. As far as I know, we are the only lycanthropes. There is no such thing as shifters, just Werewolves. We have been given many names over the course of humanity. We have been around just as long as they have. But the stories about people turning into anything other than a wolf? Well, those are just fairy tales."

"So, no vampires? Pixies? Angels? Demons?"

"Angels and demons are not my forte. As far as I know, the accounts of angels and demons come from humans doing amazingly good or amazingly evil things, with the help of a little magic they may or may not have figured out they can tap into. Some call them witches. All human, just with the ability to control the flow of magic that surrounds everything in this world. Vampires," he shuddered when the word escaped his lips, "they are very real, and we do not, under any circumstances, have anything to do with them. The idea of natural born enemies is very real. Mostly because their venom can kill us, and our saliva can kill them. It is the only real weapon to use against either Were or vamp, besides decapitation or stopping our hearts."

Mackenzie had stopped cleaning and just stared at him. She hadn't known any of that. She was kind of hoping that he would deny the existence of all other supernatural creatures she had read about, even if that hope wasn't well founded.

"Wow. So all this time, humans thought these creatures were just stories told to scare us, were real?"

"One, we are not creatures. Not like you are thinking. We, you and I and the rest of our pack, of our kind, are Werewolves. You need to try and accept that you're one of us, not a creature, not a monster, and definitely not a human. Two, many of the stories written are either made up or about one of the few who went off the deep end. We keep control of our own and if someone messes up so badly the humans begin talking about them, they are dealt with. Little red riding hood's big bad wolf? That was Michelangelo, and no, not the artist, he was banished from his pack. The humans hunted him down, just like in the original story. We have our own storybooks, if you are interested. The real stories behind the humanized fairy tales."

"Thanks."

They finished cleaning the room up together without talking. When the last bits of broken trinkets had been swept up, Mackenzie brought out the vacuum. She figured she might as well finish her chores since her temper tantrum had already woke up the entire house. Geoff returned to sitting on the couch and when she approached with the machine, he diligently lifted his feet in the air to allow her to clean under his feet.

"Mackenzie?" Her name being called from the doorway startled her. When she flipped the switch to turn the vacuum off, she realized that it was Margret. Geoff had mentioned her earlier, but it wasn't until then that she realized she must have returned from getting Analise settled in California.

"Welcome back!" Mackenzie called with a big smile. She was grateful to Margret for finding her and helping her. She even coached her on what to say to her mother when she finally roused the nerve to call. She still had to do that.

"Thank you, dear. Would you mind if I had a word with Geoff?" Shaking her head, she quickly wrapped the cord around the machine and pushed it through the door, while Margret slipped into the room.

Mackenzie put the vacuum away in the closet around the corner and passing the just barely open door to the living room on her way to the stairs, she overheard her name.

"I see you and Mackenzie are spending more time together."

"That's what you wanted, you asked us all to befriend her and be there for her. The tempering is a hard time, and she has so many questions."

"Be careful, Geoff. You know how emotional pups are. I can count on you to be there for her without being with her, can't I? You know how important she is."

"Yes, ma'am."

~*~

Racing up the stairs, Mackenzie didn't know if she wanted to be grateful for overhearing that conversation, or cry because now she knew Geoff was off limits. Throwing the door open, she didn't even care if she woke Teresa up. The girl could deal with it.

From the resonating crack shook the wall from the doorknob slamming into the little table that stood next to the door for their keys and other necessary items when leaving the house, woke Teresa up. She sat up, without saying a word, and just stared at Mackenzie.

The glare Mackenzie sent Teresa's way told her she was not in the mood to hear anything about the noise.

"You okay?" Teresa could be really cool when she wanted to be. In the two weeks that Mackenzie had been in the house, she spent most of her time with Teresa or Natalie. She tried befriending the others, but she just felt out of place. Teresa had a temper, but honestly, who in the house didn't? She liked to say the reason she had less control of hers than the others was because she was a redhead. Genetically speaking, she was just a firecracker. Mackenzie couldn't help but laugh at that, and then wondered what her own problem was because her hair was plain old brown.

"No. Every time I start to think that I can handle this new life I was thrust into, something jumps in to bite me in the ass. I mean, first I turn into a massive wolf, and that hurts a fucking lot. I don't even want to think about the next cycle. When I do change, I am a monster that rips animals to shreds. I lost the life I had planned. I am terrified to talk to my mother, let alone see her. I find out I am going to live for hundreds of years, that I won't be able to have kids, vampires are real and hate me just because I drool once a month, and apparently, my chances with Geoff are null and void because Margret doesn't want him to get involved! WHAT HAPPENED TO MY LIFE?"

Throughout her tirade, Mackenzie paced the floor in front of the window, ignoring the spectacular view. Her brain was on overdrive with everything she had learned. She could heal from just about anything—except vampire bites, beheading, and having her heart stopped. She had a group of people surrounding her that accepted her for who she was and wanted to help her. It sounded like it would be a great life. If only she could focus on those things, and forget the rest.

The creaking sound that came from the springs compressing and releasing broke the silence in the room. Teresa padded across the room and put her arms around Mackenzie, resting her forehead in the center of her back, hugging her tightly. Mackenzie relished the comfort of another person for just a moment before pulling away.

She gave Teresa a small smile and took a drink of water that she kept in a bottle on her nightstand. "Sorry. I know I need to grow the fuck up and deal with this, but damn it, I never answered the question: 'What do you want to be when you grow up' with the word Werewolf."

"Don't be sorry. There are a lot of us who were changed and left to figure it out on our own. We all have been through exactly what you are going through now. It's a lot to take in. Just be glad that Margret found you, like she found us. She is amazing, taking in all the new pups that have nowhere to go. Once you have been here a while, she will even get you started on the training, to make you a better fighter, both in human form and wolf form."

"What do we need to know how to fight for?"

"Well, as young as we are, we won't be fighting for a long time. She tries to keep the pups safe. But we are a large pack and sometimes other packs want to control ours. If they take Margret out, our pack belongs to them. After you have been in a pack for a year, you take the oath. Once you take the oath, the magic that makes us who we are, binds us to our pack leader. Not like a slave or anything, more like a strong urge to be loyal to them. The strongest can deny the pull, but with Margret? Why would you want to? She is amazing."

"So what happens when they attack and they don't kill her?"

"She kills them. It isn't pretty, and she doesn't like it. She often mourns their lives in her office for days on end after, but when a wolf starts a fight, the only way to stop it is by death."

"So, the whole pack either dies or becomes loyal to Margret?"

"Yeah, basically. That's how we got the Alaska land. A pack traveled down here, to take our place. Margret is very old and so is this pack. Just about everyone knows about us, and they know that we have ideal land and that Margret's funds cover all the necessities. Not every pack lives like we do. Hell, most don't. Most just meet up wherever they can. They are a pack, not a family, and they are jealous of us."

"Wow." Mackenzie couldn't help it but she was completely in shock over the information, but knew she shouldn't have been. That is one thing that the books got right, in order to take over a pack, the pack leader had to die. It was in everything she had ever read—both in her textbooks and in all paranormal novels. Why did she think that Margret's pack would be all sunshine and rainbows, and that everything would be as happy as can be?

"Don't worry, it doesn't happen often. It hasn't even happened since I have been here. I was just told about it when they started my training. I still can't turn on command, so I'm not learning how to fight as a wolf yet, but I can remember the training I do know, at least. It's not always a good thing."

Teresa's voice lowered and her eyes glistened over, staring out the window. Mackenzie realized that she wasn't as tough as she wanted everyone else to think. Even after four years, she still struggled with her wolf.

"How long until you can control the wolf? Not just remember what it does?"

"I have no idea. For some, it happens in a few years. For others, it takes a hell of a lot longer."

"Have you ever..." Mackenzie didn't know how to finish her question. No one in the house except for Geoff and Margret knew that she had killed someone. If she asked Teresa about it, she would know.

"Ever what?" Teresa moved to sit next to her and took Mackenzie's hand in her own. Taking a deep breath, she decided to trust that Teresa wouldn't look at her differently. They were just talking about how neither could control their wolves. If she wanted to make the most of this new life, she had to let other people in.

"Ever killed someone?" It was a faint whisper, Mackenzie knew that Teresa would hear her, but she wasn't ready to share with anyone who might be walking by.

"Yes, and turned someone. Natalie. I turned Natalie."

THE TEMPERING
133

Chapter 13

Bundled up in a winter coat, even though she was boiling underneath, Mackenzie and Geoff walked along the snow-covered streets in town. After almost a full month, Mackenzie was growing bored in the house and had finally convinced Margret to let her get a job. The woman's answer was yes, but only if Geoff agreed to work with her.

The conversation hadn't been easy. Margret couldn't understand why, with everything they had available in the house, that Mackenzie could get bored enough for a job. She had no need for money, there was plenty of socialization in the house, and if she wanted a movie or a game or a book, Margret would provide it. It wasn't until Mackenzie explained that she needed to get out of the house, to do something that would make her feel normal. She needed this to be happy and Margret was all about keeping her happy.

"Mack, seriously? Can't we just pretend to be normal by going on road trips or throwing parties? A job?" Geoff had begun to shorten Mackenzie's name to Mack the previous week. She usually hated nicknames, but because Geoff had given it to her, she decided it wasn't so bad.

"Yes, a job. Think about it, you will have money that you don't need to ask to use. What if you wanted some porn?" The shocked look on his face made Mackenzie burst into a fit of giggles. "Well, you are a guy, after all! I mean, come on. Are you really going to ask Margret for something with the title of 'Bleach Blonde Busty Babes'?"

"Blondes? Nah, my collection is all brunettes. And the guys in the house have a list. We don't ask, we write it down, and it shows up. That simple. No embarrassment required." The fact that he mentioned her hair color made her grin like a fool. It shouldn't. They were discussing his choice of porn after all, but at least he preferred her hair color. Even if according to Margret, she was off limits.

"Look, a help wanted sign!" Mackenzie wanted to change the subject before she further embarrassed herself and the white sign posted in the window of the local coffee shop saved the day. Geoff stepped forward and held the door open for her, and she realized that with him growing up in an era where being a gentleman was not only expected, but also demanded, it certainly had its perks.

The small shop had a few tables that were all full and a line that ran along the sidewall, wrapped around the back, and stopped just short of the door. The powerful, and rather delicious, scent of coffee filled the air. Grabbing a hold of Geoff's elbow, she tugged him toward the line.

"But aren't we just getting applications?"

"Don't you want some coffee? I do." Then she did something she had never even attempted to do before. She gave him the puppy dog eyes that she had seen so many girls do in the past to get their way.

"All right, fine. Would you look how long this line is, though?"

"Well, that just means they need a lot more help! This is a good thing. Now stop complaining and enjoy my company." She was still attempting to flirt, hoping that being away from the house would make Geoff forget about Margret's request that he keep the relationship completely platonic.

"Have you given much thought about tonight? The others are going to scope out the camping spot in a few hours. I thought you might want to join in."

Being reminded that in just twelve short hours she would succumb to the wolf, losing herself in the process was a complete downer. Taking a deep breath to control her raging emotions, she placed a hand on his arm, not at all relishing in the fact that she could feel his muscular curves, and looked up into his eyes.

"Can we not talk about that now? Later, sure, but not now. This is our normal moment. Just you and me getting coffee and looking for jobs. Normal."

"What happens if a customer pisses you off and you lose control? What happens if you are asked to work the night shift on a full moon? What happens if someone sees you accidentally break something you shouldn't be able to or sees you heal if you cut or burn yourself?"

"You couldn't let me have a moment? Fine, we won't get a job. But damn it, I wanted coffee!" She was fuming. He had ruined her moment. She could feel the sadness taking over and quickly left the shop, kept her head down and walked toward the long road that led to their house.

"Mackenzie! Wait!" She considered stopping, but then decided fuck it. He could chase after her if he wanted to.

~*~

Eventually, Geoff stopped calling her name and just walked behind her. She was glad he hadn't tried to walk with her. All she would see was someone who was babysitting her. Was he even really her friend or was that because Margret asked him to pretend?

As soon as the thought slipped into her mind, she dismissed it. Margret wasn't cruel. She wanted Mackenzie to have friends. She was doing everything she could to help Mackenzie adjust.

The snow crunched under her feet as she cut across the lawn instead of walking all the way around to the driveway. She knew that Geoff wouldn't follow her. He didn't like his pants to get wet. She couldn't care less.

Her to-do list had three things on it. Go inside, get undressed, and relax in a hot bath to forget all that had happened in the last hour, and to ignore what was coming in the next few.

When she opened the door, she heard a bunch of voices coming from the dining room. Thinking it was a family meeting, she stuck her head in and saw only half the house. Margret was at the head of the table and along the sides were the oldest members of the house.

"Tonight stick with your pups. Do not let them kill anyone." When one of the members gave a little cough to interrupt Margret, she realized that Mackenzie was at the door.

"Is Geoff back, too? Can you send him in and close the door behind you?" There was a smile on Margret's face, but she knew that the questions were not really questions at all, but orders given out in a polite way. Nodding her head, she did as she was told.

The front door swung open, the glass rattling as the heavy wood struck the wall. Geoff stood in the opening, his face distorted in anger and his chest rising and falling in rapid succession. Mackenzie could tell he was pissed and trying to calm himself down. She really didn't care, though.

"Margret is having some sort of meeting in the dining room and asked for you." Turning to head up the stairs without waiting for a response, she felt a tug on her arm. She allowed him to turn her around, coming face-to-face with him, only inches apart.

"Do not ignore me like that again. All I was trying to do was to help you. You would be destroyed if another incident like before happened, and you know it."

"How about you let me move on? You told me not to get hung up on it. To accept it as part of my new life, and as hard as it was, I was trying, damn it. I don't need you to remind me the very first time I get to go out and be around normal people. You said I could control it. How the hell am I supposed to learn to control it without being in the situation to begin with? If you were there, you could have helped me. Or is that it? You didn't want to be there? Was it so bad to be out having coffee with me? We might not have even gotten the jobs. I just wanted to try, damn it!" Mackenzie was just an inch from his face and shaking with her own anger. He stood there and let her get it all out. He never once moved or yelled back. Her yellow-green eyes locked on his brown ones that would change in a matter of hours.

They stood there, staring at one another; not a single word spoken after both had their say, for what felt like hours to Mackenzie, but was only mere seconds. Her eyes broke away from his just long enough to travel his features and land on his lips before darting back to his eyes. Wetting her lips, she hoped with all that was within her that he would take that moment to lean in and kiss her. She didn't care that they had just been yelling at one another, all she cared about was the physical pull she felt.

Geoff lifted his hand slowly and traced a line along the side of her face. When she leaned into his touch, he brought his hand down, along her arm, leaving a trail of flames behind. Just as his fingers threaded through hers, a throat cleared behind them.

"Geoff. Cycle meeting. Now. Mackenzie, go get ready with the others. We will be heading out in the next hour or so." Margret stood with her arms crossed and she definitely had the 'mom look' on her face. Geoff's fingers disappeared from her hand and he walked off without as much as a goodbye.

Shaking her head and hoping she hadn't just imagined the entire encounter, Mackenzie returned to her room.

Chapter 14

Hiking out to the meeting point in the snow, a full five miles through the woods, was actually much more enjoyable than Mackenzie thought it would be. She hadn't expected to see Natalie and Teresa excited for the night. She couldn't help but wonder how Natalie had gotten over the fact that Teresa was her attacker.

Attacker wasn't the word the wolves liked to use when someone was turned and then actually cared for after. They preferred to say, "sire." Teresa was her sire. They only call it an attack when the wolf does so with the intent of killing, then can't finish the job, and just runs away. "Runs away like a little scared bitch" is how Teresa explained it. "We may not have control of what we do when we are wolves, but we damn well know what we are doing as humans."

Mackenzie spent most of the day wondering if she would have been able to forgive her attacker if they had in fact stayed around to be her sire. She knew as well as any of them that she couldn't control, or even remember, her time as a wolf. Maybe they couldn't either.

A snowball hitting her back brought Mackenzie out of her thoughts and returned her to the family hike. Every member was goofing off and having a good time, almost as if none of them would be turning into giant bloodthirsty beasts in just a few hours time.

"Hey!" Looking over her shoulder, she saw Geoff trying to catch up to her. Mackenzie stopped moving forward and bent down to tie her shoe. While she was down there, she packed a tight snowball and as Geoff moved closer, she stood with her back to him.

"Mackenzie. Look, I need to talk to you." Geoff had put his hand on her shoulder to get her to turn around, and when she did, she had a big grin on her face. "Oh, good. You're not still mad."

"Who said that?" Mackenzie lifted her hand so swiftly that Geoff didn't have time to react and she smashed the snowball on top of his head. While he stood in shock for just a moment, she ran off laughing.

Joining in on the ongoing snowball fight gave Mackenzie a chance to forget what was coming and just enjoy herself. Natalie and Teresa teamed up with her and as soon as they broke through the last copse of trees to the large clearing, the girls started pulling fallen logs to the center while the rest of the group went on with their own tasks.

Within an hour, the pack transformed the clearing into a bonfire party and everyone was just enjoying life while waiting for the moon to reach its highest point. Mackenzie tried to join in on the fun. She tried to fill herself on hot dogs and hamburgers because Margret had confirmed her theory that a full human stomach could help with the cravings as a wolf. She played the silly games with the rest of her family, but every time she allowed herself to really enjoy what was going on around her, guilt slammed through her chest. How dare she enjoy life when she had already taken the life of another and when there was nothing to stop her from doing it again?

The watch on her wrist began to tick louder. Each passing second, each millimeter the moon moved in the sky sent waves of panic through her. The earth hummed beneath her feet. Every heart beat in the clearing, and that of the animals nearby, was louder. She was more aware of every distinct smell of the forest. Taking a deep breath, she tried to zone it all out.

"Hey, I'm with you tonight." Opening one eye to look at Geoff, she sighed. Could she not get away from him? Hell, did she even want to?

"What does that mean?"

"Well, Margret likes to pair up those of us who can control ourselves with those who have yet to overcome that particular barrier. If things get out of hand, I step in and stop you."

He had the power to stop her? Where the hell was he last time? He sure showed up quickly after the sun rose. Why hadn't he saved whoever the hell it was she had killed?"

"You can stop me?" Mackenzie's voice turned icy, but her eyes were burning. Squaring off with Geoff, her heart was racing and her muscles were contracting. She wanted nothing more than to release every bit of anger and tension into his face with her fists. Over and over again.

"Yes. Margret told me to. Said you couldn't handle another accident." He didn't move away. Maybe he thought she was challenging him. She wasn't. She wanted someone to stop her. She just wished he had stopped her before and was furious to find out he could have and didn't.

"Where were you last time? You came through the trees so soon after sun up. You had to have seen what I was doing. You could have stopped me!" Her voice had raised a few octaves and they were earning looks from some of the pack. Before sobs could rack through her body at the memory of what she had done, Geoff's hands were on her shoulders.

"I wasn't all that close to you. You ran off. You were hunting and I didn't know you and you didn't know me. I wasn't exactly ready to be chewed in half in case you were some wicked fighter and older than we thought. When I let you get ahead of me, I heard the screams. It was too late. Then the sun came up. I won't leave you this time."

Not knowing what to say to him, Mackenzie looked to the sky. It was almost time. Stepping away from Geoff, she began to undress. Modesty was a thing of the past and within minutes, the clearing was full of humans, naked and bathed in moonlight. All stared at the sky, waiting for the wolf to take them.

Howls filled the air as nineteen wolves padded around the clearing. Mackenzie was on high alert and took in the group with caution. With hackles raised, she backed up, keeping her eyes narrowed on the danger in front of her. There were others doing the same thing, but most were watching the retreaters. As the trees became denser and the clearing was no longer in view, Mackenzie turned on all fours and ran.

The thundering of her own heart only sped up as she pushed herself faster and faster. The earth easily moved under her paws and the wind sang as it whistled by her speeding body. The wolf that had taken over Mackenzie needed to run and play. It jumped against trunks of trees, using them as spring boards to cross long distances without touching the ground. Massive jaws clamped down on fallen logs that were thrown about, only to be chased. The ice-cold pond served as a pool and minor hunting ground as fish after fish were caught and eaten.

A snapped branch pulled her from her playful mood into protection mode. Her ears stood up and her head whipped around to look to the dark forest on the other side of the pond. Her eyes locked with another pair, and sniffing the air, she smelled another. A growl rose from her chest and she ran. She attempted to close in on the intruder, but with every twist and turn through the trees, she would lose sight of the wolf. She relied on her nose to track it down.

Frustration pushed her harder, faster. She would catch it and she would kill it. Within moments she was on its heals. The wolf running from her stood no chance. She was ready to leap forward with her mouth wide open and teeth ready to strike when another scent invaded her muzzle. Something better. The smell was intoxicating. Planting all four feet to stop her momentum, she let out a loud howl. She told the entire forest that she was hunting and they better not get in her way.

The wolf she had been chasing just moments before had followed her. Her tail was being nipped and scratched at by the intruder on her hunt. Not wanting to ignore the call of the blood, Mackenzie pushed on, digging her claws deeper into the almost frozen ground, launching her further with each stride. Over and over, she did this until she was no longer in any threat of losing her kill. The wolf that had been following her was long gone and the scent on the air grew more potent with every stride.

Her prey sat beneath a large tree, covered in a heavy cloth, with a single lantern beside it. The wolf didn't wait to inspect the area. She didn't care that the lantern was lit when her large body knocked it to the side, and it didn't care that as its jaws clamped down on the shoulder of her kill that a piercing scream filled the night air.

She didn't feel the heat coming from the fire that had taken to the blanket at the feet of her and her prey. Not one of the victim's fists that pounded into her side was enough to deter her as she tore flesh from bone, relishing in the tang on her tongue. The howl from the trees of the wolf she had beaten to the wondrous meal, alerting the forest to her destruction, only egged her on to finish her meal before having to defend it.

What did stop her was the rising of the sun.

Chapter 15

The blood stained snow blanketed around Mackenzie's naked body, as the fire licked at her skin. The sensation was strange, being burned and frozen all at the same time. When her body was finally able to obey her commands, she quickly moved, tossing the snow on top of the burning blanket.

She didn't understand why there would be a burning blanket so close to her unless she had made her way back to camp as a wolf. Then she realized she wasn't at camp. Slowly, turning her head to the right, she saw everything.

Dropping to her knees, she stared, speechless as Geoff hovered over a body. Feeling its neck and dropping his head to put an ear beside its mouth.

"I'm sorry. I'm sorry. I did it again. Oh God. Not again." Mackenzie began to chant the same thing over and over. The tears refused to fall, but the desperation of the nightmare was ever present. The thundering of her heart was the only sound she heard until the whole world went dark.

Screams pierced through the darkness and a quick succession of slaps against her face woke her. Geoff kneeled over her, worry in his eyes.

"Hey, there you are. Are you okay?" As much as she wanted to get lost in thoughts about what his concern for her meant, or that they were literally inches from one another without a single shred of clothing on, the cries behind him were drawing her attention.

"Who is screaming?" Then she realized she hadn't killed the person at all. She just almost did, leaving them to a fate she wasn't sure was any better than death.

Trying desperately to look around him, Geoff grabbed her shoulders and forced her to look into his eyes.

"Don't. Just go back to camp and get Margret. Tell her you need her to come quick. That someone was bitten badly but they're still alive."

All she could do was nod her head. She knew she had done it. Geoff was too old and too controlled. Plus, she was the one covered in blood with a stomach sloshing full of things she would rather leave a mystery.

Standing and running a few feet into the trees, she stopped briefly to look over her shoulder. There, lying in the snow, writhing about, and crying out in pain was a man. He had blonde hair that looked to be matted in blood, his pale skin was turning a slight shade of blue from the cold, and there were broken glasses lying beside him. She couldn't tell what color his eyes were, but she knew if he survived, that within a few days they would match her own.

~*~

Running through the trees while naked was not for anyone who couldn't heal themselves. Mackenzie felt every stinging scratch and cut on the way back to the camp ground, but every injury followed by the tingle of her skin knitting itself back together.

The clearing where the fire pits had been set up had a few pack members getting dressed and talking lively with one another, laughing and playing around. She was disgusted by their lack of concern for the night before. Perhaps they could control their beasts, but not everyone could. Their kind— her very pack— was killing helpless animals and people all over the world. Mackenzie didn't think she would ever be able to see the change as her pack mates did.

Never slowing from a full sprint, the others finally took note of her blood-covered body and horrified look on her face. They ran to her. When she finally stopped in front of her pile of clothing, she hastily pulled them on, without even bothering to wash off the evidence of the most vile thing she had ever done in her life. It didn't matter that she couldn't remember it. It didn't matter that she had no control. She ruined his life and fated him to the exact same.

"Where is Margret?" Mackenzie asked through a shaky voice. *Do not cry. Do not cry. Keep it together. I am strong. I can do this.*

"I don't know. She hasn't made it back yet. She was with Natalie last night." Mason, one of the older members was looking at her with worry. "I can help. What's wrong?"

He gripped her shoulders and turned her toward him to keep her from scanning the tree lines, hoping to see the swaying of the low branches and leaves, indicating someone's return.

Looking up at him, she realized he had been one of the members at the meeting the day before. That meant that Margret trusted him. He was there and Margret wasn't. He would have to do.

"Geoff said to get Margret. I hurt someone. Real bad." Heart thundering and stomach dropping, she felt light headed. Here it was, time to tell the pack how bad she was at being a wolf. How much trouble she is and to watch them run away or kick her to the curb. They didn't all know about the person from the last cycle, but Margret did.

"Let's go. Show me the way." Then they were running. She had thought that she wouldn't be able to keep up with him, but more than a few times Mason called out, asking her to wait for him. Maybe age had nothing to do with strength and speed, as the legends assumed. Maybe the younger are the stronger and faster. But it was not the time to worry about those things. She had to get to the man.

Halfway back she heard sobs. Coming to an abrupt halt, while waiting for Mason to catch up, she scanned her surroundings. She knew the voice that echoed through the cries, begging for forgiveness and screaming apology. It was Natalie. This meant that Margret wasn't too far off.

"Natalie! Are you there? What's wrong?" Momentarily veering off course, Mackenzie slipped between trees, following the sounds that were pouring out of her friend.

When she came into view, Margret was with her, holding her and rocking, much like a mother to an upset child. She was petting her hair and whispering in her ear. Mackenzie almost didn't want to interrupt, knowing something horrible had happened.

Looking around she saw them. A couple, torn to shreds and lifeless laying on the forest floor, and a small child, shaking and bloody.

"Margret?" she whispered. Mason had finally caught up and let out a single curse word when he saw the scene around him.

"This isn't the time, Mackenzie."

"There's another one. But, he isn't dead." Margret's head snapped up and looked to her. For a split second, a smile ghosted across Margret's face. Then it vanished so quickly and was replaced with a look of complete worry that Mackenzie wasn't even sure she had seen it to begin with.

"Mason, take over here. The child is alive, and you know what to do."

Mason's eyes widened and he forced a swallow before nodding his head in acceptance. Natalie wailed even louder and Margret stood. "Let's go."

~*~

Mackenzie was afraid to ask Margret what she meant when she told Mason that he knew what had to be done with the child. She had a horrible feeling that poor kid wasn't going to make it out of the woods, but she didn't want to believe it. These people were supposed to be a good pack, loving and welcoming to all. At least that's what she had been led to believe.

"How much further?" Margret asked after ten minutes of silence. Only Mackenzie didn't have to answer because the screams echoing through the trees answered for her.

"There." Mackenzie pointed to the large copse of dense trees where she had attacked the man.

Geoff had heard their approach and darted out, flagging them in his direction. "Quick, I don't know how long 'til the knitting completes and he can run his ass out of here."

When the blonde-haired man came into view, he was leaning up against a tree. His face was scrunched up in agony. Geoff covered his body with the charred blanket. Any added warmth in the freezing temperatures would help the man.

"How did this happen?" Margret asked, looking between them. "I thought you were supposed to stay with her? These wounds are severe. He is going to be lucky to finish healing before his body just decides it's had enough."

"We knew Mackenzie was fast, but Margret, I. Could. Not. Keep. Up." He said each word slowly and pointedly. It was as if they knew something she didn't and between waking up to another grave mistake, seeing the other dead bodies, and not knowing what was going to happen to that child, she was tired of being on the outside of information loop.

"What the hell does that mean? What is going to happen to that little girl back there with Mason and Natalie, and what is happening with him?" She was yelling and gesturing wildly to get their attention.

"You need to calm down. You are just really fast. Some are really strong, some are really sly, and you are really fast. It's a learning curve. It just means next time we need to assign a faster wolf to you, that's all. The child? Well, that is for another day when you aren't upset already, and this man will be okay if we can get him back to the house soon. He will start the change within hours and he needs to be somewhere safe." Margret had said matter-of-factly.

Mackenzie wanted to argue. Wanted to jump up and down screaming like a petulant child who had just gotten a 'because I said so' from their mother. But her energy was gone. Due to the emotional strain of the morning mixed with the fact she still didn't know everything she needed to about her new life, she was willing to trust in Margret and let her handle things. So far, she hadn't said or done anything to make Mackenzie question that trust.

"Geoff, pick him up. Mackenzie, stay behind and clean this up as much as possible. Get rid of the lantern, the blanket, the blood. Make it look like nothing happened here, then get back to the house without being seen and clean yourself up."

Chapter 16

Geoff tried more than once to pick the man up,
but each time he would fight back as best as he could.
After a few minutes, Geoff growled his annoyance and
knocked him out with one swift punch.

"What the hell? What did you do that for?"
Mackenzie demanded. Geoff threw the man over his
shoulder and turned to look at her. She could tell he
was doing everything he could not to show his
annoyance at her attitude, especially since it was her
fault they were in the situation.

"How else would he have allowed me to carry
him? You do your job; I do mine. I will see you back
at the house." Mackenzie watched as Geoff and
Margret padded through the trees, going faster than a
normal pace, but slow enough not to harm the man any
further.

When she was finally alone, she sank to her knees. The cold snow seeped through her jeans and soaked her skin. She took one look at the carnage around her and sobbed.

After a few minutes of weakness, she wiped the salty tears from her cheeks and stood.

The snow was the easy part. She used the charred blanket to carry clean snow from one side and covered the rusty colored snow. Mackenzie had to try time and again to throw the lantern high into the tree before it would stay. Crying in frustration, she grabbed the blanket and wrapped it around as many rocks as she could find between the 'scene of the crime' and the stream. Throwing it as far into the center as possible, the only thing left was the man's bag, which she knew she would carry back with her. He would want it. He would want a piece of his life that most likely would be ending, one way, or another.

~*~

Walking through the front door of the massive house felt like a walk of shame. Every head snapped in her direction and whispers echoed all around her. She didn't have to ask anyone where her victim was; she just followed the trail of people, through the front entryway, along the hall, through the kitchen, and out to the back den.

Margret sat next to the still unconscious man who lay on one couch while Geoff and Tanya, a woman who stood at least five inches taller than Mackenzie, and had green hair and more tattoos than empty skin, unfolded the pull out bed from the inside of the other couch.

Mackenzie hadn't spent much time with Tanya. Honestly, she kind of scared her, but in that moment, she looked to Mackenzie with sympathy and understanding, not the usual annoyance.

"He should be waking up soon. We will have a short amount of time to talk to him before the change begins. Go shower. If he sees you covered in his blood, it will only make it worse."

Margret didn't give her a chance to argue, standing and leading her out of the room then closing the door behind her.

Natalie lay on her bed when Mackenzie appeared. She was staring at the ceiling, still disheveled and covered in mud and blood with a few stray leaves in her hair. Teresa was next to her, arms wrapped around her waist with her head on Natalie's shoulder. Seeing the two of them still together and close after such a tragedy made Mackenzie realize that the pack was still a family and they still loved each other. No amount of fuckups could take that away.

"Mackenzie? You okay?"

Not able to actually answer, she just shook her head and headed for the shower. Peeling off the clothing that had begun to stick to her skin with dried blood, she climbed into the shower. Steam gathered around her as the hot water washed away all evidence of her crime. The red stained water swirled around the drain and disappeared from sight. All that was left was the memory. Too bad she still couldn't remember the night before.

When the water ran cold, Mackenzie left the confines of the bathroom, dressed and returned to the den. The wolf that had bit her left her without so much as a second thought. She wouldn't do that to the man on the couch.

His eyes began to flutter as a low groan escaped his lips. Every muscle in Mackenzie's body went rigid. Fear pummeled her even though she knew that there was nothing he could do to physically hurt her. She was terrified of seeing her own eyes staring back at her. When deep blue eyes locked with hers, she let out a sigh of relief. That is until he screamed and tried to get away from everyone in the room.

Backed into a corner, he was screaming. "Don't come near me! Where the hell am I? What are you?"

The last one was directed at Mackenzie. He had to have seen her change back. She was a monster. Even if she felt close to normal living with the pack, to anyone else, she was still a freak, a monster, a murderer.

"I'm sure you have a lot of questions. But we need you to calm down." Margret took the lead and Mackenzie was more than happy with that. She found that she couldn't speak. Her voice ran off with her humanity, it seemed.

"CALM DOWN? Why the fuck would I calm down? SHE WAS A FUCKING ANIMAL!" His body shook and even though he was yelling, trying to be brave, the amount of fear rolling off him was palpable.

"You were bitten and survived. Your wounds have healed. You are turning. If you want any kind of explanation, you need to calm down and listen."

"You people are insane! I'm going nuts. That has to be it. I am still outside freezing to death. Hypothermia has made me hallucinate!"

Mackenzie stood from the couch and walked over to Geoff, keeping her eyes on the man who still muttered to himself. Placing a hand on Geoff's shoulder, she leaned in to whisper in his ear. She had every intention of speaking to him without the man hearing, but the scent of him, his hair tickling her nose, and the low rumble that filled his chest when her body slightly touched his made her lose her train of thought.

A throat clearing by Margret with a pointed look shook Mackenzie from her daze and she managed to complete what she set out to do.

"Change. You can do it without the moon, right? Show him. Prove to him what we are saying is true."

A slight nod of his head was the only response she was able to get from him. She wasn't sure if the moment had affected him as it had her, but looking at the terrified man told her it wasn't the time or place to worry about it.

"What is your name?" Geoff asked as he moved closer.

"Liam Hardy," the blonde replied. His voice came out stronger, more confident than before. Mackenzie wasn't sure if it was because he was trying to prove his courage or strength to another man, but whatever the reason, it was better than the quivering voice.

"Liam, you are not hallucinating, you are not insane, and we are not lying to you. You were bitten under the full moon and survived," Margret said, then motioned to Geoff. At that moment, Geoff turned and Liam passed out.

Chapter 17

Moving Liam from the floor where he passed out to the pull out couch proved to be more difficult than previously. The change had begun and his skin was flushed red and hot to the touch, and his body writhed about.

"Is this normal?" Mackenzie asked in a whisper not wanting to wake Liam. She figured sleeping was probably the only way to keep the pain away.

"Yes. Every bitten Were goes through this. You did, but the body shuts the mind off for a reason. His bones are breaking and healing. Cartilage is shifting or growing. Muscles are stretching. It's a whole process that the body goes through. The only thing to do now is wait."

"Okay. I'll be right back." Waiting might be part of the process, but maybe she could make him more comfortable. He may not recognize what she was doing, but she did.

Grabbing a bucket of cool water, a washcloth, and some blankets, she went back to the den. Margret and Geoff stood off to the side, whispering with one another so low that even with her super hearing, she couldn't tell what they were saying.

"I am so sorry, Liam. You can't hear me, but I won't leave you. We can figure this whole thing out together. You are not alone." Her voice was soft and she knew the others could hear her, but she didn't care.

Dipping the cloth into the cool water then ringing it out, she placed it on his forehead.

"Mack? Come on. Let's leave Margret to deal with this. You need to rest." Geoff stood so close she could feel his breath on her neck. As much as she wanted to turn around to see how close he was and to go wherever he asked her to, asshole or not, she couldn't leave Liam. He was her responsibility. She would be his sire. He needed her.

"I can't leave him. Not yet." Tears slipped from her eyes but for the first time in ages, she didn't wipe them away or force herself to stop. Someone needed to grieve for his lost life even if no one knew it was gone yet.

Within hours, Liam began crying out in what could only be described as half growl and half cry. His body shook with shivers as the first wave of fever broke. Mackenzie moved quickly to remove the cool cloth. As she grabbed the warm wool blanket to cover him, she noticed that the sweat had soaked his clothing.

Without a second thought, she removed the shirt that Geoff had put on him when he was brought in and threw it across the room. Liam's chest rose and fell quickly with each labored breath. The defined abs and pecks were something to be admired, but before she could add to her pile of guilt where Liam was concerned, she covered his body with the blanket.

Footsteps echoed in the hall outside the closed den door. She knew Geoff hadn't gone far after Mackenzie turned him away. She could hear him muttering to himself, trying to find the words to change her mind.

She wouldn't allow herself to stray from her duty. She wondered if he actually understood what she was going through. He wasn't bitten after all. He never had to deal with the blackouts or losing everything important in his life, like she and Liam had. He knew what was coming. He could plan for it.

Feeling her irritation growing with every footstep, she walked to the door. When he stopped moving, she took a deep breath. Flinging the door open, Geoff stood in front of her with a big grin on his face. "Good, you're ready to give him some space. Let's get out of here."

Mackenzie's eyes narrowed at him. "What?"

"I am not going to get out of here. I want you to give ME some space, Geoff! I will not leave him like that bastard left me!" Slamming the door in his face, she moved back to the couch, glanced down at Liam and sat.

A few choice curse words could be heard as Geoff walked down the hall but it didn't matter. She could smooth things over with Geoff later, but right now, Liam needed her. A soft knock on the door alerted Mackenzie to Margret's presence.

"Sweetheart, are you sure you want to stay in here? All it is going to do is make you keep thinking about what went wrong. What is done is done and we will all be here for him from day one. Maybe you should find some alone time to forgive yourself." Margret's voice was soft and her eyes danced between Mackenzie and Liam. As much as she wanted to believe her, Mackenzie just didn't believe she could ever forgive herself.

"I can't, Margret. I need to be here when he wakes up." Returning her attention to Liam, she heard the door softly click closed.

The light filtering into the room through the large windows began to turn a golden color before disappearing. Moving from her perch on the side of the couch to turn on a small light, she was able to stretch. With her muscles wound tight, she was beginning to feel uncomfortable enough to find a new place to rest. Her bed was beginning to sound like a good idea before Liam began to cry, now in a much deeper octave. Why should she be in comfort if he was in agony? She decided that she would stay where she was.

The laughter and joy that could be heard floating throughout the house irritated her. They acted as if a man turning into one of them happened so often that it didn't require any kind of consideration or sorrow. How could they just not care?

When the scent of sizzling chicken filled the air, her stomach growled loudly. Looking longingly at the door that led to the kitchen, she sighed and sat back down next to Liam. Food would be there when he awoke.

"Mackenzie?" Geoff's soft voice said after a light knock on the door. "I brought you some dinner."

Looking up, she saw the sincerity in his actions. He could be a jackass, but he did care if he took the time to put up with her mood swings and still bring her dinner. Still not quite ready to let him know she had forgiven him, she sighed in an exaggerated tone, hoping he would think it was in irritation.

"Thanks, I guess. Just put it on the table." The fried chicken smelled delectable and her mouth began to water. She practically ran to the table, her grumbling stomach leading the way. Geoff stood off to the side, leaning against the bookcase with a little grin on his face, watching her devour the plate of food. Realizing she was being watched, she slowed down her chewing, swallowed, and wiped her mouth. She began to eat like a proper lady then looked over to Geoff.

"Does this mean I am forgiven? I know I can be an ass, but I brought you chicken." The smirk remained fixed on his face and as much as Mackenzie wanted to smack it off, she couldn't help but smile back at him.

"I suppose. Thank you for dinner." Geoff nodded his head and left the room without another word to leave her to her bedside vigil.

~*~

The sun rose and fell once more before Liam gave any indication of waking. His limbs had lengthened and became more taught. His skin cleared up and his blonde hair looked slightly longer and had more highlights.

The moaning and thrashing about had stopped just an hour before his eyelids began to flutter open. Mackenzie jumped up from his side and stood back, not knowing what the best course of action would be. Should she stay right next to him, hold his hand and tell him what had just happened, or should she stand back and give him space to deal with it himself?

Before she could make up her mind, standing halfway between his side and the wall, he yawned, sat up, and stretched. Mackenzie froze, waiting for some kind of response from Liam. After rubbing his eyes and scratching his nether region, he finally looked up and locked eyes with her. The yellow green shade of his irises sent a pain through her chest as if an ice pick had found its way in to her overheated body. He was a Werewolf.

"What happened? Why am I here and why are you here?" His voice was steady but the acidic tone wasn't missed. He was not happy to see her. He remembered that she was the one to attack him. She knew that she had to explain, to let him know what he was.

"You changed. You're a Werewolf now. I'm sorry. When you change at first you have no memories and no control, I didn't mean to. I really didn't." She had been planning on being cool, calm, and collected while talking to him, but every icy glare he sent her way dug deeper into her heart, riddling her with guilt. Every word she spoke was filled with regret and tears.

"Get away from me. You are insane! This whole thing is crazy! I am not a Werewolf!" Liam stood and ran from the room. Wiping her tears, she followed after him, hoping someone would stop him along the way.

Reaching the front door, she found it wide-open, snow flurries blowing into the entryway. Liam stood outside with Margret and they spoke quietly. Not wanting to interrupt and scare him further, she stood and watched, trying desperately to hear what they were saying.

Liam walked away from Margret, who stood watching him before returning the house. As she passed Mackenzie, she reached out and squeezed her hand, and said, "Come on. Let's go talk."

Nodding her head, Mackenzie followed Margret through the house and into her office. She had never been in the office before and had believed it would be some big opulent room, but it wasn't. It fit with the decor of the rest of the house, very down-to-earth and homey. There were papers lying about and a large desk with chairs on either side.

The only thing that made this room stand out above the others was the very large, very old painting of a woman that Mackenzie didn't recognize. The brush strokes were stunning and the colors so well preserved that she was mesmerized by it. The woman had dark hair, and was standing in the middle of a clearing wearing nearly nothing—with woods on one side of her, a cottage on the other, and in the distance, a spectacular stone castle.

Margret smiled when she saw that Mackenzie was taking an interest in the painting. She walked back around to stand next to her and admire the ancient work.

"It is stunning. Where did you get it?" Mackenzie asked in awe.

"That's my mother. Wasn't she beautiful?"

"Absolutely breathtaking."

"She really was. Powerful woman, powerful wolf. She is everything I aspire to be. She loved everyone within her pack, the largest in history. But, that is a tale for another day. Let's talk."

Nodding her head but not being able to look away from the painting for another few seconds, she was able to take in the similarities between Margret and her mother—the hair, the eyes and even the shape of their faces. It made Mackenzie think of her own mother. The one she had yet to contact since running away from college. She had to be worried, and that was never something she wanted to do. But how does someone not only tell their mother the three hardest words, 'you were right', but then follow it up by, 'If I had listened to you I would still be human'. Mackenzie wasn't sure any mother would be able to handle the second one.

Sitting in the chair opposite Margret's, Mackenzie crossed and uncrossed her legs, laced her fingers together then unlaced them, and finally began strumming her fingertips along the wooden arm rests.

"Mackenzie, please calm down. Liam's reaction is normal. The only thing we can do now is to give him what he wants, which is space. When he starts to notice the changes, he will be back. He knows what happened to him. I explained the signs to look for and warned him of the danger of being around humans close to the full moon. As a man, his strength is almost double your own and you remember how hard it was to control it."

"But he shouldn't have to do it alone. It was so scary, not knowing what the hell to do."

"I know that. But he does know what is going on and he knows how to find us when he has questions. If you force him to talk to you, it will only make it worse. After his first change when he sees that you had no control, things may get better. Or it may take a lot of time. But as long as you never hold his anger against him, and are there for him when he needs it, everything will be fine."

Not knowing what else to say, Mackenzie nodded and stood. She took one last look at Margret before glancing to the portrait and leaving the room. She didn't want Margret to see how weak she was so she held it together until the door softly clicked closed behind her and the tears fell. Wiping them away again, she growled in frustration at herself. She was supposed to be done crying.

Each step up to the third floor felt like walking through quick sand. Her entire body was aching. She was exhausted from forcing herself to stay awake while Liam was changing, and not to mention the emotional toll his anger with her took on her body.

The bedroom door stood open and Teresa and Natalie were nowhere to be found. Mackenzie hoped that Natalie was managing her wolf mistake better than she was, but she really doubted it. She knew Natalie. Natalie was kind-hearted and soft. The reality she awoke to that morning had really shaken her.

Walking across the room to her bed, she began peeling clothing off, one piece at a time and leaving a trail from the door to the foot of her bed until all she wore was her bra and panties. Climbing under the covers, she fell asleep.

Chapter 18

A gentle rubbing along her back woke her from a dreamless sleep. The view through the window showed a sky that had turned dark with stars shining brightly above the trees. Rolling over expecting to see Teresa or Natalie perched beside her, she nearly screamed when she saw Geoff instead.

Pulling the blankets up to cover herself, even though he had already seen her in the nude on more than one occasion, she scooted back away from him. There was just something much more intimate about him seeing her in bed in just a bra and panties than him seeing her naked in the wild after a change.

"What are you doing in here? I'm not dressed!"

"Yeah, I know. What's the big deal? I've seen you with much less on more than once now. Plus, you left the door wide open."

"Twice. It's been twice and it would be never if I had a choice about it. Get out!" With one hand holding onto the blanket, and the other pushing against his chest, that may or may not have been perfectly sculpted beneath his super thin t-shirt, she groaned. It was like trying to move a boulder that had been sitting in the same spot for a hundred years—firmly planted and rock solid.

The grin on his face, while he watched her trying to remove him from her bed, sent her temper flaring. Dropping the blanket to use both hands, she climbed onto her knees and when his eyes went wide with surprise at the site before him, stunning curves, supple breasts, and wild brown locks.

She shoved him.

Falling to the floor with a resounding thud, Mackenzie's scowl faded into a smile of victory. Geoff never stopped staring at her. The way he looked at her set her body ablaze. Every inch of her was dying to be touched. She knew he wanted her, and she was more than happy to surrender.

Margret took that moment to walk past the door and cleared her throat. Mackenzie looked to the open door and saw her, standing with her hands on her hips and a scowl on her face. It didn't take a genius to know she was not happy with the scene before her.

"Margret, it's not what it looks like!"

"So you are barely covered with Geoff sitting on the floor staring at you like you were made from his favorite candy?"

"Well, yes, but No! He woke me up then wouldn't get out of my bed so I made him."

"Yes, that sounds so much better. Geoff, no men are allowed on this floor and you damn well know it. A word, please? Mackenzie, get dressed."

Geoff stood, still focusing on Mackenzie, licked his lips, and backed out of the room. What had just happened? She was so angry with him, but with a single lustful glance, she had turned to putty. Was this another side effect of the Werewolf thing? Increased strength, speed, temper…and lust? Or was it just as simple as a man and a woman being completely attracted to the other? She laughed at herself. As if it were only sexual attraction? Whatever it was, she needed it to cool off.

Picking her clothing off the floor, she traipsed into the bathroom for a cold shower to remove any lingering thoughts of Geoff.

~*~

Mackenzie felt much calmer after her frigid shower. Dressed in jeans and an oversized sweater, hoping to hide away beneath them, she sat on the floor in front of the large window. She had taken a book from the shelf in the library and was reading, hoping to lose herself in someone else's romance and drama instead of thinking about her own. And of course, not a Werewolf, vampire, or any other supernatural being involved. Who needed to read about it if they were living it?

Just when the hero was about to ravage his busty blonde heroine with his thirsty eyes and pulsing member, the door behind her creaked open then quickly shut. Knowing exactly who would be sneaking into her room, she quickly hid the book beneath the pillows she had arranged for her "reading nook" as Teresa had started to call it.

"I'm not supposed to be in here."

"So why are you?"

Each footstep he took closer to her, thundered out and her heart raced. She couldn't just hear him, but she could feel him getting closer. The instant calming effect that she felt being around the others was null and void when Geoff was in the room.

"To ask you to come up to my room to watch a movie with me, get your mind off things." She knew she was setting herself up for one of two situations. One, he was being a friend. A friend that would actually watch the movie and want to obey the orders Margret had set forth for the two of them. The other was she was setting herself up for much more than that. Watching a movie in his room. With him. Alone. She wondered exactly how much of the movie they would actually see after the looks he gave her earlier.

"Yeah, I think that's a good idea." At least, she really hoped it was.

He held his hand out to help her stand, but when she was firmly on her feet, he didn't let go. *Score one for a whole lot more!*

. Walking through the halls holding hands with Geoff garnered a whole lot of looks from everyone they passed. Mackenzie couldn't understand what was so shocking and was more than a little embarrassed by the gawking. She knew of other couples within the house. Was she so horrible that Geoff couldn't possibly be interested?

"You would think they never saw you hold a girl's hand before," she whispered. Moving herself closer to Geoff to go around a little table in the hallway, he slipped his hand from hers and lightly placed it along the small of her back. Thick sweater or not, she could feel the heat.

"That's because they haven't. Come on. I have my own room so no more prying eyes." Geoff opened a door at the end of the hall, allowing her to enter first. His private room was as large as the room she shared with Teresa and Natalie. Not one piece of furniture matched another and there was clothing scattered all over the floor… and chairs… and bed… and dresser. He did have a very large television mounted onto the wall in front of his bed.

"Um, it's nice?" Mackenzie didn't know what to say. Should she compliment him on his confidence in himself for not caring what others think of his living space?

"It's a pig sty. At least I know it. Let me clean off the bed, and you can look through the DVDs and pick out a movie." Geoff ran over to his bed and began throwing things to the floor. Mackenzie shook her head as she realized his version of cleaning off the bed meant making the floor worse.

His DVD collection was varied and haphazardly thrown onto a bookshelf. As she read the titles, she habitually began standing them up with the titles facing out. Eventually coming across an action movie she had wanted to see, she grabbed the box and turned to see Geoff standing and watching her.

"Organizing for me?"

"Um, no?" She looked anywhere but at him. She was embarrassed at being caught cleaning up after him. Maybe he liked his movies in a disaster of a pile along his bookshelf.

"Forget it. Trust me. I know my habits. No matter who cleans up after me, it will look just the same within a week. Still want to watch the movie with me even though I am a horrible housekeeper?"

"Yeah, just do me a favor and don't help me with my room," she chuckled, and then stopped. Looking at him with confusion, she said, "Wait, you helped me with the cleaning in the den before, what was that?"

Mackenzie had sat on the now clear bed and handed Geoff the movie. He began setting up the system and spoke without taking his eyes off the machines in front of him.

"That was me helping out the new girl. I do my chores just like everyone else, but our rooms are ours. So I do as I please in here."

"Yeah, about that, how did you get out of sharing?"

The bed beside her dipped when Geoff sat down. Even though more than five feet of open space existed between them, he sat close enough that their legs touched.

"I'm sort of third in rank in the pack. Margret then Peter, who stays in the California house, then me."

"Wow, so that's why I'm off limits." Mackenzie looked away, feeling really dumb for thinking she ever had a chance. Chemistry or not, for all intents and purposes, he was a boss and she was an underling.

"Why would you say that? Did Margret say something to you?" His hand reached over and took hers, lacing their fingers together. Turning his body toward her, his eyes darted about her face. Mackenzie could only think he was searching for answers.

"Not to me. I heard her that day with you. Then earlier when she freaked over seeing you in my room."

"She isn't happy with the idea of you and me. She thinks I'm letting my "male urges" rush me into things. In our world, we have hundreds of years to decide who will be our mate. We don't rush into things. And Margret doesn't believe in 'lustful unions' as she calls it."

"Lustful unions?" Mackenzie couldn't help but laugh loudly at that. "She seriously thinks sex without being in a long-term, committed relationship is a bad thing. I guess that makes sense, old school views for a woman who is hundreds of years old."

"You realize I'm old school, too, right? I have no intentions, no matter how tempting, of being more than your friend while we get to know each other. Even if those friends make it clear we are looking to someday be more by doing this," he held up their joined hands, "or by spending time together watching a movie alone," pointing to the screen, "or because of this," and he leaned in and softly placed his lips upon her cheek. "Is that okay?"

Barely being able to speak, she breathed out, "Perfectly."

The two went from sitting up watching the movie, to laying on their stomachs, to on their backs with Mackenzie's head on his chest and his arm wrapped around her, laying sideways along the bed to see the movie.

As comfortable as she was, she couldn't stop thinking about Liam. She knew she was crazy for worrying about another man when she was wrapped around Geoff, but she couldn't help it.

"Do you think Liam will hate me forever?"

"No. He will see that, while he may not have pictured his life going this way, you gave him a gift."

Pushing herself up, so she could see his face, she said "A gift? How the hell is this a gift? I ruined his life. He may learn to live with it, to make it work, but it's no gift."

Mackenzie could see the anger cross his face, and the breath he took before sitting up himself. He stood from the bed and paced back and forth for a minute that felt like an hour before turning to her.

"You are still young. This life? This is a gift. If you still think so horribly about what you are, and you despise it so, what are you doing here with me? Can't have a human because you know you can't be around them? You already nearly broke a little girl, killed another, and now changed a third. Is your interest in me just because you know you won't kill me?"

"Damn it! NO! And do you have to fucking throw that shit in my face? You don't think I think about that all the damn time? Why would a life that has me hurting and killing people be a gift? Why would turning into a fucking wolf and not being able to control what I do, or even remember it, be a gift? Do you honestly think I would forgive the one who turned me? I had just hoped that by trying to be there for Liam he would maybe forgive me. I asked you because you have been around a long ass time and seen plenty. I know that Natalie gave in to Teresa, but is that normal? But, instead of answering my questions, you go off on me."

Geoff didn't answer her. He began pacing again, back and forth, turning and looking at her like he was going to speak, then shaking his head and pacing again.

"Would you stop and talk to me?" Mackenzie had lowered her voice so she wasn't yelling anymore. She really didn't want to fight but she just had no idea how turning Liam would in any way make his life better.

"Think of it this way, you gave him friends and family that won't die for hundreds of years. You gave him strength and speed. Once he learns to control it, you gave him a new outlook on life. I promise you, once you can control your wolf, you will appreciate this world more than ever before. By turning him, you made our pack stronger. When he comes back to us— and he will—our pack will have one stronger male to defend it. Accidents happen and with the other packs wanting our territory, the more members we have the better. Can we just finish the movie, please?"

Geoff lay back on the bed, but instead of cuddling up to his side again, Mackenzie stayed sitting up, arms wrapped around her knees and stared at the screen although she no longer paid attention to the movie.

~*~

Catcalls and howls followed by rapid knocks on the door woke Mackenzie from her sleep. Groggily, she rubbed her eyes and rolled over, coming face to face with Geoff. Jumping up she looked around and realized she had fallen asleep in Geoff's room. In his bed. With him. She was thankful for the fact that they were both still fully dressed. With the swirling emotions the night before, she wouldn't have been surprised if she had mauled him in the middle of the night, acting out her very graphic dream.

She reached out and hit his chest to wake him. "Geoff!" When his only response was to mumble and throw his arm across the bed, she picked up a pillow and hit him in the head. Safe and effective while still allowing her to keep her distance— a good two feet away.

"Gah! What was that for?" Rolling over to finally look at her, Geoff heard the sounds being shouted about in the hallway and sat up. "Shit."

"Yeah, shit. What the hell am I going to do? They all think that we slept together, Of course, they do. We came in holding hands, shut the door, and never left. What else will they think?"

"That we fell asleep watching a movie?"

"FAT CHANCE OF THAT!" One of the boys from the hallway called. "We heard the moans in the middle of the night!"

Mackenzie's face flushed as she recalled her dream. It was very likely that they did indeed hear moans. She had always been very vocal in her sleep, either talking or crying or moaning. No one ever wanted to share a room with her.

Geoff looked to her and tilted his head to the side, silently mouthing the word moans at her in question to what they were talking about. Not wanting to admit to having those kinds of dreams, she shrugged her shoulders, hoping he would buy it. If she was flushed with embarrassment at the accusation, it didn't mean she was admitting anything.

"Shut it, Rob! And mind your own damn business!" Geoff called out. Mackenzie could hear the groans of disappointment from the boys being told their fun was over and the retreating footsteps that followed signaling the coast was clear.

"Thank you."

"Don't worry about it, and I will have a talk with them about manners later. Ready for some breakfast?"

"I think I should change clothes at least."

"You are probably right. Give me a minute to change and I will walk you out?"

Not wanting to leave him just yet, despite their argument, she nodded and watched him walk into the bathroom.

Wandering around his room, carefully treading as to not accidentally step on something or trip and fall flat on her face, she looked around, hoping to see something to tell her more about Geoff. He had pictures tacked to the wall and by the type of photos, she could tell he had been collecting for a while. One photo was placed inside a plastic zip lock bag before being tacked to the wall. It was sepia toned and faded. The edges were slightly damaged and the clothing

Geoff and the other man wore in the picture screamed early nineteen hundreds. To say that freaked her out a bit was an understatement, but to look through them all and kind of see his life unfold, with the same people throughout, it was no wonder he felt that the bonds made were a gift.

The side of his bedpost had carvings into it. No pictures, just notches. If she didn't know him better she would assume the worst and think the thirty-two slashes was evidence of former lovers. Her fingers traced the lines, feeling the rough wood on some and the obviously older and more worn marks on others.

"What are you doing?" Geoff asked from behind her, startling her enough to make her jump, then effectively, trip. He reached out and caught her in his arms, just before she hit the floor.

"Thanks. I was just taking a look around. That is okay, right?"

"Yeah. I told you we all make mistakes and have accidents when turned. Those are my mistakes. Thirty-two of them over my lifetime. You won't ever forget who you have harmed Mackenzie, but you will learn how to manage the after math and forgive yourself. You wouldn't blame a wolf for attacking a deer, or a bear for a fish. A Werewolf craves human blood. As a bitten Were, you will crave more than a born. It is just the way it is. Come on. Let's get you to your room."

"I think I might go alone. I don't need everyone on the girl's floor watching my every move, too." In all honesty, she just needed to be alone to think. Another bomb had just been dropped on her and she

had no idea what to do with it. Had those mistakes
been kills or new pack members?

Chapter 19

A week had passed since the night she had spent with Geoff. Seven full days of friendship that bordered on the line of something more and it was driving Mackenzie insane. They would hold hands one minute, and then he would find something more interesting and ditch her the next. He would walk her to her room and kiss her cheek goodnight, but would never allow himself to brush his lips against hers.

Mackenzie and Geoff sat on the couch in the den late one night, the only light filling the room was from the fireplace, the glow of the Christmas tree lights, and the television. Mackenzie couldn't concentrate on the explosion of cars on the screen, only the ones going off inside of her, begging her to grab his hand. She was growing steadily more tired of only being his friend.

Perhaps with Christmas just around the corner she could get around the house's no gift policy and give Geoff herself. But really, that would be more of a gift for her than for him.

Giving herself a mental pep talk, she bit her lip, held her breath, and reached out, taking his hand in hers. She waited for him to pull away and reject her as he had before when she attempted to be bold and kiss him first, but he didn't. He looked over and smiled at her, squeezed her hand and turned back to the television. Letting out the breath she had been holding for far too long, she settled into the couch, and into his side.

They stayed that way for another hour, and while Mackenzie wished she could stay there forever, her growling stomach made Geoff chuckle and pull away.

"Mack, go grab some food. I can pause the movie. Can you bring me back a soda?"

"That's probably a good idea. And yeah, gimme a minute." Standing and stretching her arms above her head, she felt her shirt rise and expose a small expanse of her stomach. Geoff had not seen any more of her skin than the rest of the house since the day in her bedroom, but for whatever reason, she saw that he couldn't pull his eyes from the little sliver of skin that had peeked through.

Quickly pulling her shirt back down, as she was still very self-conscious about certain aspects of her body even with the wolfy genetics making her leaner than she had been, Geoff turned back to the movie and Mackenzie left the room as quickly as she could. When he looked at her like that, the friendship boundary seemed ridiculous. They were adults, and it's not like the rest of the house had a no sex rule. She heard more moans and bangs than she ever did living in the apartments back at college. She wondered if it were his position more than his honor that kept them apart. He may be from a different era, but he had lived through a good number of all the progressions, too. He had to have picked something up from that.

Mackenzie was lost in her thoughts of Geoff, and how to call an end to the friendship truce when the front door swung open, banging against the wall behind it. Without any lights on in the entryway, all she could see was the outline of a tall figure filling the doorframe and her heart raced with adrenaline at the possibility of a fight.

"YOU!" The figure bellowed. Mackenzie lost her fight in the 'fight or flight' mechanism in her brain and began retreating, hoping Geoff would hear and come out of the den. Most of the others were either playing video games or already in bed, but she would take anyone to stand beside her in that moment.

"Me? Who are you?" Mackenzie yelled at him. The footsteps coming from three separate directions let her know that she had been heard and wasn't going to be alone for much longer. Thank goodness for family. If only Margret was there, but it was Alaska's turn to have the pack leader residing with them.

Laughing without a bit of humor, he stepped into the house and flipped the light switch that was just next to the coat rack. When the light illuminated the area, Mackenzie had to hide her eyes before adjusting to the new brightness, but when she was able to pull her hand away, she saw that Liam had returned and he was standing directly in front of her.

She heard the others arrive behind her and instantly felt better about standing so close. He was angry and he had every right to be. She also knew that when she was getting used to her new body, there was no controlling the temper or the strength that came with it.

"I really am sorry, Liam. I know that isn't enough. I know it doesn't matter that I had no control over what happened and have no memory of it. You have every right to be angry, but everyone here can help you. I will be here if you need anything—need to just talk, or to yell and scream, even. I can answer what I know, but the truth is I am still learning, too."

"Why would I want to talk to you?" His hand shot out faster than she had anticipated and gripped her neck. His fingers pressed into her skin so tightly that it cut off her breathing. Her hands went on top of his, trying with all her strength to remove them, but the fear inside her didn't allow her to concentrate. "You bit me. You tore my flesh from my bones. You ate pieces of me! Then you bring me here to make me heal instead of letting me die like I should have—as a human! Why can't I die?"

As he shouted, she felt herself being lifted up, when her feet no longer were on the ground, her air supply was completely gone. Knowing she wouldn't die from strangulation didn't help when her brain still told her that breathing was important. Finally, she fell to the ground and was pulled back by Teresa, holding her tightly in a hug while Geoff and Mason restrained Liam.

Rubbing her throat, Mackenzie finally realized what he had said. "What do you mean, why can't you die?"

"Forget it, just let me go. I can't be here around her without turning into a fucking monster and attacking a woman, if she is still even considered that."

Completely insulted, she left the room to allow the boys to handle Liam. Teresa walked with her all the way to their room with an arm around her.

The next morning, Mackenzie stayed in her room. She didn't want the looks and whispers as she walked by and she certainly didn't want the questions. She wasn't okay. She thought she was getting better. She was able to only think about Liam once a day until he stormed in the night before reminding her exactly how bad things were. Since then, she could only think of Liam and how to get to the point of being able to be in the same room together, without him trying to kill her. At least not until he learned more about werewolves and only then, if he didn't try to off himself first.

While she despised everything she had done since turning, she never once honestly considered trying to kill herself. Just the thought of dying scared the bejesus out of her. The fact that Liam was so hateful of what he had become that dying was the better option dumbfounded her. But then again, she had considered the idea that he would have been better off if the sun had just waited another minute to rise, allowing him as he put it, to die as a human. She too hated what she was, but she didn't want to die.

The door behind her opened and Natalie came in carrying a banana and a yogurt. She set it on Mackenzie's desk then joined her in her little book nook, staring out the window at the trees in silence.

"He's still here," she said eventually without looking away from the window. Worry sank Mackenzie's heart and stomach and tears tried to spring from her eyes. She deserved his hate, but it didn't make it any easier to handle.

"Oh. Well, I guess that is a good thing. He can figure out how to handle everything from the start."

"You can't stay in here forever. He knows you live here and he chose to stay, just don't be surprised if he is pretty quiet when you're around. The strength and stuff kicked in pretty wicked this week, I guess. His little brother had to be taken to the hospital. Broke his arm by accident while arm wrestling. He was even trying to be gentle and let the little guy win."

Mackenzie couldn't help it. The tears flowed from her eyes and she wasn't able to stop it. Wiping them away, she growled out and threw the book she was reading across the room.

"Damn it. His brother's arm is my fault even if he is the one who did it. I bit him. So I guess I get to add that to the list of fuck-ups that are now piling up on my life list. I don't want to keep crying. How did you do it? How did you forgive Teresa for changing you? How are you so put together after the last moon?" Mackenzie had yet to bring up Natalie's wolf night, but she had to ask. She couldn't control her emotions and Natalie seemed to be doing perfectly okay.

"It took Teresa and me a while. It really did. Margret made us share a room and you see how well that works, but more than that, I was able to see her remorse over time. Then I was able to realize that I had no control either, that I had no idea what I did while I was turned. It just takes time, and even knowing that she didn't turn me on purpose, I still wanted to hate her for a long time. But I got to know her, and couldn't.

"As for how I handle mistakes like the other night? I allow myself to grieve for them. I allow myself to be angry or hurt or sad. I cry in the shower and wash away the tears. It's kind of symbolic for me. I have to forgive myself eventually. Until I have complete control, my wolf and I are not one in the same. She did those things and as the tears go down the drain, I allow the emotions that come with killing someone go, too."

"So you think he will get it?"

"I do."

"Guess I should be heading out for a run. Want to go?" The sun was shining and the trees looked to be standing pretty still. It was a beautiful day outside and perhaps it could help alleviate her ugly mood.

Natalie was right about one thing. Liam avoided her at all costs. For weeks, it was as if she didn't exist to him. Not only would he leave if she was there, but he would completely act as if she didn't exist if something forced him to stay.

He worked with Geoff regularly on controlling his strength and while Mackenzie was happy that he was getting the help he needed, she was jealous of the time she no longer had with Geoff. Christmas day came and went, and everyone kept to the no gift-giving rule. She had at least hoped to spend some time with Geoff, but he was busy with Liam. Why they put up decorations but didn't do anything else was completely beyond her. But that's just how it was.

Mackenzie was starting to feel the pull of nature. The full moon was approaching and all she wanted was to be outside. If only she could do so with as little as possible coming between her and the earth beneath her feet, the wind on her skin, and the sunshine on her body as she could. But the December weather wouldn't allow it. Sure, she ran warmer than most and she would heal from anything, but that didn't mean that she wanted to feel the sting of the cold.

Dressing in long yoga pants and a long sleeved t-shirt was the least she dared wear. Sitting on the floor in the entryway, Mackenzie was lacing up her running shoes when the front door opened, letting in a gust of icy air. Looking up, she saw Geoff and Liam all buddy-buddy as they walked in. Apparently, they too had felt the pull. It shouldn't have surprised her; most of the pack had already been in and out of the house that day. They were all feeling it. Most were getting the excited buzz going and were playing around; others—much like her—were finding ways to handle the pull while still keeping their cool, afraid of the night to come.

Liam had a huge smile on his face. Mackenzie was able to see a half-crooked grin with beautiful white teeth and a dimple, just on the left side. Reaching up to her own face, she felt for hers. She also only had one but hers was on the right. Her mother always told her that the doctor who delivered her forgot to poke the other side. It became a running joke her whole life. At one point, she had even seen one of those carnival psychics who told her that her true match would complete her in every way by being her exact opposite. When she asked what they had meant, they wouldn't tell her. She kept trying to figure it out. If she were aggressive, would they be meek? But if that were the case, she would never even give them the time of day. When she returned to the carnival a week later, the Psychic told her to think smaller details. Where she was dark, her match would be light. Where she was more of a scholar, he would be more artistic. Where she was right-handed, he would be left. He will be the other half to make the whole and everything will fall into place after meeting him.

Mackenzie shook her head from the memory. She hadn't thought about since she was fifteen. Just because Liam was pretty to look at and had an opposite dimple did not make him right for her. Hell, the man couldn't even stand to be around her. Geoff. That is who she wanted and he wanted her, too. At least, that is what he led her to believe even if he hadn't tried to move much further than a kiss on the cheek. All he needed was time and they had eons of it.

"I'm telling you, the pull of nature is strongest right before the full moon. You will do anything to be outside. This one practically fell out of her window two cycles ago trying to get to the fresh air." Geoff laughed and gestured to her. Irritation rose as she stood eying him and wondering if she were going to actually be able to get a word in before Liam ran off again.

"Uh huh." Liam said, but refused to look in her direction. His stance had changed from the happy man who just finished a run with a pal to what felt almost like an angry ex-boyfriend pretending she wasn't in the room. His arms were crossed and he studied the pictures on the wall then looked back through the open door.

"Well, since I apparently am not here anyway, I am going for a run so I don't have to sleep in a window as you so like to tell everyone." Storming out of the house, she slammed the door behind her and hit the road running. Geoff had some nerve telling Liam about that night. He had told her he wasn't going to say anything. It's not as if it were a bright moment in figuring out what the hell was happening with life. That was a moment the two of them shared, at least that's what she thought. They may not have been able to stand each other much that day but still, she was really embarrassed about damaging the quaint little B&B.

She knew she needed to let it go. When the full moon was close, she had more and more trouble containing her feelings, the good, and the bad. She did not want to over react when she returned to the house.

She wanted to just ignore both men and take a long bath and rest before the following day when it would be completely hectic around the house preparing for the moon.

Taking a deep breath, she let herself connect with the world around her. The wind was soft, but still rustled the leaves of the evergreens gently. The sunlight fell down upon her, warming her body from the outside while her working muscles warmed her from the inside. The scent of the damp soil beneath the snow and the moist wood in the trees anchored her to the earth. It was as if everything around her stopped and she was one with her surroundings.

As she headed back toward the house, reality began to sink back in. In a little over twenty-four hours, she would return to her other life. Her wolf. She just hoped and prayed with everything she had in her that she didn't harm anyone else.

Walking into the house, her nose was welcomed by the smell of burning wood in the fireplace. If she had to pick her favorite scent, that would be it. So many memories of a burning wood stove at her grandmother's house had just made that scent make her think of love and warmth.

Wanting to sit in front of the fire, Mackenzie pulled her snow-covered shoes and socks off and headed for the den. As she walked in, she saw Teresa and Liam sitting on the couch in front of the fire with Geoff on the floor and a few others spread around the room. Not sure if she should stay or go, she leaned against the doorframe and listened as they spoke.

"This is your first cycle. It's going to be painful. And after the pain, you won't remember a thing."

"Can't I fight it? Can't I just tell my body NOT to change?"

"No. You can try to fight to keep your mind active, to be able to remember what you did, but you won't have control. And even remembering what happened takes a long time. Natalie just started being able to remember what her wolf does last year. And now, she is just starting to gain a little control. And even when she has it, it's only for a few minutes at a time." Teresa placed her hand on Liam's shoulder as she spoke. Mackenzie knew all of that. But no one had told her to fight against the blackout. Maybe they were just trying to help Liam with his fear and it would never work, or maybe they just didn't tell her. Teresa would never intentionally keep that from her. Maybe she just never asked the right questions. One thing was for certain, this cycle, she was going to do everything she could to try and keep a hold of her own brain when the wolf transformed the rest of her body.

Chapter 20

The day passed quickly. Too quickly for Mackenzie's liking. She felt as though she had just woken up, but there she was, sitting around the campfire with the rest of the pack in the middle of the night waiting for the moon to claim them.

Liam sat with Geoff on the other side of the clearing, shooting daggers at her with his eyes. He was nervous. He may not have said so, but his body spoke volumes. His legs were bouncing and he couldn't seem to focus his eyes on anything but her and even that was only every so often.

She needed to talk to Geoff. She wanted to speak with him earlier, but every time she tried, he was with Liam. Mackenzie had given Liam a full month of tip toeing around and making sure he had the space he needed, but she had needs, too. In that moment, she let her own needs win out over his.

Standing, she centered her eyes on their circle. If Liam wanted to get up and walk away before she got to them, that was his choice, but she was going over there. With long purposeful strides, she crossed the clearing and stood directly behind Geoff. Liam looked to her in shock and disgust, as if she were some freak who walked up to the cool kids table. They may be young, but they were not children any longer and it was time he started acting like an adult.

"Geoff, can I steal you away for a few minutes?"

"Mack, the moon will peak soon. Can it wait? I need to be here when Liam turns so I can stick with him. We don't know how fast he will be." She rolled her eyes. She wasn't an idiot. She could see where the moon sat in the sky. She didn't want Liam to hurt anyone and knew he needed a follower, but honestly, Geoff wasn't the fastest one to be able to help. He hadn't been able to stop her.

"Are you sure you're going to be able to help him? You were supposed to be with me last moon and we all know how well that turned out."

The entire circle stopped talking and turned their attention on Mackenzie and Geoff. She was fuming and every nerve in her body was on edge. She was set to turn in a few minutes time and he chose then to piss her off?

"Hey now! You will not speak to me that way. You are different. You are extremely fast and we had no way of knowing that. That's why tonight Mason will be following you. He is our fastest besides you. If you have any hope of not hurting anyone again, he is it."

"I out ran him as a human!"

"She did, man. I think we need two with her. I told you last night at the meeting. I really think Christy should help me." Christy was the only other female in the house that was a born were. Mackenzie had found out that the Alaska house had most of the borns there because there was plenty of room for children. If the day came that Christy wanted to have any herself, she would transfer houses.

Christy stood from another fire pit circle and walked over. She was smiling at Mackenzie even though they never really had a chance to talk more than typical pleasantries.

"I can do that. Teresa doesn't really need me anymore and if she is as fast as Mason says, then he is going to need the help."

"Fine, it's settled." Geoff had stood and called out, "We have about five minutes!"

"Then give me three of them. Please," she whispered. She didn't like being passed off but for once, she was able to control her anger and plead with him. She needed him and she had thought they meant more to each other than just a leader and an underling. When his face softened, she knew she was right.

"Okay. But we have to be quick."

The two of them stepped away from the group and in a whispered voice, Mackenzie quickly went through the overheard conversation.

"You can try, but Mack, I never had to fight it. I don't even know where to begin. I never had anyone to tell me what was going on. I got an anonymous letter in the mail before my thirteenth birthday warning me of what was to happen. When it actually happened, I just gave into it. I let the wolf take over and there was no pain. I don't know if that will work for you or not. I have always been able to control it since. It's part of me. The best I can tell you is to think as many human thoughts as you can throughout the change. Don't focus on the pain, just allow it to happen and keep your mind on anything you think will keep you attached to your human self. It's about time. We will talk after, I promise." Then he leaned in and kissed her cheek and the usual warmth spread through her.

"Thank you."

He smiled in response and returned to Liam. Everyone undressed and watched the sky. Mackenzie was going to try to ignore the pain and allow it to just happen. As the moon reached its peak, the cacophony of cracks and pops and screams of the others' transformations filled the air. When her first bone broke she wanted to scream out too, but instead she thought of her mother. Her over-powering, crazy mother who wanted nothing but for her daughter to succeed even if her standard of success was lower than most. She thought of the holidays and birthdays with her and cooking in the kitchen together. She thought of her grandmother and the wood burning fireplace at her house. She thought of Geoff and all the times they almost moved to that next level. Each thought became fuzzier and fuzzier until they stopped completely.

The wolf was free.

~*~

Sunlight bathed Mackenzie in the early morning hours. Rubbing her eyes and sitting up with apprehension to see where she had managed to go the previous night, she discovered that she was lying by a river on top of a large boulder. Her feet were dangling into the frigid water, which was slightly pink from the blood that was dripping into it from beneath her. Closing her eyes, she attempted to remember the night before and see if she knew whether the blood that covered her was anything to worry about. She was hit with brief flashes.

Geoff's body conforming into a four-legged beast before bursting with fur. Their eyes locking and his head cocking to the side before running after a pure white wolf. Trees racing by her, so fast that they held no form other than blurry lines of brown. A deer running, then on the ground bleeding with its flesh torn away. And water. Lots of water.

She had done it. She wasn't sure if she was remembering in order or not, or how much else had happened. But seeing Mason and Christy sleeping soundly along the edge of the trees told her she hadn't needed their intervention. She didn't remember them, but that was okay. She remembered something. Yelling out in celebration, her fellow pack members slowly sat up and looked to her with smiles.

"What's up?" Mason called out.

"I REMEMBER SOMETHING!" Mackenzie started dancing around on her rock before promptly realizing the reason Mason began to laugh at her. She was still nude. It was one thing to see one another after a change, quite another to be jiggling it all around.

Losing her footing, she fell backwards into the water. The soft chuckle turned into a riotous laugh, from both Mason and Christy. Maybe she didn't like her as much as she originally thought.

"Come on, let's get back to the clearing," Mason said. Climbing out of the water, she nodded in agreement keeping her eyes anywhere but on her wolf-sitters. She was in no rush to see the laughter still playing at their mouths over her embarrassing fall.

Chapter 21

Once everyone had returned, it was obvious that this cycle had been a successful evening. Everyone was smiling and joking as they dressed. All except for Liam. He walked back into the clearing with Geoff but refused to speak to anyone. He was covered in blood and his eyes were red-rimmed. She knew what he was feeling. She had been there just a few months before. She knew he was moments from losing it when he reached down and scooped up a small handful of snow and tried rubbing his skin raw.

Someone needed to go talk to him, to be there for him. There were plenty of people around and no one could see how upset he was. Geoff had even left his side to get dressed himself and joke around with the others. Could she be the one? Would he allow it? Or would he be even angrier with her now that he truly knew what she had done to him?

Mackenzie stood, watching Liam. Watching and waiting for him to acknowledge her, She wanted him to give her some clue as to whether or not her approach would be welcome. He could scream and yell at her, or cry or just stand there, as it didn't matter. She just wanted him to know that he wasn't alone in this. She shifted her weight back and forth. She bit her lip—then her nails. And just when she thought he would never look her way, he did. Only he didn't look at her, he looked past her. Then he ran.

Sighing, Mackenzie went back to the group and Geoff found her side. When he laced his fingers through hers and smiled at her, she hoped that since the first cycle of Liam's were-life was over, she might get Geoff's attention back. Liam may have still been new, but there were plenty of others in the house he could talk to other than Geoff.

"How'd it go? Mason said the only fatalities were a few deer and some fish." He leaned over and whispered in her ear. "Gotta say, that's a new one. Never been fishing as a wolf before." His warm breath tickled and sent shivers down her spine.

"It worked. I remember a very tiny bit." She wanted to scream it from the rooftops again, but instead shared with only him. He was the one to help her make it happen. Without his advice, she didn't think she would remember a thing. When she looked up to him, instead of seeing pride in his eyes, she saw skepticism. "What?"

"Are you sure? I mean, I know you want to remember, and maybe you are hoping what you think you remember is real, but Mack, it takes a bitten years to gain even flashes."

"I'm telling you, I remember. I saw you change. You looked at me, turned your head, and then ran off after a white wolf. Am I making that up?"

"That's incredible! We have to call Margret when we get back to the house. She is going to want to know exactly what you did. If we can get all the new bittens to mature as fast as you are, we can get them trained that much sooner. Our pack will be stronger than any others. Our numbers are high, but so many of you all are too new to have control, and we can't train wolves who have no control. This is amazing!" He pulled her for a hug. While his arms were wrapped around her, Mackenzie felt so wonderful. He had initiated the hug. He was so pleased with her and so happy in that moment, she thought it would be the perfect time to move things forward.

Pulling herself back just a bit to look into his eyes, she saw him smile at her. Taking that as her cue, she stepped up onto her tiptoes and leaned in. When her lips touched his, she thought it would be the best moment in her life until he pulled away so quickly that she hadn't the chance to actually feel the warmth of him.

Geoff released her completely and looked around at everyone who remained in the clearing, watching them. Not only was she rejected, but also he had done so in front of everyone.

"Mackenzie, I told you, we have to take things much slower than humans do. Not only do we have a lot longer to make it happen, but also I am in charge here and I do not need anyone thinking I am less of a leader for being with you. Not that there is anything wrong with you, there isn't. You're great. It's just I need to be able to stay neutral about everyone should something happen. Margret has already practically forbidden it unless we are certain that we will be mates, basically till death do us part kind of thing. I don't know about you, but I think we are still getting to know one another and I cannot say that yet. I like you – a lot. But we need to be sure."

"Fine. Sorry," Mackenzie said quietly, desperately trying to keep the tears at bay. He reached out to grab her hand but she pulled back. She was hurt and she didn't need his hand. Turning away from him, she found Teresa and Natalie, and the three of them walked back to the house. Her two best friends knew that no words were needed. All she needed was their companionship.

~*~

Mackenzie stayed in her room for the remainder of the day. The sun had set and Teresa and Natalie had left long ago, wanting to socialize with someone who would actually speak to them without snapping. She understood, of course. It wasn't their fault that Geoff embarrassed her by turning her down but that didn't make her any less irritated at the world.

Mackenzie hadn't even bothered to get out of bed to turn the light on when the room became dark at the same time as the sky. The only light illuminating the space was from the moon and the muted TV that she had long stopped paying attention to.

"What the hell am I doing?" Mackenzie muttered to herself. Deciding to stop acting like such a schoolgirl, she threw off her covers and headed for the door. She wouldn't pout or pine after Geoff any more. No. That was it. She was done. He had to come to her if he wanted to talk.

As she reached to grasp the doorknob, a knock sounded from the other side. Startled, Mackenzie jumped back. With one hand on her pounding chest, she used the other to open the door and stood face-to-face with Liam. Not sure if she could take any more drama for the night, she sighed and dropped her hands.

"What is it?" She had no energy left to argue or show any attitude to the man whose life she had changed forever and who hated her more than she thought was possible.

"Um, can I talk to you?" His eyes stayed trained on the floor and his voice was just barely above a whisper. Anger, hatred, cursing, all of that, she was prepared for. Friendly and wanting to talk? That was new.

"Yeah, I guess so." Still standing in the doorway, she looked at him, even bending her knees slightly to see into his face and try to get his attention.

"I just—God. I just wanted to tell you I get it. I don't like it. I still hate this and am so angry that I can't even look at you, but dammit, after last night? I get it. I thought I had done so well up until the moon. That you were just out of control, but I've got nothing. I have no idea what happened last night and all I know is that I woke up covered in blood. Geoff said that it was an animal, but how the hell do I know? What if it wasn't and they just don't want me to freak out? I am freaking out!" By the end of his speech, he was no longer whispering but yelling and finally looking at her. His nostrils flared with every breath and his yellow-green eyes were wild. She could see the muscles in his forearms tensing and releasing with every clench and unclench of his fist.

"Liam, I know. I do. I am so sorry. If Geoff said that it was an animal, then it was. He wouldn't hide it from you. Trust me. He let me see each and every mistake I've made." Her voice was calm and soothing, but she was anything but. Her brain was racing a mile a minute on whether or not he was going to lose it and attack her again. She tried to listen for the others to find out how far they were. Just because he came to tell her he understood didn't mean he had his temper or strength under control when he was in such an emotional state.

"I just need to talk to someone who knows what it's like. I know they all do. Well, most of them, but it's been so long for them that they all just brush it off as normal to wake up covered in blood."

Seeing him lose all the anger in his face and fight back the tears that she knew he would never want to spill in front of her, she relaxed. He wasn't going to do anything. He really just needed to talk.

"The first time I woke up and saw what I did I was so mortified that I cried for hours after apologizing to the bear that lay at my feet. I ran away. I couldn't handle it.

"I tried to stay at home. I tried to ignore everything. I thought you all were insane but when the doctor couldn't figure out my eyes or my strength, I started to allow myself to wonder. Then, with Ben, I just..." Liam sank to the floor, resting his head against the wall opposite her bedroom door. He pulled one leg up and wrapped his arms around it.

Sliding down the doorframe to mimic his position, she just sat there. Being around the others gave her a sense of calm that she didn't have anywhere else, but being near Liam, when he wasn't glaring at her or calling her names under his breath at least, left her with more than just the calm of being around her own kind. She couldn't explain it, but it was more than that.

"I couldn't stop myself from hurting my little brother. What would have happened if I stuck around? I ran. I had to. But not far enough. It's great here, but I am terrified of going into town. My family lives two towns over. What if they happen to come here? I never told them I was leaving. I just left." As Liam spoke his hands were wringing together and his leg bounced, Mackenzie could tell how difficult this was for him to open up to her.

"I haven't talked to my mom since I left for school. I thought she was just some unsupportive irresponsible person that did more harm in my life than good. I have never missed her more than after my first change. She may not have been perfect, but she was mine and she loved me. Her goals and dreams for me weren't my own, but that didn't mean she didn't love me. Amazing the things we realize when it might be too late. I know I should call her, tell her I dropped out, but I just can't. How do you tell your mother that not only was she right, but that you aren't even really human anymore?"

"Exactly! I have no idea. Geoff said that there were other houses farther away. I wonder if any of them have a place for me." The thought of Liam leaving just as they began to talk saddened her. She wanted to be there for him. She never wanted him to feel alone or scared if she could help it. If she was his sire then she needed to be there for him. But she didn't want him to feel trapped either.

"They might, but Alaska is full of little kids from what I know. California might be an option. But you could stay here. I know it isn't ideal, but maybe once you get more control you could still see your family, and don't tell them? Just let them know you needed space and moved out. You could still go see them once in a while."

"Says the girl who won't even call her own mother."

"Point taken." Mackenzie remarked with a forced grin.

"What college?"

"Huh?"

"You said that you left college. Where were you going?"

"Oh, right. Harvard." The look on Liam's face was priceless. His jaw literally dropped and his eyes widened. After a second, he started laughing loudly and shaking his head. Mackenzie couldn't see what was so funny. Her future was changed just as much as his had been and she hadn't laughed at him.

"What? What is so funny?" She glared at him and when he took the time to actually look at her, his laughter dried up.

"Oh, God. You were serious? Shit. That sucks ass, Mackenzie."

"Ya think?" Her stomach took that as its cue to announce to the world that it had been neglected for far too long. The rumble echoed off the empty hallway, and both Mackenzie and Liam laughed loudly.

"Come on, let's get something to eat." Liam stood and held his hand out to help her stand. Slightly surprised by the action, but not wanting to stunt their growing friendship, she placed her hand in his and pretended not to notice his slight flinch at the contact.

As soon as she was on her feet, though, Liam released her hand. They walked silently down the three flights of steps, politely ignoring the stares that followed them. They could of course hear the whispers wondering if they should follow. Mackenzie actually appreciated it as they were all worried about her safety, but from the look on Liam's face, he didn't feel the same.

"Ignore them. They will stop worrying once they see you don't want to bite my head off anymore. Just think, they will be just as protective of you if the need should ever arise." Liam nodded his head but said nothing.

The two walked into the kitchen and began to grab everything they needed for a late night meal in silence. Mackenzie didn't have to tell him to grab the plates while she pulled the cups from the other cupboard. He grabbed the sweet pickles instead of the dill, without her even mentioning that the dill pickles that Margret bought for the house were much too sour for her taste.

Mackenzie made their sandwiches and Liam poured the tea. It was as if the two were in a synchronized pattern that allowed them to work together seamlessly. It wasn't until a throat cleared from behind them that they even looked up from their tasks.

Geoff stood in the doorway, watching them. Mackenzie was still angry with him, but that didn't stop her insides from turning in circles or her skin from flushing with heat in his presence.

"Hey, you hungry?" Liam grunted out between bites, not noticing the obvious tension in the room.

"Nah. But can I talk to Mackenzie for a bit?" Liam looked between Mackenzie and Geoff for a moment, before standing and nodding his head.

"Yeah, sure. Hey, Mackenzie, maybe we can talk some more later?"

She smiled at him and nodded before he walked out with his plate in hand. Her gaze returned to Geoff. Mackenzie crossed her arms and sat back in her chair, waiting. If he wanted to talk, then he needed to talk. She had nothing to say.

"So, Liam came around like I said he would, huh?" Geoff's grin was too damn cute. Mackenzie hated that it was so damn cute. She couldn't understand why he had that affect on her. Most of the time, she welcomed it, but dammit, she was supposed to be mad at him.

"Uh huh."

"You want to talk about what happened earlier?"

"You want to apologize?"

"Me? I don't think I was the one who did anything wrong. I have told you before, if there is ever going to be you and me, and I really do want there to be, we have to take things slow. I know that your humanity is so recent that a few weeks time seems like forever when your hormones are in overdrive, but really, it's nothing."

"Oh, right. I'm the one to blame. I am twenty years old! I'm not a virgin, so why the hell should I have to go back to celibacy because Margret told you to take things slow? Is she in charge of your body? No one sure as hell told me that rule. And it's not as if I tried to jump your bones right there! I kissed you. I didn't even use tongue. All you had to do was not push me away. A peck, that's all it would have been. But keeping up your golden boy routine is so much more important than embarrassing me in front of everyone."

"Do you really think it would have been just a peck?" Geoff took a giant step forward, coming face to face with her. So close, she could feel the heat radiating off his skin and smell his grassy scent. Every nerve ending was on high alert as his words washed over her. "If you think I could stop with just a peck, you are mistaken."

"Is that right? All you have ever managed to do was ogle me or hold my hand. Prove me wrong." Mackenzie spoke with such confidence. She knew she was pushing him, but if it got his lips on hers, she was all for it.

"Mackenzie," he growled out. His eyes were fierce and the caramel brown color caught the light in such a way that had her transfixed. If she had been able to look anywhere else, she would have seen him wet his lips ever so slightly.

She couldn't even form words in response, only a growl escaped her. Before she knew what was happening, Geoff had his hands in her hair, gripping tightly as he pulled their bodies together and smashed his lips against hers.

With a racing heart and flaming skin, Mackenzie pressed herself closer to him. Her hands began to explore the contours of his back and found their way under his shirt. She needed to feel his skin on hers. Geoff walked them backwards, never removing his grip on her or his lips from hers, insistent on tasting every inch of her mouth. When the counter dug into her back, she pulled away slightly, just long enough to take a breath and hop up, allowing Geoff the room to stand between her legs and press himself more firmly against her .

Instead of waiting for Geoff to initiate the kiss again, she pulled him in fiercely. The moment his tongue touched the tip of her lip, she opened wide to him. Their tongues tangled together as his hands explored every inch of her body he could reach. Moaning into his mouth, Mackenzie rocked her hips forward, encouraging him. He thrust back into her with every movement. She had never felt as alive as she did in that moment.

Geoff let his lips wander away from hers, kissing along her jaw, nipping the skin over to her ear, suckling her earlobe, and then trailing kisses along her neck. Mackenzie pulled her hands from his back to his chest, running her nails along his skin the whole way. His skin erupted in goose bumps under her touch.

Mackenzie gripped the bottom of his shirt and ripped it from his body, letting the tattered cloth remains drop to the floor. She retreated so she could take in his beauty and was met with a steely glare. Geoff took a deep breath and two steps back, leaving her sitting on the counter breathing heavily in a lust-filled stupor.

"I told you I wouldn't be able to stop at just a simple kiss. You didn't believe me. Mackenzie, this cannot happen yet. There are reasons we must wait that I cannot tell you. I'm sorry. You know I want to. God, you know I do. But this cannot happen again. We have to prove to everyone that we are more than just lust-filled Weres."

"Are you seriously telling me you have never had sex? Not once?" She couldn't believe they were having the conversation. He was two hundred and forty years old, for crying out loud. And a man!

"Of course, I have, but I was mated. She died in one of the pack wars." Instantly feeling like a jackass, Mackenzie hopped off the counter and went straight to him. Placing her hands on his chest and looking up into his eyes, she could tell that he was telling her the truth. Why would he lie about that?

"Oh, Geoff. I didn't know. Why didn't you tell me? How long has it been?" Mackenzie realized that everything made sense. His standoffishness, his ridiculous no touching rules, his fear of commitment.

"It was a long time ago. Henrietta died over a hundred years ago."

"That is a long time. So no sex in a hundred years?" Geoff gave her a little laugh before removing her hands from him and walking to the refrigerator.

"Not with another Werewolf. I am a male, Mack. Human or not, we do need something more often than once a century." Instantly irritated again, she huffed. So it wasn't the act that was out, it was the act with someone he actually had a future with.

"Uh huh. So while I am waiting around, if you get horny, you just go out and find some human girl? What about me, huh? What if I get an itch I need scratched? Do I get to go out, too?" Mackenzie could see his entire body stiffen. He didn't like that one bit, but she honestly didn't care.

"As much as I don't like it, if we are not dating, I have no say in what or who you do, now do I?" Taking the milk from the fridge and drinking directly from the jug before putting it back, he turned to her again and said, "You know that I think we could be good together. It's up to you if you want to wait for me or not."

Mackenzie stood there and watched him walk out the door.

Chapter 22

After the most amazing kiss and most irritating conversation with Geoff, Mackenzie decided to give him plenty of space. The next morning she went for a run with Natalie, ate breakfast with Liam and Mason, then hid away in her room reading her books until the late afternoon. When she couldn't stand to sit still for another moment, she went downstairs and sat in the game room while the boys all fought over controllers and players in some video game.

Liam sat next to her, and by the end of the game, he had stopped flinching every time his arm grazed hers. She smiled to herself, taking it as a good sign. She couldn't think of any friendship where the people involved were terrified of touching the other.

"Mackenzie?" Teresa's voice yelled over the obnoxiously loud television set and hollering boys. "Are you in here?"

Mackenzie smiled picturing Teresa on her tiptoes looking around the room for her. There was no way that she would be able to see her sitting on the couch surrounded by all the male pack members. The boys were all hooting and hollering and bouncing around playing whatever shooting game had been on the television screen for the last hour.

"Yeah, T, Gimme a sec." Climbing out from behind and between the others was no easy task, but she did laugh a few times when she fell or accidentally knocked one guy into another's lap.

Smiling when she reached Teresa, she realized that she was actually happy. It may have taken her a while to get to that point, but knowing where she and Geoff stood, having Liam talking to her and having a group of people to not only call friends, but to call a loving family was amazing. Yeah, the Werewolf thing sucked ass and she wished that she could have all of it without the beast, but that just wasn't possible. If she could just keep working on it, maybe the next cycle she would remember more, and by the next maybe all of it. Who knows how long until she could control her wolf?

"Hey! What's up?" "Margret came back early. She and Geoff are in her office. She wants to see you," Teresa said.

"Hmm." She didn't know what else to say to that. Why had Margret come back early? Had Geoff told her about their little (okay, not so little) moment in the kitchen? Or about her memory of the last cycle? Sighing, she knew the only way to find out was to go in there. She hadn't done anything wrong, so why did she feel like she was being summoned to the principal's office?

"Good luck," Teresa said with a chuckle as she ran up the stairs. Mackenzie rolled her eyes and turned down the long hallway that led to Margret's office.

The large wooden door stood wide open and Mackenzie could hear Geoff and Margret talking happily inside. Apparently, the California house was doing well and some member named Jamie has found a mate.

."Knock, knock," Mackenzie said, poking her head into the room. Margret looked up with a wide smile and raised her hands, beckoning her into the room.

"Come in. Come in. Geoff called me and told me about what tremendous success you had at the last cycle. That is just so wonderful, Mackenzie!" Margret enveloped her in a hug.

"I thought so. I don't remember everything, but a little bit here and there. I thought it was a good start." Mackenzie released her pack leader and pseudo-mother figure to sit in the chair that was on the opposite side of the room from Geoff. She hoped it wasn't too obvious, considering the chair was the more comfortable out of the two in the room.

"A good start? Mackenzie, that's a GREAT start! Most bittens don't remember anything for at least a year, some take longer. How did you do it? Maybe we can train the others." Margret had grabbed the other chair and dragged it right in front of Mackenzie's chair. When she sat, she leaned forward with her elbows on her knees and her hands curled up under her chin. For the first time, Mackenzie saw another side to

Margret. She wasn't sitting like the regal woman she had come to know, but more like a schoolgirl eager to learn.

Glancing up at the large painting of Margret's mother, Mackenzie could imagine how the beautiful woman had looked down at her own child all those years ago. Smiling at the thought, she turned her attention back to Margret and gave her all the details.

"So you didn't fight the change and just thought of important human memories? That seems really simple. Can you think of anything else? Maybe you did something, ate something, or drank a new herbal tea? We have tried everything from supplements to hypnosis and none of it has worked."

"No, none of that. Geoff just told me not to fight it and try to hold onto my human thoughts, so I did. Except I didn't think I want to be human, I just thought about the special parts of my life. Nothing else was different."

"That is amazing. How did you just give into the pain of the turn?"

"I don't know. I just did. I guess it's like when you go in to get a tattoo. You know it's going to hurt but you are hopeful that the end result will be worth it."

Margret stood then and started pacing the room. Mackenzie took that moment to look to Geoff, to get a read on him. Would he act any differently now?

His body was angled away from her, his head slightly down while listening to Margret mumble as she paced the room. But his eyes were not were she expected them to be. No, he was looking at her and when he realized she had seen, a smile played at his lips that he quickly licked.

Just seeing his tongue dart out made her mind dizzy with thoughts of what it could do to her. Then she remembered more than just the hottest kiss she had ever had the pleasure of being a part of but the conversation that followed. They were years off. It did her no good to get hot and bothered when nothing could or would come of it. That is, unless she cornered him again.

Lost in her own naughty thoughts, she nearly missed the excited chatter between Margret and Geoff. Snapping her head back up to pay attention, she only caught part of the conversation.

"I knew it. I knew she would be different!"

"Margret, maybe we should talk about this in priva..."

"Don't you see it's in the blood? The blood!"

The two of them were standing very close to one another and Margret looked wild with excitement while Geoff just looked plain old nervous. He kept glancing between Mackenzie and Margret and trying to get Margret to listen to him. Whatever they were talking about was important but not to be spoken of in front of her.

"Hey, guys, still here. What blood? Why am I so different?" Mackenzie stood herself and waived her hands around a bit to gain their attention. When Margret looked at her, she was white as a ghost.

"Oh, I just had a feeling you would be amazing as a wolf. Sometimes gut instincts are a strong and reliable source."

"Okay..." Mackenzie wasn't buying it, and Geoff hadn't offered any explanation himself. He refused to meet her eyes and when Margret finally took notice of the body language between the two, her eyes narrowed at Geoff.

"Mackenzie, you should be celebrating with your friends. I hear that you and Liam are finally talking. Why don't you see if he wants to go to a movie or something? Invite a few people. Just grab some money from the kitchen."

Knowing she had been dismissed, she said a quick thank you before giving a small wave and a smile to Geoff. She knew that he was about to get a lecture about being inappropriate with the pack members without mating and blah, blah, blah. She felt bad for him, but only slightly. At least it wasn't her.

~*~

Mackenzie left the office and heard the door being closed as she rounded the corner to collect some people to go to the movies with her. She wasn't really interested in going, but she figured it was better than sticking around and getting pulled into the "this is inappropriate" conversation.

Liam was more than happy to go as long as they didn't go to the closest theater, which was in his hometown, but instead went to the one that was over an hour drive in the opposite direction. Teresa and Natalie jumped on board, and as they were walking out of the house, Geoff was released from Margret's office.

"Hey, you want to come?" Mackenzie asked as she pulled on her coat.

"Can't. I have things to do. But Mack, just remember, long term." He reached out and grabbed her fingers for just a second before disappearing down the hall. Slightly flustered, she watched him go.

"Earth to Mackenzie!" Teresa was snapping her fingers in front of Mackenzie's face and laughing all the while.

"Yeah, sorry, let's go."

They all walked out the door and piled into the small two-door car that was in the garage for the pack's use. Teresa was driving and Natalie had called shotgun, forcing Liam and Mackenzie to squeeze into the back together.

The only way the two could manage to fit comfortably was with his long legs in both floorboards and hers lay across the tops of his thighs. She thought that it would be awkward or just emotionally uncomfortable for Liam, but he actually just went with it. Not once adjusting or flinching away, and by the time they had reached the theater, his hand was actually resting on top of her thigh.

"Hey, are you and Geoff together?" Liam whispered once the girls had gotten out of the car to stretch. They had yet to pull the release lever to allow Liam and her to move from their tangled position in the back seat.

"Not really. There is something there, but as of right now and the immediate future, nope."

"Oh. I just thought with the time you to spend together and the kitchen thing last night, that maybe..."

Instantly on high alert, she tried to sit as upright as possible and look at him.

"Last night? You, uh, you saw that?"

"You mean the kiss worthy of a late night pay-per-view movie? Oh yeah. I had come back to put my plate away. Then instead, I made a quick exit."

"Yeah. Thanks for that. What you didn't see was Geoff's own quick retreat moments later. He is good at those. Werewolf politics or some shit that basically says he and I are a no go unless we plan to be together forever. And forever is a bit fast for me."

"Wow, yeah. Not cool."

A banging on the window behind Mackenzie's head made her jump and the girls outside laugh hysterically before moving the seats forward to let them out.

"Ha, ha, very funny. Can we please go see the movie now?" Mackenzie crossed her arms and pouted at her friends before laughing because she just couldn't fake being angry with them.

~*~

Leaving the movies, Mackenzie couldn't help but wonder why Liam had been so interested in her and Geoff. Was he concerned with the fact that one of their leaders was fooling around with a pack member? Was it really as big of a deal as Geoff was making it out to be?

"You guys, next time, I get to pick. I do not want to sit through another sappy romance movie that is so predictable you know right from the beginning what is going to happen."

"Sorry, but when you go to the movies with three girls and not another man in sight, you are going to be out-voted. Want to see blood and guts and gore? Go with the boys," Teresa said, bumping into Liam's shoulder, forcing him into Mackenzie's side. A quick smile was exchanged between the two.

"Hey, I like blood, guts, and gore sometimes. It's not just a guy thing."

"Good, then maybe we can come back next week and see *Death's Revenge*?" Liam asked. He looked to her with apprehension and at first, she didn't understand why, then it dawned on her, he hadn't asked anyone else.

"Oh, um, yeah sure. Maybe Mason and Terry would want to go to?" Mackenzie figured it would be best to do a bit more friend things before anyone tried moving anything past the friend zone. She knew that Geoff wasn't really going to happen, but that didn't make her care about him any less.

"Oh, yeah, okay. No problem."

Teresa and Natalie watched with rapt attention, not saying a word. When Liam had gotten into the car, both girls grabbed Mackenzie's arm, and with a stern look, they said in unison, "Later."

Mackenzie knew they wouldn't let it go until she did the whole 'boy talk' conversation. She really did want to talk to someone, but she wasn't sure if talking about what had happened with Geoff would be all right or not. She couldn't deny that being around Liam was nice. They got along great and there was a sense of something more there that she didn't understand.

Teresa leaned into her ear and barley whispered, "You know, sire and sired usually have some killer chemistry."

"T, not now. Later. I promise." But that one shared secret had given her so much to think about on the ride home.

Chapter 23

Dinner in the house was a celebration that night because Margret returned early. Everyone loved her and loved when she was around. She always cooked dinner when she was there and for most of the pack that was enough to grant her sainthood.

Barbeque ribs and baked beans overflowed the platters and bowls in the middle of the table as the plate with ears of corn on the cob was being passed around. The dining room was full of chatter and everyone managed to make it down to eat as one big family. That is, everyone except the one person Mackenzie really wanted to see.

Geoff's chair beside Margret was empty. Mackenzie kept watching the doors that led into the room, in between conversations and eating. When she spotted Margret watching her, she looked instantly to her plate.

"It is so nice to be back with you all. You know you are my children and I love you dearly. I will be staying here for the next month, cycling with you all, and helping you as much as I can. Geoff has had to leave to the Alaska land to help out there. He will be back after the next cycle." Margret had the attention of the whole room. They hooped and hollered when she told them she was there to stay and no one seemed all the upset with Geoff's absence. That is, except Mackenzie. Watching Margret's face, trying to decipher if Geoff really was needed to help, or if he was being punished for their relationship, provided no answers. She would just have to ask.

Everyone lingered around the dinner table long after the food had vanished. Margret spoke about the pups in Alaska, and how another pack had challenged the California members of the pack while she was there. The room erupted in chatter, questioning the safety of their brothers and sisters. Mackenzie couldn't help but wonder how Analise had held up.

"Is everyone okay?" Mackenzie asked above the noise. The room fell silent and everyone turned their attention back to Margret. She actually voiced what everyone wanted to know, but for some reason didn't ask.

"As you all know, when a pack challenges another there are always casualties. We lost four of our family, but the other pack fell and are being trained as our own. I hope you will welcome the new members with open arms when you meet them."

"Who?" someone called out.

"Nicholas, Bradley, Brea, and Lance." While Mackenzie didn't know these people, she grieved for those who did and was grateful that Analise was not among them.

"I hope you made that bastard feel the pain before you ripped his head from his body!" Mason said with a steely glare. Mackenzie could tell he was trying to hide his emotions. His eyes were red-rimmed and he kept taking deep breaths before turning his glare to the floor.

"He paid for attacking our family. His pack members are now mine. We lost four of our own, but won ten more. We will forever miss our fallen, but we are stronger now than we were before. Our land in California has increased to cover the forest to the north of our previous boundary."

Mackenzie sat in her chair long after everyone else left the room. She couldn't understand how Margret could show not an ounce of real grief. Could she be just holding it together for the sake of the pack?

So lost in her thoughts, she hadn't heard anyone come back into the room, so when two large heavy hands were placed on her shoulders from behind, she nearly jumped out of her skin. Quickly turning around to see who it was, she was able to breathe a sigh of relief. It was only Liam.

"You scared the hell out of me!"

"Sorry," he said, though by the way he laughed through the word he wasn't sorry at all. "I just wanted to check in on you after all that. That Margret is something, isn't she?"

"Yeah, she is. She has been so kind, welcoming me into her home, helping me that morning she found me. I hate to say it, but something just doesn't feel right when she's here anymore. Everyone else loves her. They consider her their mother. I just get a bad feeling and I don't know why."

Mackenzie began watching the doors, hoping they were speaking low enough not to be overheard. That was one thing about living in a house with so many other beings with super-sensitive hearing, unless you learned to whisper, no one had any privacy.

"You should go ask her about Geoff. You know you want to."

"I do. But I don't think she will answer me."

"Can't hurt to ask." Liam gave her a brief smile and patted her shoulder before leaving her alone once again. Mackenzie knew he was right. But actually approaching Margret was more difficult than actually thinking about it.

~*~

Mackenzie could see a light shining from the crack beneath the office door. Standing in the dark hallway, she took a step forward before turning around and retreating. She did this ten times before the door swung open with Margret standing just before the opening, the light creating a halo around her whole body.

"You have been pacing out here forever. Spit it out." Margret spoke so matter-of-factly. She had to have known that Mackenzie wanted to ask about

Geoff. The irritation on her face was evident and Mackenzie almost decided to drop the topic and walk away. But she knew that if she did, she would kick herself all the way back to her room.

"Where's Geoff?"

"Mackenzie, I told you all at dinner. He went to Alaska to help with the influx of pups. There are more than normal coming into their strengths. They needed another leader and I needed to be here for you. I will be the one shadowing you on the next cycle so I can see exactly what is happening with you. That way, in the morning you can tell me what you remember and I will know for sure if it really happened or not."

Caught off guard by the fact that Margret didn't necessarily believe her about the last cycle, she stilled. She had been so excited for her just a few hours prior.

"What? You think just because Geoff believes you that I am going to, also? I am not calling you a liar. I just need to see it with my own eyes before I give the other pups any false hope of being able to control the wolves sooner than normal. You understand don't you?"

Mackenzie just nodded. She did understand to an extent, but just because Margret said she wasn't calling her a liar, didn't make it feel any less so. The two stared at one another for another minute before Margret sighed.

"If that's all?"

"No. I mean, that's not all. Why are there more pups than usual in Alaska? Did something happen?" She knew she should have left well enough alone, but things were not sitting right for her. The California attack, Geoff leaving, and then an influx of pups?

"Alaska is where we put the majority of our born Weres. They can start families and raise their children in our way of life without prying eyes or human customs. This time of year usually has more pups coming into their wolves. Kids grow up, Mackenzie, even Werewolf kids. It's how life works."

"Oh. Right. Of course. Can I get the phone number for the Alaska house? I would really like to be able to talk to him." She felt like an idiot. She already knew there were kids at that property. Why had she assumed the worst?

"I don't think that is such a good idea. If he didn't give you his phone number, then it isn't my place to. Mackenzie, I know the two of you are attracted to one another, but you have to know there is no future for you two. You are a bitten. And that does not make you less of a Werewolf or a person, but you already know that means you are barren. You cannot have children and Geoff is a leader amongst our pack. He needs a mate that can bear his young. He knows this. He told me he spoke to you about the fact you cannot be together without being mated. There are plenty of other men in our own house as well as the California house that will make a good match for you. But you and Geoff can only be friends."

Mackenzie was speechless. She had known a little about the mating but Geoff never told her he had to mate with someone who could give him children. She knew that he had no children yet. At least, that was what he told her. She knew he had been mated before, perhaps his last mate died before she had the chance to give him an heir.

"Oh." Not knowing what else to say, she turned around to go up to her room. Just before she got to the stairs, she turned back around abruptly to see the office door almost closed.

"Margret, One more thing!" The door swung back open to the pack leader leaning against the doorframe watching her. "The California pack? How was Analise? I haven't heard from her since you two left here."

"Analise has decided that pack life isn't for her." Margret took a step back and closed the door, leaving no room for further discussion.

~*~

Taking the stairs slowly, Mackenzie kept replaying the conversation with Margret in her head. Margret wasn't being mean or rude, but she was very matter-of-fact and didn't hold anything back. She may not be less of a wolf or less of a person, but according to Margret, she wasn't good enough for Geoff because she couldn't bear children. For the first time in a long time, she did feel like less. Less of a woman.

She walked into her room and saw Teresa and Natalie curled up on the bed, watching something on the television. They both looked up when she came in, but neither spoke to her. Mackenzie was sure that her mood was evident and she didn't blame them for not wanting to deal with the mopey roommate. She just had to pull herself together. Geoff was gone.

Apparently, they had zero chance unless he was willing to go against traditional Werewolf customs and politics. Just because of that and the fact that her first friend in the pack was no longer in the pack, didn't mean she didn't have things going for her.

Grabbing a pair of pajamas and heading to the bathroom to take a long hot bath, she reminded herself of everything she did have. She had two really great friends right outside the bathroom door. She had a budding friendship with Liam. She had a built in pseudo-family and she had found a way to speed up the process of controlling her wolf, even if Margret wasn't sure she believed her.

What Mackenzie couldn't understand was why she seemed so excited that morning, only to act as if she didn't believe it that night.

The warm water soothed her body and her mind, and by the time the water had cooled, she felt much lighter. There was nothing she could do about Margret except wait until the next cycle to prove to her that she was being honest. There was nothing she could do about Geoff being gone or the fact that Analise had chosen to live alone rather than in the pack. What she could do was get dressed and go watch a movie with her two best friends in the house.

Chapter 24

The following morning loud knocks sounded from the opposite side of the bedroom door. When Natalie groaned at being woken, Mackenzie knew it had to be very early. Peeking her head out from under the pillow, the sky glowed with a pink hue.

Mackenzie knew there was entertainment coming when Teresa was the one to climb out of bed first. Murder in her eyes, she stalked over to the door and flung it open.

"What the fucking hell—" Teresa's obvious anger deflated in less than a second when she saw the perpetrator was none other than Margret herself. Mumbling an apology, Teresa retreated, allowing Margret to enter the room. The three girls all quickly and not so subtly looked around the room, hoping that they had kept the mess to a minimum. They were usually tidy, but the movie the previous night had turned into a marathon, complete with junk food and manicures.

"Girls, I am sending everyone out of the house today. It is supposed to be unusually nice outside and you have all been cooped up indoors for too long. I know a certain gentleman has been hoping for some time with a certain young lady," Margret said with a little grin in Teresa's direction. The blush that emanated from Teresa's skin suggested she too knew who the certain gentleman was. Natalie, on the other hand, looked completely torn. "Mackenzie, Natalie, I hoped I could convince the two of you to take Liam for a run with you. Spend some more time with him. He was closest with Geoff and Mason, and with Geoff gone and Mason dealing with pack business around here, he needs to be with someone he is comfortable with. Plus, I think the sire bond is something to explore."

Mackenzie knew what she was doing. She had told her just the night before to explore other options in the opposite sex. She wasn't sure she was happy about being set up with someone who she had just started to be friends with, but at least Natalie would be there too.

Teresa began buzzing around the room getting ready for whatever she and the mystery man would be doing. Watching her flit around, Mackenzie couldn't even believe it was Teresa. She had never even seen her leave the bed before nine, let alone do it happily. She smiled as she watched her friend. She was happy for her, but that apparently didn't work for Natalie.

Grudgingly, Natalie and Mackenzie readied for the day as well, but it proved difficult with all three crowding the bathroom. They had never attempted to do so before and they soon figured out why. A single sink and limited counter and mirror space had the girls pushing and shoving to declare their own area. Unfortunately for all of them, it took longer than if they had taken turns.

Teresa headed out first, leaving Natalie sulking. Mackenzie watched her friend and wondered if maybe the sire bond between the two was stronger for one than the other.

"Nat?"

"Not now, Mack. Please?"

"Okay, but I am here, ya know. No judgments, no comments, just an ear to listen."

"Thanks." Natalie stood up and wrapped her arms around Mackenzie, squeezing her tightly. "You are a really good friend. I am so glad that you joined our family."

Mackenzie just nodded and hugged her tighter.

Liam, still rumpled from sleep, met the girls at the front door. Both girls took in his appearance and laughed. His hair was sticking in all directions, there were pillow lines along his face, and he still wore his pajama pants.

"What? I'm here, aren't I? Why am I here?"

"Because we were banished from the house for the next few hours apparently and you were lucky enough to be assigned to the two of us. Are you sure you want to run in that?"

Liam looked down at himself and ran a hand through his hair, then looked back to the girls. "I have my running shoes on."

"Okay, then. Let's go!" Natalie called out before charging out the door. Liam and Mackenzie followed behind her, pushing themselves to catch up.

The brisk morning air chilled her nose, but the speed with which they were running began to warm Mackenzie from the inside. The three running partners said nothing. The only sounds came from their feet on the pavement, their heavy breaths, and the few animals still skittering about.

After an hour, the three ended up in the middle of town. Mackenzie looked around to see if anyone had noticed them, remembering Liam's worry about being seen by someone who knew him.

"We can go if you want," she whispered, leaning up close to his ear so only he would hear her. She didn't know how much he wanted to tell Natalie and it wasn't her story to tell.

"Let's grab a bite to eat first. It's still early. I doubt anyone will be here," he whispered back in the same way. The closeness brought a smile to Mackenzie's face.

Liam held the diner door open for the girls and followed in behind them. Taking a corner booth in the very back of the dinner, they ordered breakfast. What had become normal to them astounded the waitress. With every stroke of her pen on her order pad, her eyes grew wider. After the fifth full meal was ordered, she began to look at them skeptically. Perhaps she thought they were just a bunch of rude kids who would run out on a huge tab, but Mackenzie knew she would be pleased when they did in fact stay and eat every bit and tip her accordingly.

Once they were alone, Mackenzie knew it was time to tell them more about her last cycle. Perhaps if they tried to do it, Margret would have more experiences to study.

"You guys, I think I figured out how to speed up controlling the beast." Both Liam and Natalie exchanged a look with the other before turning back to her. She cringed when the word beast slipped from her mouth. She knew the rest of the house detested her use of the word to describe the wolf. She hoped her friends in front of her would ignore her personal views of their circumstances and focus on her intended meaning.

"What do you mean? I know you said you thought you remembered bits and pieces, but you think you made that happen?" Natalie asked in hushed whisper. Liam sat next to her silently. He stared at the table and Mackenzie hoped that he wouldn't return to the 'I hate her' mentality. She rather like hanging out with him.

"I know I did. Geoff told me not to fight it. To allow the change to happen and to somehow keep my own mind. When the moonlight hit me, and the pain started in, I swear every time I think I'm going to die, but I gave into it. I thought of everything in my human life that I loved. My mother, even though she and I never really saw eye to eye once I grew up, my grandmother, and... feelings I wanted to remember. I stopped fighting the wolf. When the morning came, I could remember bits and pieces. Not much, but enough to know that it was working."

"You think it will work for us? What if that had nothing to do with it? What if you can just do it faster? I can already remember. I wonder if I would be able to control it for more than a few minutes?" Natalie asked.

"The only way to know is to try it. Can you guys keep this between us? Margret wanted to make sure what I was saying was true before telling anyone. Didn't want to get anyone's hopes up. But after the last two cycles, I thought you two would want to know there was a chance."

"But the pain, how do you…how do you just, just let it happen?" Liam asked, still intent on studying the table.

"You focus on something else. What is the one thing that keeps you honest? That reminds you of how good it can be to live. I don't know how else to explain it."

Everyone became lost in their own thoughts as the food was placed on the table. Less than an hour later, every plate was empty and still not a word had been spoken. Mackenzie was terrified that she had just scared them off, but as Liam paid the bill and the girls split the tremendous tip, Natalie looked up with unshed tears in her eyes. "Thank you."

Smiling at her friend, and then looking over her shoulder to Liam, she knew she had done the right thing. "You're welcome."

Instead of running back as a group, Natalie decided she wanted to shop alone for a while. "You guys head back. I just need some girly products and

Liam shouldn't have to be subjected to that from any female he isn't dating. And no offense, but you are just not my type." Mackenzie couldn't help but laugh because she finally knew what type that was.

"Are you sure you don't want us to hang around some other shops and we can all head back together?"

"No, you two go on. I will be fine. I want some time alone anyway. See you back at the house." With that, she disappeared into a store with mannequins in the windows decked out in sweater dresses and stunning bags.

"Hey, I didn't, you know, make you mad back there did I? I thought you would want to know. I mean, I am really glad I figured it out because just the idea of years of not knowing and not controlling myself part of the time just scares the hell out of me." Mackenzie stumbled through her thoughts. She was just trying to help but she didn't want him to go back to ignoring her.

"No, why would I be mad? No offense, but I never want the wolf to hurt anyone. Animals are one thing. I ate animals before you bit me. Hell, I had a steak that very night. I eat animals now. The only difference is that as a wolf, I hunt it and eat it without going to the store and buying it already butchered. But I never want to hurt a person. I don't want to wake up and find out I killed someone or turned someone. If what you said works, I won't know how to thank you."

"You could forgive me?" She had finally said it. She knew it was her fault that he had become like her. It was her fault that he had to leave his real family, her fault his brother was hurt, her fault he despised his life so much.

"I already have. I told you I know you didn't have control, that it was the monster that hides inside of us."

"But some part of you, some part has to still blame me. Hell, I still blame the bastard who bit me and I don't even know who it was. The fucking wolf attacked me and ran off after I bashed its face in with a rock. I don't even know why now. At first, I thought it was because I hurt it. But I know how fast we heal now. I think the rock should have just pissed it off more. It should have killed me. But it didn't. It ran off."

"Do you think it was young and couldn't control itself or did it know what was going on?" His question was one she had asked herself a million times. She wished she had the answer.

"I have no idea and I doubt I will ever be able to ask."

The walk back was a slow one, neither wanting to rush back to the house, just enjoying the companionship. Mackenzie looked up at Liam and wondered if what Margret said were true, that Geoff could never really be with her, if she could ever have a future with Liam. Immediately, after the thought passed through her mind, she chastised herself. If Geoff had wanted to follow the traditions of the packs, then he would have told her. He would never lie to her or lead her on. He cared for her. She knew he did. Even if he did get his manly urges off with unsuspecting human girls. Mackenzie briefly wondered if he was doing that at that exact moment.

Jealousy flared through her and knowing it was wrong but knowing it wouldn't stop her anyway, she turned to Liam.

He was extremely attractive. She had realized that immediately. She wasn't blind after all. He had that cute geek chic look going but more of the Clark Kent variety because she knew what lay under his shirt. She knew now that they finally were speaking and were on friendly terms that he really was a nice guy and made her laugh. She also knew there was something about being around him that made her feel different.

"Hey, do you know when that movie is playing?" She asked.

"Next week you mean? I hadn't checked yet. Still need to ask the others."

"You should look for this weekend. You don't have to invite the others."

Liam looked surprised by her statement, and in all honesty, so was she. She knew she was hung up on Geoff. But Geoff couldn't or wouldn't be with her. Liam was perfectly nice and perfectly handsome, and perfectly available.

~*~

Days went by without word from Geoff. At first, Mackenzie felt really guilty for making plans with Liam, but with every passing day that Geoff didn't call, she felt less and less bad about going out with Liam.

It was nice to actually have a date. Not a movie in the living room or sitting next to one another at a table with the whole pack, but an actual date. Dress nice, put on some make up, and go out together without anyone else around. Not having to hide the smiles when they looked at one another in front of the pack was new and exciting as well. She was actually able to talk to Teresa and Natalie about everything because the idea of a relationship with Liam not only wasn't taboo, but also encouraged by Margret.

On more than one occasion, Mackenzie had seen Margret smiling at her and Liam. She had even given Liam extra money to turn their movie into a real date night with dinner as well. Liam wasn't supposed to tell Mackenzie, of course, but he had anyway. She was pleased, but also a little nervous. What if it didn't work out between them? What if they were destined to be really good friends and Geoff was the one for her? Would going out with Liam jeopardize everything she and Geoff had? But every time that thought entered her mind, she would swat it away. Geoff told her he couldn't be more than a friend until they were ready to pledge forever to each other. Forever was a very long time.

Music blared through the speakers in Mackenzie's room as she danced around with Teresa and Natalie. Clothing scattered the room as she tried on everything she owned twice, and Natalie's once and she still hadn't found anything that she wanted to wear. Standing in front of the closet mirror in nothing but her underwear and bra, she held up two pieces of clothing, going back and forth and throwing them to the floor in frustration as well.

"That's it! I am going like this. Let's do my hair and makeup and be done with it." Mackenzie announced through a fit of giggles.

"Hey, I'm sure Liam won't mind. His job is half done that way," Natalie shouted before jumping away from Teresa's swinging arm. Another round of laughter sounded from the girls until finally Mackenzie sighed, looking around at the destruction surrounding her.

"I have no idea why I am so worried about this. He sees me every day. I bet I can just throw on some jeans and any old shirt and it would be fine. I mean, dinner at the little diner and a movie. It isn't a big deal. Let's just pick something."

"Mackenzie, maybe you should try this?" All three girls jumped at the sound of Margret's voice in their room and turned around to see her standing there holding up a beautiful deep green sweater dress and brown boots.

"Those are so pretty, but are you sure it will fit?" Mackenzie all of a sudden found herself transported back into her old body, her old feelings, and her old mentality that anything pretty was too small.

"Yes. I am. Try it on."

Teresa ran over to Margret and grabbed the garment and practically forced it over Mackenzie's head. It fit like a glove in all the right places and flowed nicely over the rest. Looking into the mirror, she didn't see the overweight girl that so often reflected back to her, but a confident beautiful woman.

"Thank you, Margret." Looking back at her pack leader, she felt a sudden urge to hug her. Maybe the bad feelings she had been feeling about Margret were wrong. Margret was looking at her like a daughter and that made her feel amazing and sad at the same time. She missed her real mother.

"Finish getting ready. Liam has been ready and pacing his room for the last half an hour. Someone is a very eager young man. Can't say as I blame him."

Margret left the room and Teresa went to work on Mackenzie's hair as Natalie turned her face into a painter's canvas. When both were done, she looked like a more polished version herself.

With every step down the stairs, Mackenzie's heart hammered louder and louder. She was nervous. Over and over, she reminded herself that it was just Liam, that there was no reason to be nervous. When she saw that every member of the house was standing at the foot of the stairs in a large arc around Liam, the nerves switched from Liam, to not falling flat on her face trying to navigate the steps in her new high heel boots.

Catcalls sounded and a few of the more immature members of the house began singing the old school yard kissing song. Heat flamed her cheeks and she knew that she was blushing. When her eyes finally landed on Liam, she had to stop walking completely. He was devastatingly handsome. He not only wore a button down shirt, but a tie to match and even though she knew he no longer needed them to see, he wore glasses. He mentioned to her that he missed them, he felt strange and less like himself without them. She told him to get a pair with plain glass if he really wanted to and apparently, he had. The dark metal frames looked very masculine and accentuated the sharp sculpture of his face.

Liam took the stairs two at a time until he stood directly before her. His eyes darted around her face before finally landing on her eyes.

"You look absolutely breathtaking," he whispered.

"So do you."

Liam smiled at her, took her hand, and led her down the stairs, through the crowd, and out the door.

The only sound in the car had been that of the radio. Mackenzie didn't know what to say, and Liam never spoke up. She never thought that their night would be filled with awkward silences. Ever since they had begun talking, they always had something to say to the other.

"Okay, what the heck is wrong with us?" Liam blurted out just before turning into the parking lot of the restaurant.

"I have no idea. Wait, this isn't the diner?" Mackenzie looked around at the unfamiliar building. It was brightly lit with twinkling white lights and green ivy growing up and down the sides of the buildings and the posts.

"No, it's not. I thought we should go somewhere new. I mean, this is something new for us. right? A date, instead of just friends hanging out?" The way he said it came across as more of a question than a statement. Liam knew the kind of relationship that she had with Geoff, perhaps he wanted to know where they stood. She wasn't really sure herself but after seeing him at the foot of the stairs, and seeing all the thought he put into the night, she really did want it to be a date instead of friends. For once, it wasn't because she wanted to piss off Geoff.

"Yeah, I like that idea."

"Let's go eat. I'm starving!"

Mackenzie laughed and shook her head, "Aren't you always?"

"Yeah, but so are you, so at least neither of us have to feel like pigs or only eat half of what we normally would because of first date jitters. Score one for dating a friend."

Dinner went well. Conversation flowed easily and Mackenzie found herself more and more relaxed. After paying the check, Liam stood and pulled out her chair, helped her with her jacket, and then, ever so quickly, slipped his hand into hers as if he had been doing it every day since they met.

The strong presence of his fingers wrapped around hers made her feel safe. The look in his eyes when gazed upon her with a slight smile and soft-hooded eyes made her feel beautiful. And the heat radiating from him only inches away from her made her want him.

Opening the passenger door for her, Liam stood close. His breath blew hot against her skin, making it erupt in goose bumps. When he went to take a step back to actually open the door, she moved with him. Gripping his shirt in her hands, she looked up into his eyes and waited. She wanted him to kiss her. She needed to know if the chemistry was there. She needed to be kissed without being pushed away. She needed to feel wanted.

Liam slowly leaned down, his eyes never breaking from hers until just before his lips briefly touched hers. Just as their lips touched, a small amount of pressure, proving to her that he had been the one to kiss her, he pulled back, but only slightly. He looked into her eyes, and she hoped he got every answer he was looking for. She wasn't moving. She wanted more. When he didn't move in to kiss her again, she took matters into her own hands and launched herself at him.

Hungry lips and exploring tongues, wandering hands and heaving chests, filled the next moments with a kiss so intense that Mackenzie only had one other to compare it to. The minute her mind wandered to Geoff, she had to pull away.

"What? What's wrong?" Liam asked with swollen lips and a look of worry on his face.

"Nothing, just, um, let's cool it down a bit. How about that movie?" She could tell he didn't quite buy it. But not wanting the night to end, he agreed. Climbing into the car, they drove to the theater to watch blood guts and gore on a big screen, holding hands throughout the whole thing.

Chapter 25

Mackenzie had never felt so wonderful at the end of a date before. Most had been painfully awkward by the time they dropped her off at her door, but with Liam, it was different. She couldn't help but think it was because they were friends first and that they could relate to one another in a way no one else had been able to do.

The house was dark upon their return, with just a slight hum of noise seeping through the walls from a few of the bedrooms. They silently hung their jackets and tiptoed up the stairs, holding hands the whole way. They didn't want to say goodbye just yet, but they also didn't want to attract an audience like the one they had when they left earlier in the evening.

He skipped over the third stair from the second floor, because it would creak the loudest, Liam landed with a thud on the next step. Fighting back laughter, the two passed the landing that led to the boys' rooms and continued their climb up to the third floor.

Liam pulled her close to him, gently brushed a few stray hairs away from her ear, and leaned in, placing his hands on either side of her hips. "Shhh. Remember, you're the one who didn't want all the prying eyes."

His words lost all meaning when she felt his breath tickle her neck, and his fingers dance along her waist. Turning her head ever so slightly, she was able to look into his eyes. Swallowing down the lump in her throat, she raised herself up onto her tiptoes and pressed a slight kiss along his jaw then pulled back. The smile that played at his lips told her their night wasn't over. When he gripped her tightly and pulled her in, covering her mouth with his, she knew she was right.

The two stumbled down the hall toward Mackenzie's room. After Liam had to catch her twice for tripping over his own feet, he simply lifted her up, holding her underneath her ass, with her legs wrapped around him.

Finally at her door, Liam braced her back against it with a thud. He pressed himself into her as she moved her hips against him. Mackenzie broke the kiss to take a breath and tipped her head to the side, giving him all the access he wanted to her neck, before gripping his hair and pulling him back to her mouth. Their tongues tangled with one another, almost in an exotic dance within their mouths.

Thrusting his hips into hers once again caused another bang against the door and a moan to escape from Mackenzie. Liam growled in response and pressed on, nipping at her lips and neck, followed by little licks and kisses to soothe the slight sting his teeth had left behind.

Much too soon, Liam stilled his hips, and slowed his kisses until all that were left were chaste pecks. Letting her legs drop to the floor, he tipped her chin up to him and smiled.

"I will see you tomorrow," he said. Mackenzie smiled at him with what she had to assume was the silliest grin she had ever mustered.

"Uh huh."

He chuckled in response before leaving her standing in awe, watching him walk away. She was grateful Liam had propped her against the door, she wasn't sure she would be able to stand on her own without it.

"Seems you and Liam have made a lot of progress in my absence." Completely caught off guard, Mackenzie snapped her gaze up to see Geoff standing a few feet away.

"Um, yeah. Where have you been? I had no way to call you or find out if you were okay." She wasn't sure how much he had seen, if he had seen anything at all. She knew that she had done nothing technically wrong, but seeing Geoff standing right there made her question all of her choices. No matter how happy they had made her in the moment.

"I was on business. Margret said she told you that. I just thought you would want to know I was back for the weekend. I had wanted to take you out but I came back to be told by everyone who saw me that you were out on a date with Liam."

"Geoff...," she started. But she had no idea what to say. They weren't together so she was technically free to see anyone she wanted. But the way she felt with him there, the way he was looking at her, as if she were his even without the title, made her feel guilty.

"Look, I get it. You have physical needs just like I do. I told you about how I fill those needs without a mate and you found yours. I just don't want to hear about it. Goodnight, Mackenzie."

She watched him go in silence. She knew that Liam was more than a physical need. She knew she needed to tell Geoff that. But she also knew that one night with Liam, while absolutely wonderful, didn't erase all of her feelings for Geoff. Groaning she opened the bedroom door to pour herself into bed and deal with her confusing life later, only to be greeted by two girls, with pillows covering their mouths to hide their laughter.

"So... that was an interesting way to end the date!" Natalie squealed. Mackenzie looked at her two friends and laughed along with them.

~*~

When the morning sun poured through the large window, Mackenzie buried herself further under her blankets. What should have been a great morning now looked much more confusing. Had her date with Liam been the only thing to happen, she would be happily skipping down the stairs to breakfast just to see if he were as joyous as she was. Or if Geoff returning were the only thing that happened, she would be thinking of ways to spend any amount of one on one time with him. Instead, she lay in bed, hiding beneath the covers, hoping that neither man remembered she was there.

After putting off the morning for far too long, she climbed out of bed and got ready for her daily run. Hoping for an easy escape, she avoided the kitchen, the den, and any other area she thought either man would be.

As she stepped out of the front door and breathed in the chilly air, she was finally able to relax. Every step away from the house, every breath of fresh air invigorated her. She knew she had to be adult about the little situation in which she found herself. Hiding away did no one any good.

Heading back to the house with a to-do list that would take her well over two hours, and that she just so happened to keep adding to, would make it so she couldn't speak to or even see either Liam or Geoff until at least lunch. A group like that would be perfect because there was no way they would want to speak with an audience.

Sneaking back into the house and practically running to her room, Mackenzie managed not to see a soul. Showering, cleaning, organizing, and finishing her book took all the time she had expected. The smells from the lunch being prepared downstairs wafted up causing her mouth to water. She could no longer deny her hunger. Taking a deep breath, she opened the door and headed down to the dining room.

~*~

Mackenzie could hear the entire pack in the talking and laughing from the hallway. When she rounded the corner into the dining room, she had hoped that Teresa or Natalie might have saved her a seat. Too bad her two supposed best friends were grinning wickedly at her, completely surrounded by full chairs.

Everyone quickly hushed and stared at her with silly grins on their faces and it wasn't until she saw that the only open chair was directly between Geoff and Liam did she understand. They were all enjoying her predicament. It was no secret how she and Geoff were becoming closer, and it was definitely no secret that she and Liam had gone out.

Both men kept their eyes trained on Mackenzie. It wasn't until she stood directly behind them and pulled out her chair that they acknowledged one another. Neither wanting to back down, they only lost eye contact when Mackenzie sat in between them. When it was obvious that she wasn't going to give the group any form of entertainment, the noise returned to the room.

Realizing she hadn't eaten since dinner the night before, Mackenzie loaded her plate. She could see Margret watching as both men tried to gain her attention. She didn't ignore either, but also wouldn't let the conversation venture toward anything that could put her in a position of choosing one man over the other. It may have been selfish, but she honestly didn't know what to do.

"Geoff, how is the Alaska house fairing with the new influx?" Margret asked. The entire room quieted down once again and turned their attention to Geoff. He wiped his mouth with his napkin and returned it to his lap.

"They are doing well. Better than we expected. That's why I was able to come back for a few days. I needed to get something and was worried that if I left it for too long, I might lose it. So I was very glad things are going well." As he spoke, Mackenzie couldn't help but notice how the girls in the room looked to her with a smile. Ever the romantics. Mackenzie didn't believe he was speaking of her, she wasn't a thing after all, and how could he lose something he never truly had?

"What did you forget?" Amanda, one of the older women asked with a grin. Mackenzie couldn't believe they were pressing the issue, until she felt his hand snake up her thigh with only inches to her girly bits and squeeze. Trying to hide her shock, not only from the group as a whole, but also from Liam, who sat to the other side of her, she too used her napkin as a cover for putting her hands below the table. She placed her hand on top of his and moved it away.

"Doesn't matter. Pretty sure it's gone now." Mackenzie's heart ached. She wanted to tell him that no, it wasn't gone. But she looked over to Liam and then back to Geoff and she couldn't tell him that. It wasn't all gone, but part of it was given to someone else.

Losing her appetite, she sat back in her chair. If she got up and left, she would be followed. If she just sat there and waited for everyone else to leave first, she could manage not to have to talk about what had just happened.

As if he could tell that something was wrong, Liam looked to her questioningly. He mouthed the words "are you okay" and she shrugged. His hand too found her leg but it felt more comforting than anything else did.

"Come on, let's go talk." Liam stood and waited for Mackenzie to follow. She looked back to Geoff who was paying close attention to their conversation before sighing. She stood up and followed Liam from the room. She was very thankful for the fact that most of the pack had already left the dining room, and they were off doing their own thing. Perhaps they would find something besides her completely confusing love life to entertain them.

Wandering to the den, they sat together on the couch. Liam looked at her for a minute and Mackenzie could see the sadness in his eyes. He reached forward and ran his thumb across her jaw before pulling away.

"Do you wish last night hadn't happened?"

His question took her by complete surprise. That was something that had never even occurred to her. Sure, she thought things would be simpler if just one man filled her night but she never wished it hadn't happened. Shaking her head, she reached for his hand.

"Never. Last night was amazing. Best date ever. Promise."

"So, is it Geoff? I thought you said you two weren't a thing."

"We aren't but that doesn't mean the feelings aren't there." Mackenzie then went into the whole conversation about Geoff being off limits. How he couldn't be with her because of pack ways and because of the fact that she was a bitten were. She told him how intense she feels around Geoff, but in a completely different way than she feels with him.

Liam never spoke while Mackenzie explained herself. He listened to her even when Mackenzie could tell it was hurting him to do so.

"So what now, Mackenzie? Do we try to go back to being just friends so you can figure out if Geoff will ever buck tradition for you? I won't be a back-up."

"You aren't a back-up! Never. I don't know what to do now. I know that this, you and me, is something. I just can't honestly be anyone's girlfriend, mate, or whatever until I know with all my heart that I am with the right person."

Liam didn't say anything. He just tugged at her hand and pulled her into his lap. They sat together for a while and planned out what movies they wanted to see or places to go. It was obvious to Mackenzie that Liam was trying to give her exactly what she needed, time with him without the pressure of defining it.

"Mackenzie, may I speak to you in private?" Completely lost in her conversation with Liam, she hadn't heard Geoff enter the room. Seemed Liam had that effect on her.

"Yeah, one sec." Mackenzie looked to Liam with worry in her eye. He squeezed her hand briefly before letting go. Mackenzie stood and watched Geoff leave the room. She sent a quick goodbye wave to Liam before following behind.

~*~

Geoff didn't look back at her to see if she were following. Mackenzie was certain that he knew she would follow him anywhere. What she wasn't sure of was if that were a good thing or not.

When he passed the office and the deserted den, she knew that he was taking her to his room. Whatever he wanted to say, he didn't want anyone to overhear it. Her heart raced at all the possibilities of the conversation, both good and bad. Truth be told, she didn't know how she was going to react with either possibility.

The stairs creaked with every step, but she didn't hear a sound. So wrapped up in her own head, going over all the 'what if's' of the pending conversation, she marched on in a fog. It wasn't until she ran straight into Geoff's back outside of his bedroom door that she snapped out of it.

"Sorry." It was the only thing she had managed to say after agreeing to follow him when he walked in and saw her sitting on Liam's lap. She had meant it just for running into him, but once the word was out, she wasn't sure what else she was apologizing for, or if she even needed to apologize

"Come on," he said as he opened his bedroom door.

Once they were inside, all sounds ceased. Geoff's room and Margret's office were the only two rooms in the entire house that were completely soundproof. She didn't know the mechanics of it, and had never asked, but they were the only places that it was truly silent. If only the door had been fully closed the night she slept in his bed, no one would have heard her moaning in her dreams.

"Are you and Liam a couple?" Geoff stood in front of her, his arms crossed and his shoulders squared. His body language screamed out power and confidence. His eyes, on the other hand, were desperately seeking validation. They darted around her face, before locking in on her eyes. She could see right through his act.

"No. I told him how much I care about you. But I also care about him. I am a confused mess right now. You are hot one second, cold the next. You keep things from me and expect me to wait around. To top it all off, I was told that because of your position in the pack, we can't ever be mated. So I am supposed to fall for someone who can never actually be mine?"

His stance visibly relaxed. When he stepped toward her, she felt herself move toward him without even thinking about it. He placed his hands on her arms, and rubbed them, looking down to where he touched her.

"I didn't tell you because I was trying to find a way around it. I want you. I want you more than anything and I will find a way to keep you and my position with the pack."

"You don't act like you want me. Everything you say and do feels like you don't want to lose me, but not like you want me. There's a difference."

"I want you."

Geoff closed the small distance between the two and grasped her firmly in his arms. His lips found hers in a hungry passion as his hands kneaded whatever flesh they could find. Walking them backward over to his bed, they tumbled down, bouncing together as they tore at one another's clothing.

Mackenzie's shirt ripped open, exposing her lace-covered breasts. A growl resonated from deep within Geoff's chest as he took in her glorious body. Mackenzie was lost to all reason as she relished in the attention Geoff was giving her body. He nipped and kissed along her jaw and down her neck, making his way to her hard nipples that were pressing against the fabric of her bra. His mouth enveloped one nipple while his hand sought out the other.

Moaning loudly at the contact, she needed more. She needed skin on skin. Clawing at his back, she was able to tear his shirt from him. Geoff pulled back long enough to remove the torn fabric from his body and stare down at her. A smile played at his lips. With a single flick of his hand, he unclasped her bra, freeing her breasts and showing him how absolutely stunning she was. Mackenzie had never been more grateful for front clasp bras in her life.

Geoff, covering her body with his own, returned to kissing her. It was rough and it was glorious. She had never had someone take charge as he was. Except for the other night with the magical kiss between her and Liam.

Liam. How could she get so caught up that she had forgotten about Liam? As Geoff lavished her chest with his mouth, his hands began traveling south. No longer completely in the sexy time haze, Mackenzie stopped his hand and sat up.

With one hand over her chest, the other reaching out to Geoff, she took a breath.

"Wait. We can't. You said so yourself, and I told you. I am so confused."

"We can. We just don't talk about it. What happens in here stays between us. I can work with that. You have wanted this since the first day we met, and now you can't?"

"That's not fair."

"You're right. Sorry. Is this about us or about Liam?" He sounded annoyed. She knew that he would be. Hell, she was irritated with herself for not giving in. It had been a very long time since she had been intimate with anyone.

"Both. You say that you want this, us, but we need to do it in secret. I understand that you have a pretty important role in the pack and that you want to keep it. And how can I sleep with you if I have feelings for someone else? I can't do that to him or to you. I can't believe I am saying this, but can we just slow down and make sure of what we want? In a month's time you may decide that I am nothing like you want for a mate and if we are already sleeping together, isn't that like cheating on the were-woman who you do end up mated to or something?"

"Something like that, but I won't. I am just glad that being with him doesn't mate you to him the way it would to me. Bittens don't get pack positions so their loyalties do not have to be tested and proven time and again. I couldn't stand to see you out of reach forever."

Mackenzie leaned forward and kissed him softly on the lips before attempting to put her bra back on. He had broken the clasp.

"Shit. That was my favorite bra!" The two laughed and she stole a tee shirt from his drawer to cover up with seeing as how the buttons on her shirt had been popped off, too.

"We'll talk later?" she asked before opening his door.

"Yeah, we will." Smiling at him, she stepped out and ran for the stairs. For whatever reason, luck was on her side and no one roamed the halls to see her 'walk of shame'.

Chapter 26

After Geoff returned to Alaska, the house was in full gossip mode. Did he leave again because of Mackenzie? Did he leave to begin with because Liam was moving in on his girl? Did Margret force him to leave to keep the two lovebirds apart? It didn't matter how many times all three of the parties still at the house protested; no one wanted to believe the truth. The stories seemed to be much more entertaining.

After two weeks of listening to the comments and speculation, Mackenzie went from annoyed to pissed off. She stayed in her room whenever possible and with Liam, Teresa, and Natalie. When it wasn't, she avoided all conversations regarding her love life, or lack there of.

The best way to avoid it all together was to go out for a run. Only a few members in the house enjoyed running as much as she did, so when it all got to be too much, she just laced up her sneakers and hit the road.

The freezing wind whipped around her and not for the first time did she appreciate the amount of heat generated by her Werewolf body. When winter temperatures could drop below zero, the added ten degrees internally helped tremendously. Taking in all the bare trees and piled up snow along the sides of the road, she was able to ignore everything happening in the house and in her heart.

Finally slowing down as the large log house came into view, she saw a car pull into the driveway that she had never seen before. When the driver exited the car, she stopped completely in her tracks.

It had been so long, she had thought he wouldn't have remembered her. How the hell did he find her? But there he was walking up to the front door of the house that she had thought was her safe haven. It was the park ranger.

Had she actually harmed a person on her first night as a wolf? She hadn't seen any evidence that said she had, but then again, she was in such an emotional state she could have missed it.

Quickly ducking behind a large tree, she watched as the man went right up to the front door and rang the bell. He looked around and shifted from side to side while waiting until finally, the door opened and he went inside.

What was she going to do? Hide in the forest all day and hope he left? Sure, that would make her seem perfectly innocent. As far as she knew, she was innocent, at least from the first full moon. What if he had been tracking her since she left and found the site in Granby where she had buried whoever it was that had been unfortunate enough to cross her path?

When he hadn't left the house after an hour, she knew she had to go in. She needed more information and she needed to talk to Margret. They might not agree on everything, mainly Geoff, but Margret was the pack leader and she would protect Mackenzie as one of her own. At least, she hoped so.

~*~

Tiptoeing through the front door, Mackenzie craned her neck around, looking in every direction, hoping not to be spotted by Margret or the ranger. When she knew the coast was clear she ran up the stairs, not stopping until she was safely in her bedroom. Slamming the door behind her, she slid down and sat with her back pressed up against the wood that separated her from what could be a really bad situation.

A soft knock from the other side made Mackenzie nearly jump out of her skin. The voice that followed, however, instantly calmed her.

"Hey, open up." Liam whispered. Crawling away from the door just enough to allow it to open a crack, she grasped the knob and pulled. Liam stood there with worry painted clearly on his face, looking down at her. "What's going on?"

"Come in and shut the door."

Liam looked around, obviously not sure if he should listen to her or not. It was against the rules for the boys to be in the girls' rooms after all, but Mackenzie tried to look as desperate and pleading as she could manage. It worked.

Once the door clicked behind him, the two took a seat on her bed. Taking a deep breath, Mackenzie looked up and saw him staring intently at her. She had been able to talk to him before. She explained how she couldn't control herself when she bit him. But she never told him about the moon before him. There really is never a good time to say something like 'by the way, I killed someone before I turned you into a blood hungry monster just like me.'

"Someone showed up here from my past. From Massachusetts."

"Okay, and you don't want them to know your here. I get that. Why not just tell Margret to have them leave? Why the cloak and dagger?"

"Because he was a park ranger and caught me leaving the woods after my first cycle. I don't know. Do park rangers investigate shit? Or are they more or less like mall cops?"

"I don't know. What happened that night that has you freaking out?" Liam's voice trembled and she knew that he was afraid of what she was going to tell him. He knew that she had no control, and that it wasn't her, but that didn't mean he wouldn't see her differently. Hell, she saw herself differently.

"Not that night. That night it was just animals. But if he was able to track me here, maybe he tracked me to the place where Geoff and Margret found me. And helped me clean up the next morning." Mackenzie could no longer look Liam in the eye. She didn't want to see him look at her as a monster again. She had quite enough of the month before and if he looked at her that way, she wouldn't be able to keep her own feelings of self-loathing at bay.

"Clean up?"

"Please, don't make me say it."

"Okay. Do you want me to see what I can find out?"

Mackenzie looked back up slowly, hoping she had really heard him correctly. He hadn't moved away or worse, left her sitting there by herself, but offered to help her. "Are you sure?"

"Until the day comes that I have more control than you in wolf form, I can't judge you. And as far as I'm concerned, until you have full control of the wolf, you weren't even there."

Closing the distance between them on the bed, Mackenzie wrapped her arms around him and relished in the warmth he provided both physically and in her heart. He kissed her forehead before standing up to dig into his pocket.

"Okay, call my cell phone and then you can hear whatever I do. I will go walk around a bit until I can find them. Sound like a plan?"

"You are a genius! Yes, that's a plan." Hoping off the bed to grab the little cell phone she had picked up just for emergencies and dialed Liam's number. The phone rang in his hand and he pushed the button to answer it.

"Okay, let's see what we can find out." He leaned in and pecked her cheek before slipping out the door. With her phone to her ear, Mackenzie sat on the bed and waited.

~*~

Mackenzie could hear Liam's footsteps and the background chatter that was almost always present during the day in the house. Closing her eyes to try and picture everything she was hearing, she lay back on her bed as her heart pound furiously in anticipation.

The loud creak that sounded through the phone told her he was on the stairs and the door opening followed by a whistle of wind into the receiver let her know that he had just passed the front door.

"Mack, I think they are in her office. I didn't see them in the living room or the den." He was whispering so she wasn't sure if the phone was up to his ear or just in his hand. Either way, she heard him and was instantly disappointed because if they were in the office, there would be no way to hear a thing.

When she started to hear a faint wisp of Margret's voice, she knew that luck was on her side that day. "The door isn't closed all the way. I'll head to the bookshelves close to the office but I don't know how much we can hear from there."

Mackenzie could see exactly where he was in her mind. He was right, unless they were both talking at normal levels and were close to the door, the chance of hearing much of anything was next to nothing.

"That doesn't explain why you are here, Donald!" Margret yelled at him. Apparently arguing was good at making others forget little details like closing doors.

"Your Majesty, I..." Donald, the park ranger, was apparently not so bold as to yell back and she couldn't really hear him. Mackenzie couldn't help but wonder what the whole majesty thing was about. "wanted to be with..."

"I understand that, but I told you, you are no longer in this house. You can't be! What if you had been seen?" Mackenzie sat up at that point. With her legs crossed, she held the phone to one ear and blocked the other with her fingers to keep out any other sounds. She needed to focus on what was being said. What on earth was going on?

"I wasn't. She wasn't anywhere around. I did as you asked. You said..." Damn it. Mackenzie stood and began pacing the room. If only the park ranger would stop doing the same. At least, that's how she pictured it, because he would be clear one moment then she couldn't hear him the next.

"A position? Never once did I say that. I hate to remind you again, but you are bitten. My mother would have had my head if I allowed a bitten on council. You know that."

"Your mother would have been proud of..." What did Margret's mother have to do with anything? The more she listened, the more she knew she herself wasn't in any kind of trouble. It sounded more as if the ranger was. Why hadn't she known he was one of the pack? Why hadn't Margret told her? But she did mention she had members all over and had been tipped off about a new pup in the area. God, she hated that term. She wasn't a goddamn puppy. She might have been a bitch at times, but she was no dog.

The creak of a door sounded and she knew they were coming out. All of a sudden, the phone filled with clunking sounds and coughing.

"Liam, what on earth are you doing out here? Did you need to speak to me?" Margret asked.

"Nope, just looking for a book."

"All right. I need to ask you a favor if you don't mind. Go on into my office, I will be right there. I just need to walk my guest out." Footsteps followed as did the sound of a chair scraping across a floor.

"Mack, I'm in the office. How much of that did you hear?"

"Enough to confuse the hell out of me. Please tell me you heard the whole thing?"

"Yeah, but it won't make it anything less confusing. I'll fill you in after talking to Margret. Oh shit, she's coming." The line went dead after that and with more questions than answers, Mackenzie moved to the large window and watched Donald the park ranger climb into his car and drive off.

After an hour of waiting to hear from Liam, her phone buzzed in her palm. When she looked at the screen, she saw an incoming text message.

She sent me to the airport to get Geoff. Snowing its ass off and hope to fuck I don't get stuck. See u soon.

Chapter 27

Mackenzie took the entire day of the full moon to center herself. She needed to stay focused on everything she loved about being human, all day long, instead of just before turning. She thought that just maybe it would help her.

The pack was just as joyous as always heading into the cycle and still she couldn't understand it. Liam didn't speak to anyone and Geoff stayed as close to her as she allowed. She could see he was back to trying to keep things platonic with a hint of something more, but she was actually okay with that. That was exactly what she had asked for, and while she and Liam grew closer, she still couldn't get Geoff out of her head.

Sitting in front of the bon fire, the flames danced about, reminding her of the burning pain that emanated from her wound the night she was bitten. The flame before her warmed her hands in a comforting way, much tamer than the fire that burned her from the inside out just four months prior.

"Geoff?"

"Yeah?"

"Why did it burn? When I was bitten, the bite burned. I felt like I was dying in a big ball of fire."

"I've only heard about the burn, but as far as I know, it's the Werewolf DNA penetrating your blood stream. It's the first step in the transformation. What made you think of that now?"

"No reason."

Mackenzie went back to watching the fire reliving her most powerful memories in her mind. Joy and sadness, anger and love. Love for her mother and grandmother, and love for Geoff and Liam. How was it possible to feel so strongly for two people? Could she be in love with two people at once? She never believed that was possible before, why now? She could have love for them both, care about them tremendously, but she still honestly believed that when she was in love with one, there would be no question as to whom she should be with.

"Two minutes, everyone! Get ready to allow the moon to guide you!" Margret yelled out joyously. She ran over to stand next to Mackenzie and smiled at her. "Okay, let's do this."

Mackenzie nodded as she removed her clothing and began running through her memories again and again. Watching the clouds shift away from the moon, it reached its peak and bathed the pack in its light. Within moments, the humans no longer existed, in their place large wolves running off into the night.

~*~

The trees blurred as she ran. The howls and heartbeats of so many other wolves resonated in her ears. Bounding between bare trees and launching herself over ravines and boulders, her paws thudded against the frozen earth beneath her.

"RUN MORE!" a voice echoed into the wolf's mind, so it did. It ran and ran until the scent of something delicious wafted on the air. Whipping its head in the direction the delectable smell came from, she sprinted toward the aroma.

A crack of a branch behind her alerted her to the presence of another. Looking back, while still pushing forward, a large gray wolf and a smaller brown one followed behind. Growling loudly, she bared her teeth at the intruders. The gray wolf slowed and nipped at the brown one with it, giving her room. That was all she needed to complete her hunt.

"DON'T!" The voice tried to convince her to stop, to leave the magnificent meal untouched. Hesitating for just a second, the wolf shook her whole body violently, her head more than the rest of her. Standing completely still for a moment more, the growling returned and the large buck never stood a chance.

With her meal complete, the wolf meandered about. Only when the water came into view did she show any signs of excitement. Bounding toward the giant boulder that acted like a dock, extending from the land and out half way into the lake, she jumped off the edge and into the water. The fish swam by, completely unaware of the danger lurking around them. One-by-one they were caught between her sharp teeth. Swimming to the surface, the wolf would gobble them down and return to the depths of the water yet again to repeat the process.

"ENOUGH!" The voice boomed into her head. She couldn't ignore the command. Dropping the fish from her jaws, she resurfaced. Swimming back toward land, the wolf calmed. When she reached the shore, her body shook, ridding it of excess water before padding out onto the rock and falling asleep under the lightening sky.

~*~

The bright sunlight penetrated Mackenzie's eyelids, forcing her to wake. Taking in her surroundings, she found that once again she ended up at the lake, on the rock. At least her wolf was becoming predictable. Glancing around her, she realized that she was alone. Either she had lost Margret in the night at some point, or the pack's leader had already left her.

Climbing down from her perch, she tried to remember everything from the night before, but she was disappointed. It was a giant black hole in her mind. Trying to think of a different way to jog her memory, something her father had said to her once, long ago, popped into her mind. Strange really, that he would have given her any kind of advice worth remembering, but she was willing to try anything.

"Trace your steps, Mackenzie. If you can't remember where you put it, start with the last time you remember having it." She spoke the words out loud, but even the fact that her father had said those to her on a good day, where they weren't running or fighting with one another, didn't make her smile. Not one memory of her father made her smile.

Thinking back to the night before, she remembered speaking with Geoff about the fire and Margret announcing the impending change. The rest was fuzzy. Like watching a VHS tape that hadn't been played in a long time and having to press the tracking buttons until pictures slowly were discernible from the static.

She could see the trees and remember feeling anxious over someone telling her to run, the anger and annoyance when they tried to tell her not to hunt that poor deer, and how she couldn't refuse the voice telling her to stop fishing. Had that been her? Had she had any kind of control over the wolf?

And who had the wolves been that were following her? She knew Margret was supposed to be following her, but the other one. He was so familiar.

Breaking through the trees to the clearing, Mackenzie found her bag and began to dress. She didn't need to wash off as her wolf had gone swimming the night before. Her mind began furiously trying to place the brown wolf. She had thought she knew what most of her pack brothers and sisters looked like when they turned, but the more she thought about it, the more unease she felt.

When she spotted Margret across the way with the park ranger, everything clicked into place. The confusing conversation with the park ranger who never was after her to begin with, the damn cloak and dagger Margret wanted Donald to pull, and the oh-so-familiar brown wolf. Mackenzie instinctively reached up and rubbed along her arm where it had been torn apart and changed her life forever.

Anger boiled inside of her and when she could no longer hold it in, she screamed out, attracting the attention of everyone around her. Liam had just made it to the clearing, running directly to her side. Her rage so prevalent in her mind that she could do nothing but focus on the man in front of her who had destroyed any chance she ever had at a normal life. She could hear Liam dressing quickly, but she wasn't going to wait for him. This was her fight and she was damn well going to have it.

Her feet felt like lead as she tried to walk toward them. She could see they were arguing with one another in hushed tones and she knew she would be interrupting but who gave a fuck. She would be heard and she would not be dismissed. Margret may be the pack leader, but that did not make her all powerful.

"WHO THE FUCK ARE YOU?" Mackenzie screamed when she got close. Both Margret and the ranger looked up with wild eyes.

"Mackenzie! How dare you speak to a fellow member that way?" Margret stood tall, and took a step forward, placing herself in front of him.

"A member? He is a fucking member? Are you fucking kidding me?" Mackenzie tried to side step Margret but had been blocked each and every time. The ranger stood behind her and coward silently.

She had drawn quite a crowd at that point. Everyone had come close, circling them. Dressing silently and never taking their eyes off the group.

"Yes, he belongs to another house and has been traveling."

"Yeah, I know. He was in Massachusetts!" Gasps abound from the group, but the ones who truly mattered stepped forward with questioning eyes. For the first time since Liam and she had begun spending time together, he and Geoff didn't give each other dirty looks, but what seemed to be a silent conversation as they stepped forward and stood on either side of her.

"I told you, I have eyes and ears all over the place. He had a suspicion you had been bitten and called."

"Bullshit! I SAW HIM LAST NIGHT WITH YOU! He is a fucking brown wolf." She spat the words out through gritted teeth. Her fists clenched and unclenched, nails digging into her palms so forcefully they cut open and healed just in time to do it again.

The group around didn't understand the implications of what she had said, all they could focus on was the fact that young pup Mackenzie could remember what had happened the night before.

"You remember what happened last night? Mackenzie that is wonderful! Tell me what you remember and we can figure this whole thing out.

Don't worry about the rest. We can talk about it later. What matters is how fast you are progressing."

"Do not try and change the subject. You already knew about my memory and you wanted to dismiss it. He was the wolf. God damn it, he was the one!" With that statement, Mackenzie lunged forward, trying to get to him. She would tear him limb from limb. She wanted to kill him for killing her human life.

Margret completely caught off guard fell to the ground as Mackenzie shoved past her. Donald's eyes were wide as he tried help her up, but was tackled by Mackenzie. She punched and kneed and scratched at any surface of the man she could reach. Much too soon for her liking, Geoff had her around the waist, lifting her off him.

Continuing her tirade, her legs kicked out wildly, hoping to make contact with Donald. A group of members had all circled around Margret to help her up, even though she didn't need it. Mackenzie only sort of felt bad for her.

"You've got to calm down. Shh, I've got you, it's okay." Geoff whispered in her ear. But it wasn't okay. He didn't just tell Margret about her, he turned her. No one understood. Not one of them! Was she the one they had been talking about in the office? If so, what didn't she want her to know about? What had she asked of him?

"No. It's not. Let me go."

"Are you going to attack him again or are you calm now?"

"I am far from calm. I need answers. God damn it. I deserve them."

Geoff let go of her as soon as her feet were planted on the ground. He nodded his head to Liam who moved closer and took her hand in his as Geoff held onto her other one. She wished she could relish in the moment that the two men who held her heart were both holding her, trying to help her, but she couldn't. Not then.

"The brown wolf. He bit me! If he was local, why didn't he stick around?" Gasps filled the area. Followed by hushed voices and whispers of disgust and shock.

"It could have been a number of brown wolves. There are only so many colors a wolf can be." Margret spoke in a slow calm voice. Mackenzie knew what she was trying to do, but it wouldn't work. Margret wasn't going to control this conversation.

"Bullshit. He did it. We heard you talking in your office. Why wasn't he supposed to come back? Which she in our pack were you referring to about him not being seen by?" Mackenzie seethed through gritted teeth.

"All of you, go back to the house now!" When no one moved, Margret finally turned visibly angry. "GO!"

They all scurried away, banished by their mother. All that was left was Margret, Donald, Geoff, Liam, and Mackenzie. Margret eyed Liam, most likely wondering why he hadn't left, but his tight grip on her hand told her that no matter how angry Margret got, Liam was going to stand by her side.

"You're right. Donald did change you. He hadn't added to our pack in many years. It was time."

"What are you talking about? What time was it? Time to bite someone new on purpose? And why did he call you your majesty?" Mackenzie looked between Margret and Geoff. She wasn't sure what to do. He had to have known, right? He was in a position of power in the pack.

Pulling her hand from his and moving toward Liam, she could see the daggers that Geoff was sending to Margret. Liam's hand stayed firmly in hers as she watched those she had thought were her family despite their flaws. But how many flaws could she forgive?

"Because I am royalty. Have you ever heard of the Royal Were Myth, Mackenzie? You were a mythology major, surely you read of her wondrous reign over all the werewolves in the world before my human father murdered her in cold blood right in front of me as a young girl. It is my time to regain our family throne. And yes, the older the wolves, the more I expect of them and recruiting new members is part of that. Without a strong pack how will I ever take my rightful place as Royal Were?"

Mackenzie couldn't believe what she was hearing. Her stomach revolted and her head spun with the new information. Her mother's portrait in front of the castle, her large pack that spread across the United States, her utter delight with being able to train wolves sooner. It all made sense.

"The attack in California? We attacked them, didn't we?" she whispered, afraid to hear the answer.

"Yes, we did. And we won. We are stronger now and one step closer. This isn't a journey for the lighthearted, Mackenzie. You were specifically chosen. There was something in you that we knew would benefit our pack. Same with Liam, do you honestly think it was all coincidental?"

Mackenzie could hear the growl rumbling within Liam's chest and his grip on her hand was bone crushing. Literally, but she knew if she released him he would attack just as she had. Looking back to Geoff, she couldn't believe he had yet to say anything. Had he been playing her the whole time? Why hadn't he told her about the quota of humans he had to bite or about Margret's plan of global domination?

"Geoff?" She whispered his name, knowing he would hear her. When his eyes met hers, they were steely and red-rimmed. Had that been because he was caught or because he didn't know?

"Why? Why did you pick me?"

Geoff wouldn't answer her. He reached out for her, but she pulled further away. A single tear slipped down his cheek. Mackenzie wouldn't feel bad for him. She wouldn't allow herself to want to help him when he had kept so much from her.

"For reasons you wouldn't understand so I won't waste the time explaining them. You have it good here, Mackenzie. You are strong and capable of a great many things. As soon as you have complete control there is a spot on council for you, you can help the others gain control faster and when we finally take our place as the royal court, you will be by my side. You will have anything you want. Come now, I know you are angry, but we must move past this. It is a time to celebrate, not fight. You now know our true path and you are that much closer to having full control."

"Celebrate? Celebrate the idea of being part of something that wants power so badly they are willing to ruin lives, and kill others for it? No, that is nothing to celebrate."

"You will be happy to know that as a council member, you will have access to any mate you wish, including Geoff. He can create offspring with a willing born, but he would be yours in heart and soul. Geoff, does that sound acceptable?"

Geoff still stayed silent. It was becoming eerie and Mackenzie could not believe the audacity of Margret to suggest that having Geoff would fix everything else.

"No. I would rather wander the world alone then to put any more people in danger. Screw you."

Margret was livid. She shook and her face turned red, her eyes glazed over before turning the yellowy-green that signaled her impending shift.

"Let's go, Mackenzie. We need to pack our things." Liam finally spoke. His voice was rough and his stance firm. She wouldn't be alone. Liam was going with her.

"Geoff? Please tell me you didn't know? That somehow she kept this from you."

"I knew about the quota. I told you I had done my share of mistakes. I just didn't elaborate. I swear, I didn't know she planned your turn."

"And the rest?" Her eyes were pleading with him.

"I'll see you at the house." It was a dismissal. He wouldn't even look at her. He watched Margret with an intensity she hadn't seen before. Shaking her head at her own stupidity, she walked away, hand in hand with Liam.

Chapter 28

When the front door opened, Mackenzie and Liam came face to face with the entire pack. None looked pleased to see them, with the exception of Natalie and Teresa, but even they weren't pleased, more worried than anything.

"What the hell, Mackenzie? We do not attack our family!" Someone from the back called out.

"He is not my family. He turned me and left me! Would any of you have turned your back on someone you bit?" The group erupted in disbelief. Liam tried to help guide her through the room to the stairs so the two could go and pack their belongings. "I don't care what you all think. But maybe you should ask those that have been around for a while how their turn quotas are coming."

"What the hell are you talking about?" Natalie asked, eyeing Teresa with caution. Teresa's eyes had gone wide as saucers when she looked between Mackenzie and Natalie.

"Margret told me I was chosen, and that Liam was chosen. I don't know about the rest, but apparently, our older members have a certain number they have to change to be in Margret's good graces. Nothing is a coincidence in her plan to gain complete control of every pack. I won't be a part of it."

"Come on, we need to get moving." Liam said and tugged on her hand. The two left the group behind as they forged ahead to their rooms.

The bedroom door opened and Mackenzie looked at what she once thought was the best way possible to live her new and unexpected life. The stunning room, with the amazing window and two roommates who became her sisters, all of it just the pretty tape used to cover up the ugly tear in the world of Werewolves.

Tears slipped down her face as she pulled out her old ratty backpack and began shoving clothing into it. The door creaked and Mackenzie whipped around to see Natalie standing there with tears of her own in her eyes.

"You're lying."

"I wish I were. She told me I had been chosen, and the night I bit Liam had been planned. They are growing the pack any way they can. The California pack wasn't attacked, we attacked them."

"Teresa said she wasn't told to bite me. That she doesn't have a quota."

"And she is most likely telling you the truth. I wasn't told to bite anyone either. They didn't care who bit Liam, just that he was bitten. She still isn't in full control of the wolf. They won't ask her to change others until she is. You can come with us if you want to."

"You know I can't. I could never leave her or my family. I will just opt out or something when the time comes. I can be one who stays behind to care for the pups or something. I've already pledged. Leaving scares me. I need them. I need Margret."

"Okay." Mackenzie wanted to be angry with her. Staying with the pack and helping to care for the young ones allows the others to go and fight and turn people. Choosing inaction is not the same as taking a stand. But the pack was all Natalie knew and Teresa was there. Her heart would be broken in two if she left. She may not agree with her, but she understood.

"Where will you go?"

"I don't know. Just far away from here."

Mackenzie finished packing her bag, just taking what she had when she moved in and a few pictures of her with Teresa and Natalie and one of her and Geoff. She slung the bag across her back and walked up to one of her best friends.

Reaching her hand out, Natalie grabbed it and squeezed. Mackenzie gave it a tug and enveloped her in a hug. The two girls clung to one another and cried.

"Can I get in on that?" Mackenzie and Natalie looked up to see Teresa standing just outside the door with a sad smile and red-rimmed eyes. They opened their arms up and welcomed her in their embrace.

"You better write to us. Let us know you're okay."

"I will. I promise."

Finally taking a step back, she waved a little goodbye and headed down the stairs.

~*~

The house had turned eerily quiet while she was packing. The stairs creaked under her feet with every third step or so. Looking around at the large house that had been her home she was sad. She had finally found a place she felt like she belonged, but it was all a lie.

The front door had been left wide open. She knew she closed it behind her so either someone left in a rush or someone came in. Desperately hoping that it was the latter, she searched the main floor for Geoff.

The office door was closed up tight but light spilled out beneath it. Could they have gone in there? Had he known all along that Margret had planned everything? Could she really have kept him in the dark the whole time? The chances were slim, but her heart needed to believe that he hadn't been lying to her all along.

"Hey, you ready?" Liam's voice called to her from down the hall. She slowly turned from the office door to see him standing there ready to go. He too had a backpack and looked exhausted. It was a lot to mentally process in such a short time, but she was ready to go. If Geoff wanted to go with them, he would have left when they did.

"Yeah."

Taking a deep breath, Mackenzie joined him and walked out the door.

~*~

"WAIT!" Geoff called from behind. Turning around she saw that the front door had opened and he was running to catch up. Liam shook with anger but watched Mackenzie to see how she would react.

"What?" she asked, trying to show annoyance in her voice even though she was desperately hoping to be able to accept whatever he had to say as the truth.

"I didn't know about her setting up certain people to be bitten. I didn't know that we were attacking the others, just that we always won and we were stronger for it. I knew she was the daughter of the Royal Were and I knew about the quotas. I told you I had more mistakes that I cared to remember but I told you about my past, about growing up alone. Margret took me in and trained me. The world was very different before and being strong was all that was important in staying alive in our world. But I told her I was leaving, that I couldn't be part of it anymore. Will you wait for me to grab a few things?"

Liam watched the interaction with guarded eyes. Mackenzie could tell that he didn't believe him, but she knew Geoff better than he did. She nodded her head at him and watched as he ran back into the house and up the stairs.

"I don't trust him."

"I know, but you trust me right?" Her eyes pleaded with him. She knew that she was making a hard situation that much worse by asking him to accept Geoff as a part of whatever it was they were now.

"You know I do."

"Then trust that I think he is being honest. We need him out there. Neither one of us has control, or has the kind of experience to make it for long, otherwise. He can teach us, help us get control faster, maybe even help us learn to defend ourselves."

"Okay. But so help me if he hurts you, or betrays us in any way, I will kill him."

"Fair enough." Geoff said from behind them. Turning quickly, the two men nodded at each other before giving their attention to Mackenzie.

"Goodbye, house." Mackenzie said and Geoff closed the door behind him.

"Where to?"

"Somewhere we can call home, I guess. I just don't know where that is yet."

The snow crunched beneath their feet and the wind whipped by them as if it were any other day. But it wasn't just any other day. It was the day that would change their lives forever for the second time. Mackenzie looked over her shoulder as they stepped into the trees, and saw Margret standing in the window of her bedroom, watching them. She had a feeling that it wouldn't be the last time she saw her.

THE TEMPERING
297

Sneak Peek
THE ENLIGHTENING,
Book 2 in The Mackenzie Duncan Series

Liam Hardy had been complaining about the cold since they had left the pack house three days prior. The snow was cold, his socks were wet, his nose was tingling from the wind chill. All of which was bullshit in Mackenzie's opinion. They were Werewolves and the heat that radiated from within their bodies made sure they never felt the sting of the cold.

"Let's head west. I'm fucking tired of the cold."

"West doesn't mean warm. South means warm," Geoff bit back. Tensions were running on high between the two men. It could have possibly had something to do with the fact that both wanted Mackenzie and she couldn't pick between the two. Or it could have something to do with the fact that they were all used to living in a huge house with all the amenities and left it behind with nothing more than a back pack each. They had been sleeping wherever they could manage and still didn't have an actual plan as to what they were going to be doing now that they were considered rogue.

"Of course it does! Everyone says California is hot. They have mild winters and hot summers. California is west." The boys had stopped walking long enough to glare at one another. Mackenzie was sick and tired of it. She wasn't their mother, nor either of their girlfriends, so why was it that she had to step in and take care of them?

"Will the both of you just chill the fuck out? Let's go south west okay? It's a little thing called a compromise, boys. Figure it out or I will leave the both of you and find my own way. Oh and Liam, you know I adore your face just the way it is but if you complain one more god damn time about your nose being too cold I will rip it off. We radiate heat. If you need to complain about something at least be honest about it."

"And what would something honest be?" Liam looked at her with a mix of adoration and irritation. It was an interesting combo that was for sure. He wore his feelings on his sleeve and was still a young wolf, much like her, whose emotions could shift in point two seconds if given a reason to. Hell, even without a real reason to.

"Let's see, we have been walking for three days and have yet to actually stay in a real building. The only food we have eaten was hunted by Wolfy Geoff so it was mangled to bits by the time he brought it back to be cooked and the two of you stink. Big time. Didn't either of you think to pack deodorant?"

Mackenzie was just as annoyed with their situation as the boys, but she didn't see any reason to openly complain at every turn. Liam did. His looks would only get him so far with her patience, and with his blonde hair, blue eyes, and sculpted abs, that was actually quite far. Geoff on the other hand was dark where Liam was light. He was just as gorgeous but also had hundreds of years of experience under his belt to help him with his maturity. If only that maturity flowed into his romantic life, they would have been together a long time ago.

"What are you talking about. We smell like roses!" Geoff said from behind her through a hearty laugh. Liam glared at him for a moment before laughing along with him.

"You might want to be careful who you call stinky, Mac. You are not too far behind us." Then Liam ran. It was a smart move because Mackenzie was right behind him.

"Sure, leave me to grab the bags!" Geoff called out after them. When Mackenzie glanced over her shoulder, she watched him lift both hers and Liam's bag onto his shoulders. His strength had always impressed her and she could imagine the way his muscles were moving and flexing beneath his long sleeved shirt. Licking her lips, she remembered just a week before when those muscles were rippling beneath her fingers as she explored his chest.

Geoff smirked at her and blew a kiss in her direction. Mackenzie shook her head to rid her mind of his gorgeous body and talented tongue. She had been the one to stop things. She had been the one to say that until she knew who she wanted, Geoff or Liam, it wasn't right to be with either in that way. Both men agreed with her, much to her surprise. She had fully expected one to tell her to fuck off. She knew that if she had been one of two girls vying for the affection of a man she might be a little pissed that he couldn't choose.

"Geoff, what's the hold up?" Liam called from a few feet in front of her. Mackenzie turned back around and took off after him again. He wasn't expecting it and since she was the fastest runner she tackled him without even trying.

"I do not stink. Let's get out of the damn woods and find a real place to stay for once?"

"I don't know, I think I like you right here." Liam whispered, keeping his hands firmly on her hips. She rolled her eyes and stood up just as Geoff caught up with them.

"Good idea. Real food should be on the agenda as well."

"Agenda? Who talks like that?" Liam asked under his breath. He wasn't taking things as well as Geoff was. Perhaps Geoff just had more confidence or maybe Liam just cared more. He had never pushed her away like Geoff had. Well at least he hadn't once he was done trying to kill her. Turning a perfectly wonderful human into a blood thirsty monster sort of dampens the lovey-dovey feelings.

"I do. Let's just go." Geoff took the lead, which Mackenzie was more than happy with. She was sick and tired of looking at snow covered ground and bare trees. She wanted a real bed and a hot shower and possibly three or four plates full of pancakes and eggs.

~*~

The motel was run down and rather sketchy looking. If it wasn't for the two men on either side of her and her super strength thanks to her new wolf genes, she might actually be afraid to step through the doorway. But they were and she was, so Mackenzie opened the door to what she guessed they considered a lobby to rent a room.

"Is this place really where we should be staying? I

mean, I bet we can find a hotel if we go further into town." Geoff was looking around in disgust. It made her laugh a little at how uncomfortable he was. She wasn't sure if he was worried about the possible crime or if he just wanted his normal accommodations of king size beds, room service, and a maid. Geoff was kind of a slob on his own.

"This is what we can afford. Seriously, it's not that bad. We have all stayed in better and after three days in the woods, anything with a mattress is perfect for me." Geoff and Liam shared a look then with a shrug went back to inspecting the area. A creak from behind the desk alerted them to the fact that they were no longer alone.

An old man with no hair on his head but a full white beard on his face hobbled into the room. He nodded at Mackenzie then found his seat. The legs of the chair screeched against the linoleum floor, sending a shiver down her spine. It was almost like nails on a chalk board.

"How many?" The old man's voice was harsh. It sounded like someone who hadn't had a drink of anything in days. He coughed a few times and cleared his throat, but nothing helped him.

"Just the three of us. One room please, with two beds if you have it?"

"Got a room with one bed or you can get two rooms."

"One bed is fine. I'm sure we can manage." Mackenzie looked behind her at Geoff and Liam hoping they would agree but they stared at her instead. Then looked at each other. Then both groaned. They knew they would either have to share the bed with her together, or sleep on the floor. She had a feeling she knew what they would choose and it was stupid.

"Room 103. Thirty dollars."

Mackenzie pulled the money from her bag and handed it over. She didn't know if either of the other two had any. She really didn't know anything about what they were doing, where they were going, or what they would do when they got there. How had they gone three days without really saying anything to each other? It was time to really sit down and talk and as much as it needed to be done, it was not going to go over well.

~*~

The springs squeaked loudly as Mackenzie sat down on the floral print blanket that adorned the double bed in the center of the small motel room. Geoff and Liam stood awkwardly in separate corners of the tiny space looking anywhere but at her on the bed or at each other.

"So," Mackenzie began. She looked up to Geoff first, his dark eyes penetrating the stain in the carpet just in front of his foot, then to Liam, who was studying the poster on the bathroom door of how to get out in case of an emergency.

"So,: both Liam and Geoff spoke at the same time, glancing at one another then quickly away.

"This has got to be talked about. Are we going to keep traveling together in complete and total silence or awkward conversations? We are all mature adults, I'm sure we aren't the first to find ourselves in this situation right?"

"Is that supposed to be a joke?" Geoff looked up, irritation in his eyes. "Three werewolves caught in a love triangle, because one can't decide between the one who gave up his home and family of two hundred years for her and the one who is tied to her by a sire bond? Which do you think is real, Mackenzie?"

"Hey! It has nothing to do with the fact that she is my sire. If you remember correctly I hated her for that exact fact!"Liam's whole body was shaking with tension. Mackenzie knew she needed to cool the situation down before he lost control, not that Geoff couldn't handle it if he did.

"I meant when three friends have feelings for each other and they don't know what to do. That has happened to so many damn people in this world that just about a quarter of all romance's are about that exact thing! And no, most aren't supernatural beings but being a wolf doesn't change the fact that we are together right now, all three of us. I meant, we need to talk about what we are going to do about our—I mean, The pack? Are they really just letting us go? Would Margret give you up that easy?" The last part was directed at Geoff. He knew the wolfy politics and he knew Margret. Probably better than anyone else.

"So we ignore the attraction, both physical and emotional, for now and focus on keeping our asses alive. As long as we keep our heads down and don't interfere with her plans I am pretty sure we will be fine. It might be a good idea to go somewhere out of her areas though." Geoff had crossed his arms over his chest and Mackenzie knew that he was still irritated with her. Who wouldn't be in his position?

"Where would that be? Sounds like she is working on taking over the whole United States." Liam sat on the floor with his legs tucked under him, his back against the wall and his head leaning back, eyes trained on the ceiling. With a quick look up Mackenzie knew he was counting the tiles. He did that when he was trying to keep his cool.

"There are other descendants of the other were 'royalty'. Margret's mother, had siblings. They never became powerful like she was, they were the younger siblings and much like human royalty, only the eldest gets to attain the crown. When Rosalinda, Margret's mother, was killed, her siblings decided it would be for the better to allow each family to run itself with a few guidelines. They sent messages out in hopes that they could all live how they wanted and be better able to hide and keep everyone safe. Rosalinda's pack had been sloppy. Arrogant. They were being spotted by humans left and right and were turning people without even a worry of who it was to be turned. If each family governed themselves, then perhaps they would learn from the mistakes of their deceased queen and would protect the secret."

"So before Rosalinda was another Queen?. Were there ever any Kings? How did they run things?" Mackenzie was fascinated. None of her research on the mythology of Lycanthropes told this story. Even Liam had leaned forward, listening intently.

"Correct and no, there were no kings. Back then, women were in charge. Only born female Weres can guarantee an offspring with the Were gene. Even now, many packs have female pack leaders. Rosalinda's mother, Gwendolynn and her court were strict with the rules governing their kind. They were diligent in enforcing the rules, both for the wolves protection as well as the humans. Then, one day, Gwendolynn was found dead along side of her was her court and her mate. Rosalinda was heartbroken after her parent's death and thought that the wolves of the world should have protected her parents instead of killing them. There were rogues that didn't want to live under a ruler. They wanted to feast whenever they wanted and mate whenever they wanted with whoever they wanted and there were strict rules about that back then. So when Rosalinda took over, she really took over. She executed any who would go against her or spoke ill of her parents. She began turning humans to create her army and even infiltrated the human royalty by marrying a duke and having an affair with the King.

"Rosalinda wanted power and obedience. She was the exact opposite of her parents in that way. They wanted harmony and safe living amongst the humans, which was the reason for the rules. Rosalinda had Margret with the Duke. She had planned on having at least one more child, but had hoped to have the King's offspring to further cement herself into the human royal world. But her wolves were becoming overly aggressive and sloppy in their procurement of new pups before she could do that. The humans began to hunt our kind. She was killed by her own husband while Margret, only a small child, was in the back bedroom.

"As Margret aged, she noticed the changes in

herself and was so grateful her father did not. When she turned for the first time, she killed him. She had always known what she was and knew that she had to keep it a secret from everyone after watching her mother bleed to death on their stone kitchen floor. She ran in the middle of the night to where her mother spoke of family living and they took her in, taught her how to be a wolf and how to be an example to those who while no longer under their rule, looked to them for guidance and support.

"After a while, she became restless. Wanting to take action against those who had been so careless to get caught and in the end get her mother killed. No one would tell her. No one knows if they were being truthful when they said they didn't know who it was, or if they just didn't want any more conflict among our kind and lied to her to keep her from starting trouble. Margret left the pack and started out on her own. She has lived on every continent and had many lovers both human and were. She believes in her birthright as a royal were and that of her children. Don't ask how many, I'm not really sure."

Mackenzie sat their completely dumbfounded. She didn't know what to say. Liam had stood and was pacing the room, looking to Mackenzie then to Geoff and would open his mouth just to close it again. Finally, he spoke.

"So, where do you come into the story?" Liam asked. He watched Geoff with trained eyes. His pacing had stopped and his body stood rigid. Mackenzie looked between the men, she knew that neither particularly like the other even though just a few weeks prior they were the best of friends. She wanted to remind them of the old saying "bros before hoes" but she refused to call herself a hoe for one and for two...what if they decided to leave her behind because she was causing too much trouble between them?

"Margret found me just after my first change when I was sixteen. I had grown up in an orphanage and like I told Mackenzie a while ago, had gotten a letter just before warning me of what was to come. I knew of Margret's plan to grow our number by setting a quota for each member old enough to have complete control. I knew she wanted a powerful pack. I did not know about her war on the others."

"How is it that you were her third in command, knew about EVERYTHING else, but didn't know about her plan to force everyone into submission like her mother had? Seems like a really big blind spot and I didn't take you for an idiot, Geoff. Well, at least not an idiot when it came to anything besides Mackenzie."

"HEY!" Mackenzie screamed out, standing from the bed. It was her turn to pace while she thought of exactly what to say. When her mind was finally made up she stood directly in front of Liam, her hand balled into fists at her side and she could feel the anger radiating throughout her body. "What was or is between Geoff and I is our business just as what was or is between you and I is our business and I will not have either of you throwing insults at the other over me. Because by insulting him you are insulting me. Do you both understand?"

They each mumbled their agreement and Mackenzie took a calming breath, counted her backward numbers, and when she felt completely in control, returned to sit on the bed. "Now, ignoring our jacked up relationship status for a while, what the hell are we going to do? Find the pack of one of Rosalinda's siblings? That seems highly unlikely. I mean, they all started off in Europe right?"

"I don't think we should look for any other pack. We become loyal to one another. We become our own pack." Liam stood as he spoke. Mackenzie knew what he was saying. He wasn't ready to trust anyone else. They could only trust one another.

"Our own pack? And who is pack leader? Who makes decisions? Who do we vow our loyalty to? Three isn't a pack. Three is just a few rogues who have nowhere to call home. We need a pack for protection you dumb ass."

"I agree with Liam. I am not ready to trust anyone else. I mean, I thought Margret was this amazing woman who saved me and could show me how to live and look how wrong I was about that bitch. No. We stick to just us."

"You two are going to get us killed." Geoff stormed from the room and into the bathroom, slamming the door behind him. Sighing, Mackenzie flopped back onto the bed and covered her eyes with her arm. With the light blocked out, she could almost pretend that the last few months of her life never happened. That she was in her tiny apartment just on the other side of Harvard Campus and that she had to write a paper on the mythology of ancient Europe. If only that could be true.

ABOUT THE AUTHOR

Growing up, Adrianne couldn't get her hands on enough books to satisfy her need for the make believe. If she finished a novel and didn't have a new one ready and waiting for her, she began to create her own tales of magic and wonder. Now, as an adult, books still make up majority of her free time, and now her tales get written down to be shared with the world.

During the day, Adrianne uses her camera to capture life's stories for clients of all ages and at night, after her two children are tucked in bed; she devotes herself to her written work. Adrianne is living the life she always wanted, surrounded by art and beauty, the written word and a loving family.

As a young adult author, Adrianne James has plans to bring stories of growing characters, a little romance, and a little magic and mythology for her readers to enjoy.

Where to find Adrianne James:
Twitter: @Adrianne_James
Facebook:
http://www.facebook.com/AuthorAdrianneJames
Blog:
http://www.AdrianneJames.wordpress.com
Email: AuthorAdrianneJames@gmail.com